ARCHER AND THE TWO PRETENDERS

Also by Colin Eston

Will Archer Mysteries

Archer Bows in

Archer's Irish Jig

Archer's Home Run

Archer at Court

Archer at War

Archer and the Stolen Boy

Saint and Czinner Mysteries

Dying for Love

The Dusk Messenger

The Pepys Memorandum

The Seed of Osiris

COLIN ESTON

Archer and the Two Pretenders

The seventh *Will Archer* mystery

Auction

"I was sitting in my study when I heard a very hard knock at my door, and immediately afterwards several ill-looking rascals who were in Highland dress, with broad swords by their sides, burst in upon me. One seized me with great violence, saying I was his prisoner and must go with him. I asked him for what offence and bid him show me his warrant. He answered not, but immediately hurried me away out of my room and house.

In the streets, through which I was dragged, with many insults, I saw to my horror houses burnt down, dead bodies of men, women and children, strewed everywhere as we passed, and great numbers of Highlanders, and Popish priests in their several habits.

My guard now brought me to a court which bore some resemblance to the court of King's Bench; only a great cross was erected in the middle; and instead of those officers of justice who usually attend that court, a number of Highlanders, with drawn swords, stood there as sentinels.

A charge of high-treason was then, I dreamed, laid against me, for having writ in praise of his majesty King George.

The court unanimously agreed that I was guilty and

proceeded to pass sentence, and I was then delivered into the hands of the executioner, who stood ready, and was ordered to allow me only three hours to confess myself, and be reconciled to the Church of Rome. Upon which a priest immediately advanced and began to revile me, saying I was the wickedest heretic in the kingdom, and had many times exerted myself against his majesty, King James III, and his holiness, the Pope. Then he added that I should have the good fortune to make some atonement for my impiety by being hanged. Whereupon the executioner immediately dragged me forth.

The first sight that met my eyes as I passed through the streets was a young lady of quality in the hands of two Highlanders, who were struggling with each other for their booty. Her hair was dishevelled and torn, her eyes swollen with tears, her face all pale, and her breast, which was all naked and exposed, bore marks of blood. This sight was a matter of entertainment to my conductors, who, however, hurried me presently from it, as I wish they had also from her screams, which reached my ears to a great distance.

After such a spectacle as this, the dead bodies which lay every where in the streets (for there had been, I was told, a massacre the night before), scarce made any impression; nay, the very fires in which Protestants were roasting were, in my sense, objects of much less horror as I was thrust up the steps to the scaffold.

A priest, after admonishing the executioner to exert the utmost rigour of my sentence, then advanced towards me and, putting on a look of compassion, advised me, for the sake of my soul, to embrace the holy communion. I gave him no answer, and he turned his back, thundering forth curses against me.

The executioner then attempted to put the rope round my neck, when my little girl entered my bedchamber, and put an end to my dream, by pulling open my eyes, and telling me that the tailor had brought home my clothes for his majesty, King George's, birthday.

The sight of my dear child, added to the name of that gracious Prince, at once deprived me of every private and public fear; and the joy which now began to arise gave me altogether as delightful a sensation as perhaps the heart of man is capable of feeling."

And, just as Mr Henry Fielding's beloved daughter woke him from his dream, so the sound of the auctioneer's gavel returns me from his shocking vision of a London overrun by Jacobite rebels, to the place in which I now stand.

Another lot sold. The sale is going well.

The room is full, but not crowded. This Soho Square residence is only in the middle rank of desirable properties, and most of the items for sale are unremarkable. Mainly old, unfashionable furniture, carpets, curtains and a few parcels of domestic odds and ends. Things that I – and many of the people here, judging by the paltry sums they realise - don't have any great interest in.

Not that I, observing proceedings from my vantage point in the window alcove, am taking part in the bidding. No, I am leaving that to my friend, Jem Bennett, sitting there in the second row, quietly biding his time.

Nor, it seems, am I the only one to employ a deputy. Even now my glance rests on my old acquaintance, Robbie, who winks back at me as I catch his eye. Today, dressed not in his footman's uniform, but in dapper dark blue, he is there on behalf of his master, Sir Francis Courtney, readying himself to bid for certain items of what might be called a 'specialist' nature in which his employer is interested.

Considering the nature of those items, I doubt Jem and Robbie are the only proxy bidders in the room.

Now, with a discreet cough and a slightly embarrassed manner, the auctioneer comes to the lot in question. The atmosphere in the room becomes expectant.

'A collection of books of, hem – er, *special interest,* gentlemen, amassed over many years by the late owner. Many of them, I am assured, are *unique* and the majority are very rare. In view of their undoubted value and – er - specialised appeal, I think I shall open the bidding at £50 for the whole collection...'

There is a noticeable indrawing of breath at such a sum. The auctioneer quickly adds, '... though I am prepared to consider offers for individual volumes.' He looks around the room. 'Anyone?'

There seems a general reluctance in the room to start the bidding or to articulate particular titles, but after some encouragement from the auctioneer one brave soul speaks up with an offer for a title which he reads from a piece of paper in his hand. His mispronunciation elicits a suppressed titter from some in the room. 'Two guineas for Lee Coal dez Fems.'

The auctioneer takes it up gratefully.

'Two guineas bid for *L'Ecole des Femmes*, gentlemen. Any advance upon two guineas?'

I notice one or two in the audience consulting notes, obviously provided by their employers who prefer to remain anonymous. Now the ice is broken, others speak up, shouting out other titles in addition to the one already mentioned. The auctioneer is becoming confused, finding it difficult to keep up.

I see Sir Francis Courtney's footman, Robbie, assessing the opposition with a wry smirk. He waits until the auctioneer has brought some order to the disparate bids and just as his gavel is about to seal the first of a long list, he proclaims, jauntily, 'A hundred and fifty guineas for the whole collection!'

Shocked faces turn towards him in amazement. So lavish a bid dumbfounds them. There is a flurried consulting of instructions but clearly none are prepared, or able, to better it. The auctioneer casts his eye around downturned faces and shaking heads, then, with some relief, declares the complete lot sold.

The auction then proceeds to individual pieces of more quality furniture, but interest has clearly waned. A good half of those present are quietly leaving.

As the lot in which I am interested will not come up until the very end of the auction, I take this as a hopeful sign and return my attention to the journal in my hand.

The True Patriot. A new weekly publication edited by Mr Henry Fielding, produced in response to the Jacobite rebels' unexpected victory over government forces at Prestonpans near Edinburgh. There are rumours that, having seized control of the Scottish capital, they have every intention of advancing into England.

His lurid and alarmist prospect of London overrun by savage foreigners and Papists is clearly designed to inflame the prevailing fears of the populace and spur the government into action.

But marauding highlanders are of only passing interest to

me at the moment as my attention is once more distracted by Robbie sliding on to the window seat beside me, his thigh pressing close against mine.

'The old boy will be cock-a-hoop, eh, Will?' he whispers, leaning close.

'Sir Francis will be proud of you, Robbie,' I tell him. 'You have missed your calling. You should be an actor. The dramatic effect of your consummate timing would impress even Mr Garrick. It certainly impressed me.'

He makes to draw me aside out of hearing of the auction. With a brief glance towards where Jem is still patiently waiting, I hold up my hand, fingers outstretched to indicate that I shall only be five minutes, and accompany Jamie outside.

'Have you heard aught from Mr Garrick?' asks Robbie once we are in the hallway. 'Sir Francis has been quite worried about him.'

'I know no more than your master, Robbie. The last I heard he's with his family in Lichfield recovering from a bout of inflammatory fever. I fear this late business at Drury Lane with Mr Fleetwood and Mr Lacy has sapped his spirits.'

'And is there still bad blood between him and Mr Macklin?'

'Macklin is as stiff-necked as ever and to make matters

worse my master and Mistress Peg have parted ways. In some acrimony, it seems. He has burnt all her letters and regards her now as little more than a money-grubbing coquette.'

Robbie emits a low whistle of disbelief. 'Phew, strong!'

'I can't say I'm surprised,' I tell him. 'I've thought for some time that he was more besotted with her than she with him. All the same it must have caused him pain, and it won't have helped his recovery.'

'Well that's women for you, steer clear of them I say!' Then, more brightly, digging me playfully in the ribs, 'And you, Master Will Archer, what have you been doing since you left us?'

'I have been back to Yorkshire to see my mother – and for certain affairs of business.'

The expression on his face clearly invites me to elaborate. But the very mention of my late business in Yorkshire serves as a reminder of why I am here...

I hastily excuse myself, bidding him farewell and promising to visit him and his master, Sir Francis, when I have opportunity. Then I return to the auction.

The numbers in the room have thinned yet further, which heartens me. There will not be so many to bid against me – or rather against Jem, for I am determined, anxious as I am about the outcome, to remain aloof from the bidding whilst he represents my interests.

All the same, my mouth goes dry and my hands clench with apprehension as the final lot is announced. I can feel my heart pounding in my breast as the bidding proceeds.

But Jem retains a cool head, increasing his offers by gradual stages until all rivals drop out.

And when the auctioneer's gavel comes down for the last time this afternoon, the final lot is mine!

I stride forward and seize Jem's hands, showering him with thanks. I know I would never have shown such calm, controlled tenacity nor achieved the prize for so reasonable an amount.

'Congratulations, Master Archer,' says Jem in return, 'you are now the new owner, with a lease of 53 years upon number 20 Soho Square.'

Change

When the crowd has dispersed and Jem is making final arrangements with the auctioneer regarding the deeds of the property, I walk around the deserted and mainly empty rooms of which I am now, for the sum of £3,670, the new tenant.

The last time I stood in this house was over a year ago when I was investigating the disappearance of Raphael Elias, the son of a prominent businessman. A case which unexpectedly revealed facts about the parentage of Charlie Stubbs, the young boy I rescued from a life on the streets and who is now my loyal companion, and whom I regard almost as a younger brother.

He was with me on my first and only time here. 20 Soho Square was then the residence of Mr Cornelius Altin, a one time bookseller whose speciality was the acquisition of erotica.

That gentleman, already physically infirm and elderly when Charlie and I saw him a year ago, but with a mind and eye as sharp and bright as ever, was found dead several months ago by the woman who came once a week to clean and cook for him. He was sprawled, neck broken, at the bottom of the staircase. He had lain there for three or four days.

The first intimation I had of his death was when Sir Francis, with whom Mr Garrick and I were staying as guests at the time, remarked upon a notice in the paper requesting any relatives or associates of the late Mr Cornelius Altin to come forward in order that his estate might be disposed of in an appropriate and lawful manner.

I could hardly have imagined when I took that newspaper from Sir Francis's hands how an advertisement, so insignificant in itself, was to set in train a series of events which would have such far reaching consequences for me and for those around me.

I mentioned to Sir Francis that Charlie and I had once met the deceased gentleman and that, misunderstanding the purpose of our visit, he had proceeded to show us some explicitly erotic works from his extensive collection.

No sooner did he hear this than Sir Francis resolved that he must possess that collection at any cost. Though his dubious desires attract him principally to juveniles of his own sex, his taste in literary and artistic works of erotica is remarkably catholic.

Mr Garrick, however, seemed indifferent when shown the advertisement, expressing no more than passing interest. With hindsight, I now realise that he was so preoccupied by the financial mis-management at Drury Lane under Mr

Fleetwood and Mr Lacy, his feud with Mr Macklin, and his deteriorating relationship with Mrs Peg Woffington, that naught else seemed important.

One of my greatest regrets will always be that I did not see what a toll these matters were, even then, beginning to take on his health.

Would I have acted differently if I had? Would I have remained in London? Not gone back to Yorkshire? Would I not have stayed away so long?

The idle regrets of hindsight!

The fact was that the day after Sir Francis drew the advertisement to my attention I received news from Yorkshire that my grandfather had died.

My previous visit to Yorkshire was three years ago and prior to that I had never met my grandfather. He existed only as a tyrant in my imagination, an unbending patriarch who had disinherited my mother upon her marriage and had shunned all contact with us even after my despairing father had taken his own life when I was but an infant.

Events during that visit three years ago had done much to alter my opinion of him, so much so that I wished I had had the time to get to know him better.

Unfortunately, events since then conspired to prevent my returning to Yorkshire. Now, it was too late. But I felt the least I could do was attend his funeral.

So it was with mixed emotions that, a few months ago, I travelled north again.

My previous trip, three years since, had been in response to a desperate plea from my estranged mother whom I had not seen since I was a child. My belief, fostered by a childhood spent in poverty, was that we were penniless, ruined by my late father's imprudent speculations and subsequent suicide.

However, during that visit I discovered how he had been fraudulently cheated of his wealth and that I was, in fact, heir to considerable property and a man of means.

With the help of a close friend who had also been a victim of the villains who had conspired to rob my mother and I of our inheritance, our fortunes were restored. When I returned to London, I left my newly recovered estates under his management, and I was secure in the knowledge that both I and my mother were now reconciled to each other and to her family.

On this more recent journey, even allowing for the sadness of my grandfather's death, I was looking forward to seeing them all again and they in turn were delighted to see me.

My childhood friend, Col St Antoine and his wife Sarah were now the proud parents of two sturdy children, a boy and a girl, with another on the way. One of the first things he did was to bring out the account books which proved how right I was to entrust my affairs into his hands.

Following the funeral, there was much to be done in sorting out my late grandfather's affairs, and so much lawyers' jargon to wade through that I was obliged to spend several weeks there. Fortunately, the unfeigned pleasure we all took in each other's company put all other cares from my mind.

However, after almost three months of dealing with shilly-shallying lawyers, and when all matters were eventually concluded, all necessary documents signed and sealed, my restlessness began to grow.

I looked at my mother and grandmother now settled back into their life at the family home, Eastthorpe Manor. I looked at Col and Sarah established at Lowfield Grange with their growing family. And I could not help feeling like a stranger. The pattern of our separate lives was too different, and London began to exert a pull which could not be ignored.

Bidding them all a fond farewell, with many promises of return, I took my leave, happy in the knowledge of their happiness, and boarded the coach bound for the capital.

I went to Yorkshire this latest time in the knowledge that I was already a wealthy man, but I returned to London an even richer one. My late grandfather had named me his sole heir.

As soon as the lawyer had informed me of this, I began to think how I might use my new fortune and a plan began to form in my mind.

Until now I had relied upon the generosity of others. Principally that of Mr Garrick, who had taken me in, saving me from a life of sexual degradation at Mother Ransom's molly house by giving me a job as an actor and nominal manservant.

The kindness, too, of Sir Francis Courtney who, for all his vices, and a less than auspicious start to our relationship, has proved a good friend and provided a refuge for both my master and his household when the quarrel with Mr Macklin led us to quit our lodgings at Bow Street.

But now, I thought as the coach rattled on its way back to London, *I can be master of my own destiny*. With funds from the banker's draft which was stowed safely in an inner pocket, I would purchase the lease on Cornelius Altin's old house in Soho Square, if it was still available Then I could offer Mr Garrick the security of a home, just as he had once provided one for me.

When I arrived in London, however, I found that Mr Garrick was no longer there. Shortly after I'd left for Yorkshire he'd fallen very ill, almost died

I learned that he was gone to the country to stay with

friends, whence he intended to visit his brother in Lichfield and relatives in Carshalton. He would not be back until summer at the earliest.

Sir Francis told me all this. And told me also that, during my absence, he had made diligent enquiries about the house in Soho Square. He had ascertained that, should no legal beneficiary be traced, the property and its contents would be put up for auction.

Fortunately the procrastination of lawyers which had so irked me back in Yorkshire, here played to my advantage. It took nearly half a year from Cornelius Altin's demise before all necessary searches had been made and a date set for the auction.

Which, in brief, is why, only a few days since I got back from Yorkshire, I am now standing in what was once Mr Cornelius Altin's library, its bookshelves now bare of books, its window denuded of the heavy drapes which once made this room so gloomy.

My footsteps echoing hollow upon the uncarpeted floorboards, I pass into the small side room where the old man kept his most precious volumes, most of which are now in Sir Francis's coach on their way to his house in Upper Brook Street.

The reading desk upon which Altin reverently displayed one of his prized erotic volumes to Charlie and myself a year ago stands alone in the middle of the room waiting, like the bookshelves in the next room and various other pieces of furniture throughout the house, to be collected by carriers' carts and transported to their new owners.

Not all the contents of the house are gone. I instructed Jem Bennett to bid for certain items which will be adequate to meet my needs as the new tenant. A few chairs and a table, some upholstered furniture for the parlour, beds for myself, Charlie and perhaps a guest, together with various necessary utensils sufficient for a basic bachelor life.

That is all I shall require. For the time being, Charlie and I shall be the only residents and during the next few weeks we shall be spending our time exploring our new abode, finding tradesmen to remedy the dilapidation of neglect, and women to scrub away years of accumulated dust and grime. Then we may turn our thoughts to refurbishing with decoration, carpets, curtains and additional items of furniture more to our taste.

I hear footsteps in the adjoining room and Jem appears at the door.

'All done,' says he, cheerily. 'I'll draw up all necessary documents in the next couple of days and then the business will be done.'

'I sincerely hope it will not be the last business I put your way, Jem. You have been a good friend to me.'

'Not nearly so good as you have been to me, Will,' he replies. 'Without you and Master Raphael, I would be a humble clerk still, scribbling away in some draughty office.'

'Instead of which you are well on your way to becoming a fully-fledged lawyer. Believe me, Jem, it is your own ability and not Raphael Elias's patronage, nor mine, that is the key to your success.'

'You are too kind, Will. Now is there anything more I can do for you, or have you finished with my services for the present?'

'There is one thing, Jem,' say I. 'I intend to spend the night here tonight, spartan as it is. But first I would rid it of the staleness and mustiness of disuse. Before you go, help me open each and every window so that a fresh breeze may blow through what is now my new home!'

New Beginnings

'What, you really mean it? A room of my own?'

'Yes, your very own, Charlie. And a proper bed, too.'

The last thing I expect is for his face to crumple and for him to awkwardly wipe the back of his hand across his eyes to prevent me seeing the unseemly wetness that wells up, unbidden.

The weakness is momentary.

'About time, too,' he retorts impudently. 'I've had enough of your snoring and your farting, your playing with yourself under the covers and disturbing me in the middle of the night getting up to piss.'

'Good,' say I, laughing. 'Well now you can do all those things for yourself in solitary splendour, and with your own pot to piss in. But just in case you miss me, I'm only in the room next door.'

We are standing in one of the bedrooms on the first floor of 20 Soho Square. I have brought Charlie to show him around my new acquisition and told him I'd like him to come here to live with me. If he wants to, that is.

'But if you don't want to, you can always stay at Sir Francis's as scullion and pot boy. Bed down by the kitchen range and have Mrs Wiggins on your back night and day.'

He pretends to consider. 'Yeah, well – 's a hard choice, but – for your sake, mind – I s'pose I could do you the favour o' movin' in 'ere with you.'

That settled, he demands to be shown the rest of the house, scampering from room to room like an excited puppy. For all he is nearly eighteen, the signs of true manhood beginning at last to bulk out his skinny frame, he is still a boy at heart, by turns awkward, mopish or exuberant.

Later, as we sit on the dusty settee in the downstairs parlour, he asks, 'How're you goin' to explain this to Mr Garrick – and to Susan? *I* knows 'ow you're a man o' property, 'cos I was wiv you in Yorkshire when all the business o' your dead pa's fortune was discovered. An' you swore me to secrecy, an' which I never said no word to no-one since. But Susan and Mrs Wiggins and Mr Garrick, far's they know, you ain't got a penny.'

'I shall tell them the truth – or part of the truth – that my grandfather left me enough money to buy an inexpensive house with sufficient left over for a modest income.'

'You're a sly one, Will, an' no mistake,' he grins. 'An' what about Susan and Mrs W? They comin' to live 'ere, too?'

'I haven't asked them yet. I'm not sure I can afford – or even need – a whole household. Like you, I'm so used to being a servant, I'm not sure I can play the gentleman just yet.'

'Yeah, well you might not get the chance. I can save you the bother o' askin' 'em, 'cos far as I can see, the answer'll be no.'

'Oh,' say I, rather taken aback. 'And why is that?'

'Mrs Wiggins and Sir Francis, they's so satisfied wi' each other – she's got a fine kitchen to work in, and 'e's got a cook what cooks to 'is taste an' is 'appy to prepare banquets for 'is friends – that she won't want to go and 'e won't want to let 'er. I 'eard 'er sayin' to Susan only the other day as 'ow she couldn't see 'erself goin' back to Mr Garrick when – or if - 'e ever comes back. So it's not likely she'll up sticks for you.'

'Yes, I can quite understand that. I don't think I would, if I were in her place. And I suppose, in that case, she wouldn't want to let Susan go either.'

'Yeah, but it's not Mrs Wiggins wot'll keep Susan there, is it?' says Charlie mysteriously.

'What do you mean?'

' 'Ow long you bin away?'

'Three months or so. What of it?'

'A lot can 'appen in three months. I knows as 'ow you and 'er were – you know,' says he with a leer. 'Nay, don't deny it, I seen and 'eard the two of you often enough.'

'It was nothing serious,' I reply, reddening.

'Aye, well it certainly ain't serious now, 'cos she's got 'erself a man-friend,' he states with an air of triumph.

I can't hide my surprise - nor a slight sense of disappointment. 'A man-friend? Surely you can't mean Robbie or Jamie?'

'Nah!' says he scornfully. 'We both know they're not interested in Susan, nor any other woman neither. No, 'e's a second footman at the 'ouse of one of Sir Francis's friends and 'is name is Joseph. Walks out together every Sunday, they does, these last few weeks, 'im and Susan.'

'Well, I'm very happy for them,' I say unconvincingly. Despite myself, I can't help feeling a tiny bit jealous.

Our kitchen-maid, Susan, has been part of my master's household from when he lodged near the theatre in Goodmans Fields, then when we shared a house with Mr Macklin and Mistress Peg in Bow Street, and latterly at Sir Francis Courtney's mansion in Upper Brook Street after the quarrel with Macklin. She has always proved a willing entertainer of my little soldier whenever he felt the urge for action. Many a stirring skirmish we have enjoyed together over the past five years. But now, it seems, that must be a thing of the past and he must be decommissioned, in that particular theatre of combat at least.

* * *

Over the next few weeks, however, Susan is happy enough to play her part in helping Charlie and me transform 20 Soho Square from a house into a home. Whilst I seek out tradesmen to patch and mend and apply fresh paint, she finds a woman to help her brush the walls and ceilings free of cobwebs and scrub the floors after the workmen have finished.

She also introduces me to Joseph, a pleasant, though unremarkable looking young man with mousy brown hair and little conversation. His devotion is plain from his foolish grin and adoring gaze whenever he is in her company, but I cannot, for the life of me, see what Susan sees in him.

Charlie sums it up quite pithily. 'You've only yourself to blame, Will, forever gadding. Happen she craves a lapdog 'stead of a roving tyke.'

By mid-April most of the work is done.

Which is fortunate, for it is then that a summons arrives from Sir William Hervey.

It is about fifteen months since I have heard from Hervey, the unacknowledged Head of His Majesty's secret service, and I had begun to wonder if he no longer required my services.

Whether that made me feel relieved or disappointed is

hard to say. Reluctant as I was when first compelled to work for him, I have since had to admit to myself that I quite enjoy the subterfuge and danger that working for him brings.

The request to attend him at Westminster, therefore, arouses mixed emotions.

Do I want to be wrenched out of my new-found security into uncertainty and possible peril?

But, knowing Hervey, do I really have a choice?

The opening of our meeting is not auspicious.

Without preamble, Hervey begins, 'I told you at our last meeting to postpone any plans you might have for purchasing a property in town, Master Archer. Yet I am informed that you have taken a lease upon a house in Soho Square.'

'With respect, Sir William, I believe it was a *request,* not an *order.'*

His chin comes up and his face becomes stony. I am on dangerous ground in contradicting him. But, despite the sweat beading beneath my collar, I plough on.

'Also, since that meeting a year last January, you have not contacted me to be of service. In addition to which, there have been several changes in my personal circumstances. Many notable things have happened.'

'Aye, an invasion of our country to name but one,' he

retorts testily.

This is typical of Hervey. He has little interest in the personal circumstances of those in his employ, unless they may be used to his own advantage. Which is how I first came to be recruited as one of his agents. I was in danger of being accused of a murder I did not commit and he extricated me, putting me both in his debt and his power.

Now, seeing his attention diverted from my supposed lapse in seeking a life of my own to a matter of national peril, I grasp the opportunity to keep it there.

'The Young Pretender?' I ask. 'I thought he had been driven back to Scotland?'

'*Retreated,* aye. But not before his army advanced within three day's march of London, with no opposition to speak of. 'Tis pure luck they decided to turn back at Derby.'

'I own, Sir William, that I am mainly ignorant of these matters,' say I, continuing to deflect his anger from my own affairs. 'Are you not satisfied that the Government is taking every measure to defeat the Jacobite rebels?'

'Whether I am satisfied or not is hardly relevant, Master Archer. My job is to look to the safety of our country, a task which I have been pursuing with the utmost diligence since I received news that Charles Edward Stuart landed in Scotland last July. For months past, my agents have been sending messages that the Jacobite army presents a real threat. Messages that have, till now, gone largely unheeded in Westminster. More concerned with factions within their own ranks, our masters seem to regard it as no more than a minor uprising by a rag-tag rabble of wild Highlanders in some remote region which is of little concern to us here in London.'

'I would have thought Mr Fielding's article in *The True Patriot* would have had some effect?'

He gives a scornful laugh. 'Aye, for a day or two, perhaps. But Henry Fielding is a writer of fiction, which is his downfall. He tends to over-dramatise.'

'Surely the fact that the Jacobite army advanced so far into England...?'

'Aye, that was a shock, certainly. And at least it has spurred Parliament into something like action. The Duke of Cumberland has been called back from Flanders to pursue the rebels back to Scotland and put an end to the uprising. He intends to gather his forces at a location near Inverness to confront the Jacobite army for what he is confident will prove to be a decisive encounter.'

'I have no doubt he will prevail, Sir William. The Duke is a fine soldier, sir. A man of courage and humanity, as I have had occasion to see for myself.'

(The occasion being the Battle of Dettingen two years since, where I unwittingly found myself after being abducted and pressed into the army by an unknown enemy who bears me a grudge. I remember the Duke, King George's favourite son, as a handsome and gallant commander of his forces.)

'Is that why you have called me here today, Sir William? Do you want me join the Duke's forces? I cannot see how my presence could be of any advantage in such momentous matters,' I say in puzzlement.

'You are right, Master Archer. You would be of no use whatsoever in the forthcoming battle. Especially as you have just proved yourself incapable of obeying even the simplest of commands.'

Am I now finally to be upbraided for my supposed fault in buying my house and my temerity in challenging him?

His tone is irritable but, catching a quickly suppressed half-smile, I dare to hope that my transgression has been forgiven. Hervey may not like being contradicted, but he admires spirit and, as he often points out, he and I are fellow Yorkshiremen and take pride in speaking directly.

No harm, however, in expressing willingness. 'In what way do you require my services, then, Sir William?'

'Two weeks ago, Alexander Ross, a cousin of Mr Duncan Forbes, Lord President of the Court of Session in Edinburgh, was murdered at his London residence. He was found by his butler in his study, shot through the head.'

'Ross – that's a Scottish name, is it not? Was he a Jacobite, Sir William? There has been much violence against suspected Jacobites of late.'

'I do not know. In fact, I doubt if anyone knows. Ross, it seems, was noteworthy only for his total lack of noteworthiness. A man of little character and no opinions. In short, a totally unremarkable man.'

'How comes it, then, that his death is of concern to yourself, Sir William? Surely it is a matter for the local Watch, or perhaps Mr Fielding's new force at Bow Street?'

'In the normal run of things, yes,' replies Hervey. 'But his cousin – the said Mr Forbes, Lord President of the Court of Session – is a staunch supporter of His Hanoverian Majesty and a valuable ally and source of information to the Government. Two days ago I received a letter from that gentleman in which he drew my attention to another of his relatives – a Mr Robert Ross – who was recently killed, apparently in a drunken brawl, at Derby during the time of the Jacobite occupation of that city.'

'Two sudden deaths in the family within as many months, that is unfortunate,' I say, sympathetically.

'But that is not all. Mr Forbes also informed me that another cousin, David, had been found dead in Manchester only the previous month – coincidentally at the time when the Jacobite army took over that town. Two deaths, as you say, Will, may be counted unfortunate, but three – especially of respectable citizens none of whom was a military man - looks like villainy.'

'Villainy which – despite what you said about the gentleman in London - might have a Jacobite connection? The other two deaths occurred in towns occupied by the rebel army at the time. Could someone loyal to the Young Pretender be trying to make Mr Forbes waver in his allegiance to King George?'

'That is a possibility, which is why I have given my word to Mr Forbes that I shall investigate. He is too valuable an ally of the Government to lose.'

'Have you inquired into the most recent killing, sir, the one in London?'

'Mr Alexander Ross, yes. His butler found the body.'

'And has the butler any inkling of who might have done it?'

'Oh yes. Unfortunately it was his night off, the night his master was murdered. But the footman who was on duty in his place gave a clear description. One which matches in every particular with a Mr Andrew Ogilvie.'

'Is this Mr Ogilvie known to show allegiance to the Jacobite cause?'

Hervey gives a curt laugh. 'Andrew Ogilvie's only allegiance is to the pursuit of his own pleasure. He is a long-standing friend of the family. And, more pertinently, Mrs Ross's alleged lover.'

'Then it would appear to be a clear case of jealousy, surely? Has Mr Ogilvie been arrested?'

'He has and, accused by the local Watch, been thrown in gaol to await trial. But there is a problem,' says Hervey, clearly enjoying the moment. 'He cannot have murdered Alexander Ross because at the time of the murder, Mr Andrew Ogilvie was dining with me.'

New Role

Jem Bennett comes to view progress upon the house in Soho Square that same afternoon.

I have just returned from my meeting with Sir William Hervey who has set me the task of inquiring into the circumstances of the two deaths that happened out of town. In view of the current political unrest, I shall be required to work incognito.

He has devised a plan whereby I shall travel north in the guise of a farmer who, suspected of Jacobite sympathies, has had his farmhouse looted and burned and his livestock confiscated by Government troops. A state of affairs which has unfortunately become all too common over the past year as rivalries have become inflamed and summary justice has been dealt out by troops on both sides of the conflict.

Thus allegedly cast adrift, I am to pursue a route via Derby where Robert Ross was killed, and Manchester where David Ross met his end and gather what information I can.

'And for greater credence,' Hervey suggests, 'it might help if you were to have 'relatives' with you. I have another agent in mind to accompany you, but more of that anon. In the meantime, I have arranged for a horse and covered wagon together with all the wherewithal and chattels a man might salvage in such circumstances.'

'The journey is imminent, then?' I say, unable to hide my dismay. 'But what of my house, and what of Charlie?'

'As for your house, I warned you a year ago that I would probably have need of you, and advised you against putting down roots. You must make what arrangements you can, but in these parlous times, I would not recommend leaving your new house empty,' says Hervey with little sympathy. Then, in a more placatory tone, 'As for young Master Stubbs, I seem to remember he is a lad of some mettle. If his discretion can be guaranteed, I have no objection to his travelling with you. The presence of another supposed family member - a younger brother, say - would add plausibility to your disguise.'

All the way back from Westminster to Soho Square, I am revolving ideas about what I can do to safeguard my newly purchased property during my absence. And debating with myself whether I want to involve Charlie in such a potentially dangerous escapade .

Upon arriving at Soho Square, I find him entertaining Jem in our sparsely furnished parlour and for the moment, all other considerations are temporarily set aside, for Jem is eager to see what improvements we have made.

Having handed over all the remaining documents, fully

signed and sealed, relating to the purchase, he accompanies us on a tour of the house, with many expressions of admiration and delight at the work that has been done.

Tactfully, he makes no reference to the sparseness of the furnishing, nor to the rooms that still remain empty. And, when we return to our humble parlour, he accepts the offer of a dish of tea.

I first met Jem, then only a humble clerk, in my quest to find Raphael Elias, the son of a city financier. Whenever his meagre wage allowed, he liked to go to the theatre and it was my connections with Mr Garrick and that life that I believe proved instrumental in his willingness to provide me with information.

Since then we have become friends and, with a grateful Raphael Elias and myself as his sponsors, he has begun training to be a fully-fledged lawyer – as well as being able to indulge more freely his interest in the theatre.

'Have you heard aught of Mr Garrick recently, Will?' he asks, once we are settled. 'The News- sheets are so full of the rebellion that there is scarce a paragraph to deal with more pleasant topics. He is recently gone to Ireland, I believe?'

'Aye, I had a letter from him a week ago. He was staying with family and friends at Lichfield, but then Mr Sheridan invited him to play at Smock Alley again, and with matters as they are at Drury Lane, I think he was glad of the chance to escape,' I say with a wry smile. 'You know that Mr Fleetwood, the manager of Drury Lane, has gone into partnership with Mr Lacy, and that the two of them are up to their necks in debt to pay off bankers who have bought the lease? My master despairs of things ever being resolved at Drury Lane whilst Fleetwood is still in charge.'

'The quality of performance has certainly suffered in Mr Garrick's absence,' says Jem. 'I went to see a play by Mr Macklin there in January. The rumours and alarms of the last few months have occasioned a renewed wave of patriotic plays, mainly about the last Pretender to the throne, Perkin Warbeck. Goodman's Fields, Covent Garden, the New Haymarket – all revived old plays on the subject. But Mr Macklin decided to write a new one, *The Popish Imposter*. A Poetic Tragedy, if you please, but 'twas more like a farce! It was terrible!'

'You were there?'

'To my dismay!' he replies with a grimace.

'It was really that bad?'

He laughs at the memory. 'Early in the first act, the King knighted a messenger who brought good news. And every subsequent messenger who arrived, the galleries called out "Knight him! Knight him!" And then there was Mistress Woffington...'

'Peg? In a tragedy? But she is a comic actress...?'

'And so she proved,' continues Jem. 'She played Perkin Warbeck's wife and, to help him escape, she changed clothes with him...'

'Aye,' I interject, 'she loves a breeches part!'

'...and was captured in his stead. When the soldiers guarding her started arguing about the reward, it ended in a quarrel where they drove each other off the stage, leaving her unguarded. Some wag from the gallery shouted, "Run away, Peg, run away!" and of course the whole house collapsed in laughter, including Mrs Peg! She was giggling so helplessly that she had to lean against the proscenium arch for several minutes before the play could recommence.'

'Not a success, then?'

'Mr Macklin may be able to act, but he's certainly no writer – not for tragedy at least! I think the play was taken off after the second night because they didn't get an audience – at least not an audience they wanted!'

'That wouldn't have done much for the theatre's finances. Mr Fleetwood and Mr Lacy would not have been pleased. But I am surprised they are having aught to do with Mr Macklin,' I say with some bewilderment. 'After last year's walkout, they refused to have him back, yet here they are presenting a play by him!'

'A legal quibble, I think,' says Jem good-humouredly.

'They would not have Macklin the actor, but they allow Macklin the playwright! I hear tell that another of his creations – an acknowledged farce this time – is to be staged later this month.'

'Mr Fleetwood must be desperate to get money in whatever way he can.'

'Yes,' says Jem with a mischievous grin. 'Since I started studying the law it is salutary to observe how often cupidity may overcome principle.'

'One thing Mr Garrick cannot be accused of.'

'How long intends he to stay in Ireland?' ask Jem. 'He is sorely missed here in London.'

'He said in his letter that he hopes to be back next month at the latest, and in much better health. He has been very unwell of late. The Drury Lane business and the Jacobite rising exercised him greatly. I am told he even wrote offering to serve in His Majesty's forces against the rebels, but his friends persuaded him that his talents would be much better directed to saving the theatre than in engaging with a Highland mob.'

'You will be glad to see him, I'll wager,' says Jem.

'Aye, if I am here. Business calls me away within the next few days and I know not when I may be back.'

'What?' exclaims Charlie who has remained uncharacteristically quiet during our conversation. 'Going away? You never told me nothin' 'bout that!'

With a fleeting glance at the look of indignation on Charlie's face, Jem rises from his seat. 'I think I had better take my leave,' says he tactfully. 'Clearly you and Master Stubbs have matters to discuss'

At the front door, he pauses and takes my arm. 'I am already enough of a lawyer not to inquire as to the purpose of your trip, Will, nor do I wish to know. But am I right in supposing it may have more to do with a certain eminent person's business than with your own?'

'No need for lawyerly delicacy, Jem,' I say. 'You know, from my involvement in the Elias case, that I work for Sir William Hervey. I appreciate your tact but, yes, it is at his behest, and, yes, there may be some danger involved.'

'You may rely on my discretion as your lawyer, Will, but as your friend I urge you, most sincerely, to be careful.'

'Thank you, Jem,' I say. 'And I shall be most grateful if you, as both my lawyer and my friend, would keep an eye upon my affairs here whilst I am away, especially as regards the safety of my house. I would be very loth to lose what I have so recently acquired.'

'Of course I shall, Will,' he replies heartily. 'Have you plans for what should happen to it during your absence?'

'I have given the subject some thought, but have as yet reached no firm conclusion. You may be assured you will be the first to know when I do.'

Then, with yet another heartfelt exhortation for me to proceed with caution, Jem takes his leave.

Charlie's disgruntlement at not being informed of my impending journey is only slightly appeased when I tell him I myself only learned of it this morning. But it vanishes entirely when I tell him that he may be able to come with me.

As soon as I tell him the purpose of the journey – to inquire covertly into the deaths of David and Robert Ross – he is full of ideas as to how he can use his skills in housebreaking and eavesdropping to accomplish it.

I interrupt his eagerness. 'This is no game, Charlie. There will be no place for japes or roguery.'

'You think I don't know that? I've seen what it's been like these past weeks here in the city. You can't turn a corner without seeing a soldier, or groups of volunteers practising to be soldiers. The nobs and swells 'ave taken fright, shuttin' up their houses in town and lighting off to their country estates. And it's still goin' on, even now the rebels 'ave turned back.'

'Aye, and 'tis worse in the country – while I was in Yorkshire, folks were scouring the papers every day for fear the Rebels might be coming our way. Folks feared for their property, for their very lives. Fortunately, we escaped it – the Pretender chose to march down through Lancashire rather than Yorkshire, but there were tales and rumours of all sorts of horrors and cruelties.'

'Yeah, but most of them ain't true, I'll lay – roastin' infants on spits! Surely not even them Highland savages would do that?'

'Perhaps not. All the same, we'll need to be cautious, Charlie. If you are to come with me, there must be no careless words or rash actions. In times like these, feelings run high and violence can flare in a second.' I see that he has gone quiet, shaken by my unaccustomed seriousness. 'The last thing I want is to put you in danger, Charlie. I'll quite understand if you tell me you don't want to go.'

'What, and miss all the excitement? Anyway, you'll need someone to watch your back, won't you?'

And so it is settled: Charlie shall play the part of my younger brother and we shall be two outcasts from the misfortunes of war, set on the road to seek whatever chance we may.

In the meantime, I have preparations to make.

First, I dispatch Charlie to Upper Brook Street with a message to Susan. Then, once he has gone, I set down to write a letter to my master in Dublin.

My Dear Mr Garrick, I write. Then, after the usual

pleasantries of asking after his health and how the season in Dublin is going, I broach my main purpose.

Mindful of your past kindness to me, I now have the good fortune to find myself in a position to repay you in some small measure.

You told me that you are like to return to London within the next few weeks and since matters between you and Mr Macklin are not yet settled and knowing that you are reluctant to impose upon Sir Francis's hospitality again, I presume that you do not have a place to stay. If that is indeed the case, I would be honoured if you would regard my newly purchased house in Soho Square as your residence for as long as you may need it.

Since you have provided a home for me all these years, it is only fitting that I should return the favour. I, alas, am called away on business for I know not how long. Should you accept my offer, you must regard my house as your own for the duration of your stay.

Then, after giving him the address at which he may find Jem Bennett who will act as my agent during my absence, I sign off with all good wishes.

When Charlie returns, I send him off again to the Post with instructions to send the letter via the Holyhead Mail Coach and thence to Mr Garrick at the Smock Alley Theatre in Dublin. Not knowing exactly how much it will cost, I give Charlie a silver florin which should more than cover it.

Later that evening, Susan and her new swain, Joseph, arrive in response to my earlier message.

Over pies and small beer ordered in for the occasion, I put my proposition to them.

'How would the pair of you regard the idea of acting as concierges here whilst I'm away?'

Susan gives me a quizzical look. Joseph merely looks blank.

'You're going away again?' asks Susan.

'Aye, and probably for some time,' I reply.

'And I'm going with 'im,' adds Charlie proudly.

'What, after all we've done to this place?' says Susan disbelievingly.

'Unfortunately so – which is why I'm making you this offer. I'm sure none of us wish all our efforts to go to waste, or worse to be spoilt by cracksmen and sneak thieves.'

' 'Twould be a shame, that's for certain,' says Susan, 'but what exactly do you want Joe and me to do? We both 'as jobs, remember.'

'I appreciate that. I don't know how far Joseph's responsibilities stretch, but I've lived with you long enough, Susan, to know that you're usually done by nine at night. Sir Francis dines early and Mrs Wiggins is snoring by ten. It would only require the pair of you to sleep here overnight. You can easily be back at your posts by morning.'

I see the dawning of possibility in Joseph's eyes. 'What, all night? Every night? Just the two of us?'

'Don't you be gettin' ideas, Joseph Hall!' snaps Susan.

'Oh - and there is one more thing...,' I continue.

'Ah, I knew there'd be a catch,' says Susan.

'Not really,' I say. 'It's just that I've suggested to Mr Garrick that he could take up residence once he returns to London. It would be nice if you could see to his needs if possible? You might cook him a meal from time to time, Susan. And Joseph might act as valet occasionally. '

'Will he pay?' asks Joseph, his eyes lighting up.

I begin to see Susan's love-sick swain in a new light. He clearly has an eye for his personal advantage!

'I'm sure he would express his gratitude for any help you could give him,' I reply. 'But I'm prepared to give you both a small allowance for your co-operation.'

'You're the money-bags all of a sudden?' asks Susan suspiciously.

'Hardly that,' I say diffidently. 'As you know, my grandfather left me enough to buy this house and a bit left over. I see no harm in sharing my good fortune with my friends.'

And so it is arranged that Susan and Joseph will look

after my house in my absence, that Jem will pay them each month and that they will make themselves available to Mr Garrick, should he take up my offer when he returns.

The Bell

Next morning, Charlie and I, dressed in our most well-worn clothes to suggest our supposed decline in fortune, and carrying only the barest of possessions, set out for the old Bell Inn at Edmonton, four or five miles north of the city, where Hervey has told us a horse-drawn wagon awaits us.

It is a fine, bright morning which does much to lift our spirits for the journey ahead, though it is not without a sense of sadness that I lock the door of 20 Soho Square and place the key in a small crevice beneath a chipped coping stone whence Susan will retrieve it later.

It takes us a good three hours to cover the distance, city streets gradually giving way to the country high road bordered by fields and eventually the scattered dwellings of Edmonton. By the time we arrive at The Bell in the main street, we are more than ready to sample its ale.

The inn is a scene of activity at this hour. Porters carrying luggage and ostlers leading horses out in preparation for the imminent arrival of the noonday stagecoach.

Charlie and I are sufficiently nondescript in our attire to pass unnoticed and we are content to merge into the background until the hubbub subsides. Ordering a jug of porter, we sit outside in the shade of a venerable old oak tree and watch the stagecoach arrive, throwing up flurries of dust as it draws up before the inn.

The landlord bustles out to welcome those passengers who are alighting here and to persuade those who are not to take some refreshment whilst the horses are changed. A picture of congeniality and good cheer with his rotund belly and apron tied up round his ample waist. Yet with an eye, no doubt, for those passengers whose purses might prove the deepest. He takes great pains to escort a well-dressed lady into the inn with great ceremony whilst paying scant regard to a dusty, black-clad clergyman who, unable to catch the eye of a porter, resignedly shoulders his battered portmanteau himself and trudges into the inn .

Charlie and I make our strong beer last, sipping it slowly as we watch the four fatigued horses being unharnessed and led away to the stables whilst fresh animals are hitched up. We observe how the care with which the porters unstrap and carry the cases and boxes whilst the owners look on, becomes considerably more cavalier once the owners have gone indoors, tossing them recklessly to one another with careless whoops and cries.

At length, new horses harnessed, fresh luggage stowed, the coachmen eased and the passengers aboard, the coach rumbles off on the next stage of its journey. As the noise of its departure subsides, quiet descends, broken only by returning birdsong and the distant lowing of cattle in the fields.

The weariness of our long walk and the soporific effect of the beer have set Charlie nodding.

'Rouse yourself, sleepyhead,' I say, nudging him to his feet. 'Time to ask after our own transport.'

The oak-panelled entrance hall is dim after the bright sunlight outside, despite the roaring fire which burns beneath a stone chimney breast, throwing out an oppressive heat.

Walking through into the deserted dining room, I waylay a passing waiter and ask where I may find the landlord. As he hurries off, he bids us return to the main hall where he promises his master will attend us directly.

Our host's notion of 'directly' is clearly flexible, for we kick our heels for a good quarter of an hour before the gentleman appears, gives us an appraising glare as demands in surly manner that we state our business. Gone is the cordiality afforded to his recent guests. The shabby pair before him obviously do not merit his attention, let alone civility.

'I was told you have a horse and cart for us to collect.'

'Out the back, next to the stable block. You'll find everything there. Just take it.'

His brusqueness surprises me. 'Is that all?' I ask.

'Why, what more would you have? My orders were to keep it safe until someone should collect it. And now you're arrived. The beast has been fed, the cart is loaded. My part of the bargain is done.'

He turns on his heel. 'You'll find it through that door there. Good day to you.'

'A right charmer, to be sure,' says Charlie as the landlord disappears.

'Clearly he does not think us worth charming,' I say as we go through the door indicated and find ourselves in the back yard of the inn.

Ahead of us is the stable block where ostlers are tending to the weary coach-horses, rubbing them down and feeding them for their brief respite before the next coach arrives and they are pressed into service once more.

In a paddock to the side of the building stands a rickety looking farm cart with a makeshift canopy of tattered canvas. Browsing on the sparse grass next to it is a jaded old nag.

'That is supposed to get us half way across the country? We've given up Soho Square for this?' I sigh, incredulously.

But Charlie is already beside the hollow ribbed beast, stroking its grey-flecked muzzle. I had almost forgotten his fondness for horses – apparently of any age or decrepitude!

An interest first sparked several years ago when I brought home a mare on which I'd accompanied Hervey for the first time in pursuit of a villain.

During our time at Upper Brook Street, Charlie spent much of his time with Sir Francis's coachman, James, in the mews. And now here he is carefully guiding this old animal between the shafts of the wagon which is to be our home over the next weeks.

It is as I am watching the tenderness with which he treats the animal that I hear a voice next to me.

'The lad seems to have taken to the poor hack, Will. Which is all to the good as neither of us, I think, would show such care.'

I turn, with a start of amazement at the unexpected, familiar voice.

So this is the other agent whom Hervey said would accompany us.

Agnes Mayer!

A New Family

Agnes Mayer – the woman who four years ago tricked me, leaving me unconscious in the same room as a dead man, intending that I should be accused of his murder.

Agnes Mayer – the woman who fled to the Netherlands, yet sent me a letter apologising for her deceit. A letter which encouraged me to believe that the affection I thought we had shared might, despite her betrayal, have some substance.

Agnes Mayer – whom I encountered again two years later in Ostend, after I'd been press-ganged into the army and who revealed that she, too, had been recruited by Hervey.

And who, over the succeeding few months, proved that my feelings for her were well-founded - and reciprocated in equal measure.

But Hervey, who had brought us together as fellow agents on that occasion, also cruelly separated us as lovers once our task in Flanders was done. I was called back to England. But she was required to remain abroad.

That was two years ago and there has been no communication between us since. Now she stands before me once again. Not this time in the silks and satins of a well-bred lady, nor with the advantages of rouge or carefully coiffed hair to enhance her beauty – but as a dishevelled, plain-clad housewife.

Sir William Hervey who, whether we like it or not, controls our destinies, has chosen to put us together once more.

A simple pragmatic solution on his part, I'm sure, reasoning, no doubt, that our previous attachment will render the pretence of being man and wife more believable. Our emotions, as our physical selves, to be used when expedient to the circumstances.

Now as we face each other on this fine Spring morning, those emotions are at war within me. My first impulse is to clasp her to my bosom, but the restraint of our time apart intervenes. I see that she, too, is hesitant.

Our long separation vies with memories of nights spent in each others' arms and we stand tongue-tied, two erstwhile lovers meeting as strangers.

She is the first to speak.

'It is good to see you again, Will. I thought this day might never come, and I never imagined 'twould be in such circumstances or in so unflattering a guise for both of us. But what our master Sir William decrees, we must obey.' She laughs irreverently, showing she appreciates the irony of the situation. 'He seems to think we would make a passable married couple. And whom he has chosen to join in matrimony, we cannot seek to put asunder. What say you, Master Archer, it is droll , is it not?'

'I hardly think it droll, Miss Mayer. Rather a proof of Sir William's ruthless lack of delicacy,' I reply. Then, covering my discomfiture with the same self-mockery that she is employing, 'But I am willing to make a fist of it, if you are.'

'We are agreed, then,' says she, hitching up the coarse fustian of her skirt like a true farmer's wife preparing to plod over the furrows. 'You shall be Hodge and I your greasy Joan.' Then her eye lights on Charlie. 'And who, pray, is the young man presently tending to our trusty steed?'

I call Charlie across and, once all introductions are done, we investigate the contents of the wagon. They are little enough, to be sure. Some blankets, a couple of pots and pans, a motley selection of cutlery and tankards. Things necessary for survival, supposedly salvaged from a destroyed household.

Together, we settle upon our plan of action. We shall assume the characters, and henceforth address each other as Seth Hodges, his wife Joan and younger brother Reuben (names agreed on in response to Agnes's initial jest).

Our story shall be that, rendered homeless by the fortunes of war and having sold any items of value, our sole remaining possessions, apart from the pitiful contents of the cart, are the clothes we stand up in - and whatever pride and dignity remains to us.

Thus resolved, we all three mount upon the coarse wooden plank which serves as a seat at the front of the cart and, with a flick of the reins, I spur our superannuated carthorse into a sluggardly saunter.

It takes us the best part of a week to cover the distance between London and Derby. This is because we are obliged to wend our meandering way among country lanes which at times are little better than rutted cart-tracks - forced by our assumed poverty to avoid paying the tolls upon turnpike roads which would otherwise have made our journey easier.

Added to which, our worn-out nag – which Agnes has christened Rosinante, after Don Quixote's broken down charger – seems to have but one speed, which is hardly better than walking pace.

Indeed, along some of the worst stretches, we all three have to dismount to lighten the load whilst Charlie who, unsurprisingly, has taken upon himself the role of ostler, leads her patiently between the holes and furrows.

It is during these times that Agnes and I often walk on ahead and are able to apprise each other of all that has happened to each of us since we parted. And over the course of these conversations, we gradually regain much of the easiness that we once shared.

This does not go unnoticed by Charlie. On the third morning, whilst Agnes is haggling over over a scrawny chicken and a few vegetables at a market stall in one of the villages upon our route, he turns to me.

'You and 'er,' says he with sideways inclination of his head in Agnes's direction, 'are you – you know...?'

'We were acquainted before, yes.'

'More than just *acquainted,* I reckon,' says he with a licentious grin. 'You and she – when you was away in Flanders all that time - did you...?'

'None of your business, Charlie,' I reply. 'But, yes, we became close. And, once this business is finished, I have hopes that we may become closer still.'

'*Finished?'* he exclaims. 'Lord, we ain't but *started* yet! There could be a whole heap of trouble before you thinks o' settlin' down into domestic bliss.' With a quick glance to each side, he sidles closer and lowers his voice. 'One man to another...' he ignores my raised eyebrow '...I knows as 'ow three's a crowd, so if the two of you, you know...' he taps the side of his nose significantly '...I can play deaf and blind, alright?'

I regard him in silence for a moment, then with a voice heavy with sarcasm, I say, 'Well that's very thoughtful of you, Charlie, but the only thing you're required to play at the moment is the part of my younger brother, Reuben Hodges, and to do that successfully neither deafness nor blindness are likely to be of much avail. We all three will need all our wits about us.'

He holds up his hands, 'Fair enough, *brother.*'Twas just a thought, that's all.' Then, abandoning all pretence at delicacy, 'Just that I'd be just as 'appy beddin' down next to Rosinante if you two wanted to play nug-a-nug in the cart together...'

'Why, you...!'

It is just as he is ducking out of range of my upraised hand that Agnes returns with the results of her haggling.

'What's this?' she cries. 'At fisticuffs? Why, what's amiss?'

'Naught of consequence,' I reply. 'A slight mis-understanding, nothing to worry your head about.'

'Aye,' adds Charlie with a mischievous grin, 'seems I got 'old of the wrong end o' the stick 'bout 'ow Will wants some *little thing* 'andled. But 'tis all sorted now. 'S that our supper you got there, Miss – sorry, *Sister Joan*?'

Early in the afternoon of the seventh day since our departure from London, we come within sight of the town of Derby. Our customary snail's pace has become even slower since we reached the peaks of Derbyshire. The landscape is rugged, wild and inhospitable. The few inhabitants we encounter in the small hamlets and isolated dwellings are unfriendly or openly hostile. Such suspicion is understandable, I suppose, given that it is only a few months since rival armies passed this way.

The town of Derby lies in a valley bottom upon the banks of the River Derwent. The tumbling weir on our left as we cross the many-arched bridge into the town, testifies to the power of the stream, the water churning and boiling with a white spume as it hurtles over the edge.

Just beyond the weir is a huge building, five storeys high, a solid square structure built of red brick from whose subterranean depths issues a thunderous, thumping roar of creaking wood and splashing water.

'It must be a mill. That sounds like a waterwheel,' says Agnes. 'Perhaps we can make a show of enquiring about the possibility of employment and thereby learn something of the town.'

Her suggestion, however, proves unnecessary for hardly have we turned off the bridge than a hurrying woman, carrying a skinny child in her arms, runs straight out of a side alley and almost collides with Rosinante. The startled beast emits a whinny of alarm and jinks sideways, almost oversetting our cart.

Charlie leaps down to calm the frighted horse and Agnes

quickly follows to tend to the woman who, knocked off balance by the impact, has fallen, sprawling, upon the rough cobbles.

The child, a mere parcel of skin and bones and pale as death, lies whimpering and groaning, clutching his hand, which I now see is covered in blood and horribly mangled.

I clamber down to assist Agnes in righting the distressed woman who is full of apologies for her clumsiness. But, seeing that we are as poorly dressed as she, her contrition turns swiftly to reproach.

Agnes, however, is on her knees beside the mewling child, gently easing his mutilated limb from the grasp of his remaining grubby hand. 'Water,' she demands, 'this wound needs cleaning.'

I grab one of the pans from the cart and hurry to the weir, leaning out to catch the water at its cleanest as it surges over the edge.

When I return, the woman, mollified by Agnes's concern and calm efficiency, is explaining how the hurt occurred.

'Caught 'is fingers in the bobbins, a-knottin' of the threads. 'Tis dangerous work and 'e weren't nimble enough. The overseer sent for me to bring 'im 'ome. Sure, if 'e loses 'is fingers I don't know what we'll do,' she laments in exasperation. 'What were you about, Sim? Ain't you been told often enough?'

'Please, ma'am,' says Agnes sharply. 'Can you not see the boy is distressed? Come now,' she continues more gently to the child, 'rest your hand on mine so that I may lave away the dirt.'

Slowly she dribbles the cool water over his bloodied fingers, gently wiping them with the corner of her gown. The boy draws in his breath sharply at first but then quietens his whimpering as it becomes clear that the damage is not as great as feared. To be sure, there are gashes upon two fingers and the little finger stands out an unnatural angle, suggesting it is broken, but there is nothing that time will not heal, aided by a dab of salve, a splint and a strip of clean linen.

Agnes says as much to the woman who, much relieved, wipes her son's tear-stained face. 'Come, let's get you home, you silly boy. We'll have you mended soon enough. My thanks, ma'am – and sirs,' she says. 'I would repay your kindness if I could, but alas I am a poor woman...'

'Think no more on't, ma'am,' says Agnes, 'we expect nothing do we, Wi-, er, Seth?'

'Nothing, ma'am, unless it be information about the town,' I reply. 'We are strangers here. What is this place,' I say, indicating the looming edifice in whose shadow we stand.

'That be Lombe's Mill, sir.'

'And might strangers like us, displaced by fortune, perhaps find employment there?'

She shakes her head doubtfully. 'These be troubled times, sir, and there be many that fate has frowned upon these last months. The town has scarce recovered, and there's a distrust of strangers since the young Prince was 'ere just afore Christmas.'

'The *young Prince?'* says Agnes disingenuously. 'You mean he who they call the Pretender?'

The woman draws her child to her and looks about her before answering in a lowered voice, 'Pretender he may be to some, but there's plenty round 'ere welcomed him – and might do so again.' Then, fearing she might have said too much. 'Not as we, 'ere in Derby, ain't loyal to King George o' course – but there ain't no love lost, if you understand me? '

'I understand you, ma'am,' say I, playing along in my guise as Jacobite sympathising Seth Hodges. 'I lost my farm and all my livelihood because of tales told against me. Tales told by people I thought we could trust. And 'twas government troops, not rebels, who turned us out with what little we now possess.'

'Truly, I am sorry for you, sir. My husband, Clem, he was taken three months ago, pressed by his employer to join the   fight against the rebels. He didn't want to, but 'e was given no choice. I en't 'eard from 'im since, so I can't think no other than that 'e's dead. And me left with three childer, and Sim 'ere the eldest, though but seven, which is why 'e 'as to work at the mill. If it weren't for Mr Bateman, I don't know 'ow we should manage.'

'Mr Bateman?'

'Mr Hugh Bateman, sir, a charitable gentleman. 'E does what 'e can for them as 'ave fallen on 'ard times with the present troubles. 'E might 'elp you find work, if you be so minded.'

'And where may we find this gentleman?' asks Agnes.

'This time o' day he's like to be at the *Mercury* office on the corner of Iron Gate and Sadler Gate. 'Tis just off the Market Place, you cannot miss it. Take the next left along Queen Street there and you'll see it directly.'

Having given us instructions upon how we may find Mr Bateman, she then hurries off with her son.

Hugh Bateman

The premises of the *Derby Mercury* remind me of the office where I first met Jem Bennett when he was still a junior clerk in the employ of Jacob Elias. The plain wooden counter, a couple of chairs for visitors on this side, a clerk busy at his desk on the other. Only here, instead of legal tomes stacked upon shelves, there are back copies of the newspaper in racks.

The clerk looks up as we enter and it is clear from his expression of suspicious distaste that he recognises us as strangers, and poor ones at that. In answer to my inquiring after Mr Hugh Bateman, he disappears into the back room and reappears almost immediately, saying that Mr Bateman will be with us presently. He then resumes his scribbling without another word.

A couple of minutes later a gentleman of diminutive stature, wearing a shirt tied up at the elbows to keep his shirt-cuffs clean, throws open the inner door, letting out a waft of oil and printing ink and a metallic clanking noise which I guess to be the sound of the printing press at work.

He is, I judge, about forty years old and a tolerably handsome fellow. Unlike almost all whom we have encountered on our journey, he looks beyond our unkempt appearance and shabby clothes and, offering all three of us a hearty handshake, is most desirous of learning our history.

Lifting a flap in the wooden counter, he invites us into an inner, more comfortably furnished room, where another door leads into the chamber whence issues the sound and smell of the printing press. I glimpse a couple of men, aproned and with sleeves similarly tied up, slotting tiny pieces of metal into grooves in long wooden trays. Their fingers are black with ink.

Mr Bateman shuts off this scene of industry and, taking up a peacock waistcoat and neat blue coat from a coat-stand in the corner, continues to quiz us as he puts them on. For all his informality, once dressed he presents an elegant, not to say slightly foppish, figure.

His manner, however, is very friendly and garrulous and he appears to be one of those men who takes a genuine interest in all about him.

As soon as he learns that we have been upon the road for a fortnight or more – (here I exaggerate slightly the extent of our travels) – he insists that we accompany him to his house where we may enjoy the luxury of at least one night in a proper bed and the sustenance of wholesome food.

'Indeed, I shall brook no refusal, Mr Hodges. I can not refuse hospitality to one who is so clearly a gentleman, however reduced his circumstances. Alas there are so many thus afflicted in these troublous times! My only sorrow is that I am unable to help more of them.'

'You are very generous, sir,' says Agnes gratefully.

'Generosity, pah!' he exclaims. 'Any Christian man would do the same.'

Though my own experience of supposedly Christian men has several times proven otherwise, I see no reason to doubt Mr Bateman's sincerity and gladly allow him to guide us to his house a short distance from the Market Place. He shows us where to put our cart on an adjoining patch of rough ground that will provide ample grazing for Rosinante, and cordially invites us in.

No sooner has he ushered us into his parlour than he summons his housekeeper, a buxom, ruddy-cheeked matron.

'Hannah, here, will provide Mrs Hodges with female attire, and yourselves, gentlemen, with shirts and linen from my own wardrobe. I regret they may not be an exact fit,' says he with an apologetic smile, 'but they will serve, I think, whilst she launders your soiled clothes – no, no, I insist! Now, if you will follow me...'

He bustles upstairs, bidding us all follow, and shows us the bedchambers he has allocated us for the night. A commodious chamber for Agnes and myself, at which Charlie gives me a shameless wink, fortunately unobserved by the others. And an adjoining dressing room with a truckle bed for himself.

'Now I pray you, ma'am, and gentlemen, to make yourselves at home. Hannah will be up directly with your fresh linen, then you may change at your leisure. When you are ready, I shall be in my parlour and would welcome your company, But pray feel under no obligation should you prefer to rest after your arduous journey. All I ask is that you shall join me for dinner this evening.'

'Well,' say I once he has disappeared downstairs, 'here's a pretty state of affairs. Perhaps it would be best if you were to have the small room, Agnes. Charlie and I can make a shift to sleep in here.'

Agnes gives me an amused look. 'Why, *Mr Hodges*, would you rebuff your new wife so soon?' says she coquettishly. Then, with a more serious air, 'Come, Will, if we are supposed to be man and wife, we must act the part. Did you not see that housekeeper? She has sharp eyes. Do you not think she will notice any discrepancy in our sleeping arrangements?'

'Aye,' agrees Charlie, with a glint in his eye, 'there's no remedy. You must face up to your responsibilities like a man – ain't that right, Miss Agnes?' Then, breaking into a broad grin, 'It ain't as if you have to go the whole way - and anyway, I'll promise to have the door firm shut...'

'Enough!' I tell him, feeling my face flush hot. 'I was

only trying to respect Agnes's sensibilities... '

Fortunately, any further embarrassment is avoided by the arrival of Hannah bearing our replacement clothes.

'Begging you pardon, sir, but I've taken the liberty of seeking out a couple of shirts belonging to my late husband. He was a man of more ample proportions than the master. They's a little worn but I daresay they'll be more your size.' She places them on the bed and holds up a dress for Agnes's inspection. 'As you may see, ma'am, this is more than a mite big for yourself, but I've brought a sash that may act as a girdle. 'Twill not be a la mode, I'm afraid, but 'twill be serviceable.'

'I am sure it will serve admirably, ma'am,' Agnes replies, taking it from her. 'I'm only sorry to put you to all this trouble.'

'No trouble, ma'am. Mr Bateman's a grand master and 'tis my pleasure to serve 'im. If it please you to bring all as needs washing or brushing down to the kitchen, I'd count it a kindness.'

'Of course I shall.'

'Thank you. Now, if you'll excuse me, I must get on with dinner.'

Twenty minutes later, changed into clean linen and the dirt of the road washed away, courtesy of the basin and ewer provided in our bedchamber, we descend to Mr Bateman's parlour.

We are the strangest trio of house-guests. Charlie and I are coatless, dressed merely in shirtsleeves, whilst Agnes, in Hannah's borrowed dress, sports an excess of bunched material that renders her almost shapeless. But Mr Bateman either does not notice, or is too polite to comment, rising and welcoming us in as if we were the most elegant of company.

Agnes excuses herself to take the bundle of dirty clothes to the kitchen and returns a few moments later to say that, if our host has no objection, she will assist Hannah with the preparation of dinner.

'No objection at all, ma'am, if that is your wish,' says Bateman gallantly.

'It is, sir,' she replies. 'Since Seth and I were driven from our home, I have sadly missed making a wholesome meal in a proper kitchen.'

'You cooked your own meals, ma'am?'

'Oh, we had a kitchenmaid who helped, but I always regarded it not just my duty, but also my pleasure to cook for my husband – and also for master Reuben, his brother. And, with God's grace, I pray the day may come when I shall be able to do so once again.'

'Amen to that, ma'am. May that day soon come.'

Once she has gone, Bateman entreats me to tell the whole history of how I came to be dispossessed. Which I do, according to our previously agreed story, Charlie putting in extra snippets of corroborative detail. To all of which our host listens with great interest and sympathy.

'But you have had troubles of your own, have you not, Mr Bateman?' I say once I have concluded my tale. 'Were not the Scottish rebels here last December?'

'Indeed they were,' says he, 'and I myself witnessed the moment they arrived. On a Wednesday, the fourth as I recall. At about eleven-o'clock that morning, two officers on horseback rode, bold as brass, up to the *George Inn,* which the town aldermen had hastily ordered to be renamed *The King's Head* for fear of reprisals, and demanded to speak to the magistrates. But the magistrates had fled two days before, as soon as they'd received news of the approaching army.'

'Just two officers? Were there no other soldiers with them?'

'Oh, yes. About thirty mounted hussars, all dressed in blue, with scarlet waistcoats trimmed with gold lace. Fine men of good appearance – not at all what we'd been led to expect from all the rumours of wild highlanders. They took up their position in the square and just sat there in silence for hours.'

'That must have been most disconcerting.'

'It was. No-one quite knew what to do. As you may suppose, we did not relish the prospect of an occupying army, but at the same time we were mighty wary of spurning them for fear of repercussions. Eventually, someone suggested ringing the church bells to make an appearance of welcoming them, and a few ostensibly celebratory bonfires were lit. Then, about three in the afternoon, Lord Elcho and his Life Guards arrived, about a hundred and fifty of them, fine figures all and well dressed, but their horses were jaded.'

'So the rebels aren't as wild and barbarous as they say?' says Charlie.

'Well, yes and no, young man,' replies Mr Bateman with a wry grimace. 'A couple of hours later the main body of the army arrived, six or eight abreast, marching – if you could call it that – to the screech of bag-pipes, that wild northern music which by all accounts raises the spirit of the martial Highlander. And a more shabby, lousy, pitiful parcel of fellows you wouldn't look to see. Old men and boys dressed in dirty plaids and shirts, many without shoes or britches. So muddied and fatigued from their long march that they were more fit for pity than fear.'

'And what of their commander, the Pretender Prince?' I ask.

'Ah, well, just as daylight was fading, some officers seized upon Alderman Cooper, who'd been too lame to run away, and commanded him to proclaim the Prince and his father as rightful heirs to the throne from the steps of the Town Hall in the Market Place. Then, at dusk, the Prince himself arrived on foot with his guards. A tall, straight, slender and handsome young man, dressed in Highland plaid and carrying a broadsword.'

'I have heard he makes an impressive figure.'

'He certainly made an impression upon the ladies of the town, I can tell you!' laughs Bateman. 'It was a source of some amusement to see how they vied with each other in making white cockades, of most delicate and costly workmanship, to present to the hero of the day!'

'But he did not make so favourable an impression upon the menfolk?'

'Hardly! Oh he was civil enough, as were most of his officers, but the fact remained that he was general of a force of thousands of men, all demanding food and accommodation...'

There is a gentle knock on the door and Agnes enters.
'If it please you, gentlemen, dinner is ready to be served, if you would care to repair to the dining room.'

Once we are seated around the table and our host has carved generous slices from the rump of beef that Hannah and Agnes have cooked, and once we have served ourselves from the steaming dishes of potatoes, swede and boiled cabbage and ladled rich gravy and horseradish sauce onto our plates, I urge Mr Bateman to tell us more of the Pretender's occupation of the town.

In recounting tales of the invaders and their effect upon the individual residents of the town, I am hoping Bateman may eventually touch upon the matter of Robert Ross's death and perhaps give us some clue as to the circumstances in which it occurred.

The Rebels' chief officers, he tells us, appropriated the best gentlemen's houses, many of which were in the Market Place.

'As for the Prince, he lodged at Exeter House in Full Street. The Earl, whose forbears were accounted Jacobite sympathisers, was not in residence. He and the Countess had removed to Burghley House, their other home near Stamford, upon hearing of the rebels' advance. It was his housekeeper, the Widow Ward, who was obliged to act as the Prince's hostess.'

'Is it a very fine house, sir?' asks Agnes.

'The finest in town,' nods Bateman. 'If you are not in a hurry to continue your journey, I could show you it tomorrow if that would please you?'

'Immensely, sir,' replies Agnes. 'Though, as Seth has no

doubt told you, the purpose of our journey is to find work, if we can. And if we may find suitable work in Derby, there will be no need to journey further. That large mill by the river, what is that?'

For the first time since we have met him, Hugh Bateman face creases into a frown. 'Alas, Mrs Hodges, I fear that work – and such work as would be fitting to a lady such as yourself – may not be so easy to come by. The town is, after recent events, understandably wary of strangers - and the silk mill is not the place for such as yourselves.'

'Silk Mill?'

'Yes, that is the building by the river, a water mill built some twenty-five years ago by Mr Robert Lombe for the production of silk thread. 'Tis still known as Lombe's Mill even though it is now owned by a Mr Wilson from Leeds, though he leaves the running of it to his partners, two brothers by the name of Lloyd. I have seen inside, Mr Hodges, and it is indeed remarkable. So many wheels and cogs and pistons and all in constant movement, 'tis like Leviathan incarnate.'

'And what of Mr Lombe, sir, is he still alive?'

'Dead, ma'am,' says Mr Bateman, dramatically. Then, in ominous tones, 'Murdered, they say, poisoned barely six years after the mill was opened.' He pauses, to gauge the effect of his words before continuing. 'He'd studied the silk-making process in Italy and saw how, with machines, it could be made on a much bigger scale and more efficiently. The Italians couldn't cope with the competition so it is rumoured they sent assassins to punish him.'

'That must have caused quite a sensation in the town,' I say.

'I believe it did, Mr Hodges, though I cannot speak from personal experience, being but ten years old at the time. Derby is a law-abiding town in the main and its citizens, thank God, are more like to die in their beds than by violent hands.'

'There were no fatalities as a result of the rebels being in occupation, then, Mr Bateman?'

Our kindly host grimaces. 'None as a direct consequence, though there was, unfortunately, much violence, as I suppose is only to be expected in the circumstances. Drawn swords, pistols clapped to the breasts of respectable citizens and their coats and shoes stolen, shops stripped of their wares. Though, in fairness, if they took people's shoes it was because they had none of their own; and no voice speaks so loud as that of necessity. And if they omitted payment, it was because they had no money. But in the main, they offered no threat to life. No,' says he with a deep sigh, 'the only violent death recorded at that time was a result of a local dispute. Nothing to do with the Highlanders.'

'Your Christian sympathy for the wretches speaks well for your impartiality, sir,' says Agnes admiringly. 'And, indeed, for the rebel soldiers who, even in such straitened circumstances, behaved with less barbarity than our own government troops, as we know to our cost. Even now,' she continues, her voice breaking, 'I cannot help thinking of poor old Joseph...'

She takes out a handkerchief and dabs her eyes.

Bateman looks discomposed – though no more so than Charlie and I who have no idea who she means. The only Joseph of our acquaintance is Susan's milksop beau back in Soho Square, and he hardly merits the soubriquet 'old'.

'My pardon, sir,' says Agnes, recovering herself. 'Joseph was one of our farm-hands. He tried to stand up to the soldiers and paid the highest price for his pains. They clubbed him with the butt of a rifle – a glancing blow for a stronger man, but not for someone of Joseph's venerable years.'

Charlie and I, now apprised of her addition to our supposed history, enter in to the fiction, nodding sorrowfully.

'Aye, poor Joseph,' says Charlie dolefully, 'he was like the grandfather I never had.'

'You have my profoundest sympathies,' says Bateman. 'This conflict is indeed a terrible thing, setting fathers against sons, brother against brother.'

'But the death you talk of at the time of the rebels occupation was nought to do with their presence?' I add, seizing my chance. 'It arose from a local dispute, you said?'

'So it was supposed,' says Bateman, happy to move to a less upsetting topic. 'It was one of the overseers at the Silk Mill – a Mr Robert Ross, if I recall correctly.'

I feel a flutter of gratification.

'The generally accepted account was that some of the workers harboured a grudge against him, which came to a head one night when they were in drink.'

'They attacked him?'

'So it was said.'

'But you are not so certain?'

'You must understand I have no proof to the contrary, Mr Hodges,' he replies guardedly, 'but I am a man who generally speaks as he finds. I am on amicable terms with several persons at the Mill, both managers and labourers, though I did not know the dead man personally. But I had heard no hint of dissension prior to the event. '

'How came it, then, that the account of his death was so quickly accepted?'

'Sir Richard Everard, our local Justice, is, unfortunately, a man of set opinions who likes matters to be straightforward. He was out of town at the time – like many others, he deemed it safer to be away when news of the rebels' advance came through. When he eventually returned to town, he was most loth to blame the recently departed rebel forces. Should they ever return, as it was felt likely they might, such an accusation could have inconvenient consequences.'

It is clear that Hugh Bateman has nothing but contempt for such craven expediency.

'A story of disgruntled workers and a drunken brawl provided the simplest explanation,' he continues. 'The victim was a single man with no family, the perpetrators were unidentified. Matter closed as far as he was concerned.'

'The man was a supervisor at the Mill, you say?' inquires Agnes innocently. 'Has a replacement been appointed, do you know? Might there be a position available for a competent and willing fellow like Seth?'

Mr Bateman purses his lips doubtfully. 'As I said, strangers are not liked. But for a position requiring such responsibility, it may perhaps be different – and for a man of your aptitude...'

His brow furrows in thought, then he claps his hands together, his mind made up. 'Very well, sir, I shall try. As I told you, I am acquainted with several in authority at the Mill. If it please you, I shall take you along there tomorrow and do everything that is in my power to recommend you.'

Lombe's Mill

Next morning, we dress ourselves in the clothes that Hannah has washed and mended. They are faded and well-worn but, now they are clean and presentable, give exactly the impression of once well-to-do people now impoverished.

Mr Hugh Bateman has excused himself earlier, with many apologies, to attend upon important business during the first half of the morning.

His absence provides an opportunity for Agnes to tell us what she learned from Hannah as the two of them were preparing and clearing up after dinner last night.

'Robert Ross had quite a reputation as a ladies' man, it seems,' she says. 'Hannah, as a regular churchgoer, takes a very dim view of such behaviour. Fortunately, like most prudes, she is not averse to gossip, as long as it's seasoned with a liberal dose of moral indignation.' She gives a knowing look. 'The mill-workers may not have had a grudge against Robert Ross, but there's a clutch of cuckolded husbands who might have done.'

'Did she give any names?' I ask, interested.

'Unfortunately not. Her condemnation of the evils of fornication tended to the general rather than the specific.'

'Alexander Ross, in London, was supposedly killed by

his wife's lover,' I say, reflectively. 'Can it be merely coincidence that adultery played a part in both deaths?'

Any further speculation, however, is brought to an end by Mr Bateman's return, punctually at 11-o'clock, to conduct us to Lombe's Mill.

'Mr Thomas Bennett, himself, has agreed to meet us,' says Bateman with no little satisfaction as we weave our way through the morning throng in the busy market square. 'He is the principal manager who acts on behalf of the Lloyd brothers. We have attended dinners together on sundry occasions and have more than a passing acquaintance.'

The five storeys of Lombe's Mill loom massively above the River Derwent, casting a dark shadow across the surrounding lanes. As we approach, I see that it is not built on the actual river bank, but on an island which separates the main river from a man-made channel that serves the water-wheels not only of this mill but of several others further along the river, downstream of the weir we observed as we entered the town yesterday .

The mill is constructed from bricks laid in what Bateman informs us, in his garrulous way, is Flemish Bond, where bricks are laid alternately longways and end-on. The whole structure rests upon a series of arches which allow the water to flow through.

As we walk alongside it, I judge it to be over a hundred feet long and to stretch near forty feet wide. Its roof rears some sixty feet above the churning, rushing waters of the mill-race.

Apart from its size, the overwhelming impression is the noise of the massive mill-wheel as it creaks and groans, at constant tumultuous war with the crash and splash of the torrent that drives it.

Bateman is reduced to beckoning us towards the entrance, his voice being of no avail against the continuous clamour.

Once inside the building, the noise is different but, if anything, even more overwhelming. A vast hall is filled with mechanical engines the like of which, for size and extent, I have never seen, and there is a constant racket of wheels and pulleys and flying shuttles. Several of these monstrous machines are so tall that they pierce the ceiling through vast square openings that reduce the floor above this level to little more than a series of bridges and connecting galleries.

Windows, set at regular intervals along the stark brick walls, admit long shafts of daylight dancing with a constant mist of fine fibres thrown up by the whirling bobbins. Within moments of entering, I feel them beginning to clog my throat.

Bidding us by means of gestures to keep close to the wall, away from the clattering machines, Bateman ushers us towards a stairway at the end of this vast cavern and having ascended two flights to the second floor, we find ourselves in an atmosphere of comparative calm.

There is still noise, to be sure, but now it is more muted, the machines here being more sedate than their discordant brethren on the floors beneath. It is now possible to converse, albeit with raised voices.

Bateman hurries us along to a room separated from the main chamber and it is here that we find Mr Thomas Bennett, the manager.

He is a powerfully-built man with a square jaw and a harsh voice, a sort of human embodiment of a machine himself. And his manner is just as direct and uncompromising.

'So, Bateman, this is the fellow you told me of who seeks employment,' says he bluntly, surveying me from head to foot. 'Well, you look as if you've more than a grain of common-sense about you. Know anything about silk-spinning?'

'Nothing, sir, but I have experience of farm management and I am a quick learner.'

'Aye, well you're honest, I'll give you that,' he grunts. 'And who be these two with you? You'll not be expecting me to employ them as well, I hope?'

'My wife, Joan, sir, and my brother, Reuben. And as for employment, they are in the same case as myself, one more of hope than expectation.'

'Again, a sound answer, Mr – what's your name?'

'Hodges, sir. Seth Hodges.'

'Well, Mr Seth Hodges, you've been direct with me, and I'll be direct with you. You're after a job as overseer. And we prefer our overseers to be single men, without ties. And most definitely without family in the Mill itself. 'Tis enough for a man to control his kin at home wi'out having to gi' them orders here.'

'Are all your overseers single, Mr Bennett?' inquires Agnes. 'And are they all men?'

Bennett looks at her in amazement. 'Why of course, ma'am. How should it be otherwise? A woman overseer! The thought is preposterous.'

'Yet you have women working here,' pursues Agnes. 'Single men in charge of so many women – they are all men of unimpeachable morals, I trust?'

Bennett laughs coarsely. 'Nay, ma'am, their morals ain't my concern. They may be saints or may, for all I know, constantly have jigging on their minds, but it ain't no concern of mine as long as it takes place off these premises! They're here to work, and damn me, I see to it they do, else I show them the door!'

I see Mr Hugh Bateman wince at his crudeness, and I silently signal to Agnes not to antagonise him further. But she chooses not to see me.

'Nevertheless, would not the women's welfare be better served if there was someone of their own sex in authority over them?'

'A woman in authority!' exclaims Bennett, ignoring her and turning to me. 'Your wife has some strange notions, Mr Hodges. Perhaps she is aiming at the job in your stead! I should look to her, if I were you.'

'I beg you'll excuse her, sir,' say I swiftly before Agnes offers a rejoinder to his boorishness. 'Joan had charge of all the milkmaids upon our farm and thinks, no doubt, that such matters might be arranged the same way here.'

'Aye, well they are not,' states Bennett brusquely. 'I regret that there will be no place for your wife here, Mr Hodges, in *any* capacity,' says he with a glower in her direction.

'And my brother, Reuben, sir?'

'He looks a likely enough fellow,' says Bennett grudgingly, casting an appraising eye over Charlie.

'I'll put my hand to anything,' says Charlie, eagerly. 'I'd be fair interested to see as 'ow them machines work.'

Clearly he has said the right thing, for Bennett almost

smiles, or at least his granite face cracks slightly. 'And so you shall, my lad. If you and Mr Hodges would care to come with me, I shall show you the workings of the place.' He takes a step forward, then turns and says acidly, 'Bateman, perhaps you might care to entertain Mrs Hodges here in my room whilst we make the tour?'

I see Agnes begin to demur, but then she thinks better of it. 'That will be most satisfactory, Mr Bennett,' says she sweetly, 'I had far rather be here with a man of refinement such as Mr Bateman than amongst your noisy machines.'

Bennett doesn't quite know how to take this. He huffs and bids Charlie and myself gruffly to follow him, which I do, with a surreptitious wink at Agnes as we go.

We venture into the clamour of the mill as Bennett proceeds to lecture us at the top of his voice.

Thus we learn how Robert Lombe, 'a man of spirit, a good draughtsman, and an excellent mechanic,' travelled to a silk-mill in Piedmont, Italy, with a view of penetrating the secret of silk throwing. When his underhand scheme was discovered, he was obliged to flee for his life with all the plans he had acquired.

Arriving back in England in 1717, he fixed upon Derby as a proper place, there being plenty of labour available and a good stream for a waterwheel to power his machines.

Bennett then goes into a detailed description of the

building. 'He agreed with the Corporation for an island in the river, five hundred feet long, and fifty-two wide, at eight pounds *per annum* where he erected the present works at the expense of about £30,000.

'The building stands upon huge piles of oak, from sixteen to twenty feet long, driven close to each other with an engine made for that purpose. Over this solid mass of timber is laid a foundation of stone.'

Before Bennett offers to tell us howsoever many bricks of whatsoever dimensions and at what cost were used in the construction, I interrupt him. 'And what became of Mr Lombe, sir?'

'Killed, Mr Hodges! Most foully murdered by the Italians from whom he had stolen the secret. An artful woman came over from that country in the guise of a friend and, by means of her womanly wiles, suborned a treacherous fellow to administer a slow poison to Robert Lombe, who lingered two or three years in agonies, and then departed this life.'

The tenor of this diatribe confirms that Mr Thomas Bennett has no high opinion of women, and I wonder what would be his attitude towards philanderers such as Robert Ross was reputed to be.

We have now progressed into the very midst of the machines upon the second floor. Mill-hands are heaving about bulbous bales of what I take to be raw silk, cutting them open and feeding hanks of feathery down into the wheels, causing fine filaments to hover and twirl in the air.

'This is the raw silk, gentlemen,' Bennett tells us above the whirring. 'It is brought in hanks, or skeins, called slips,' says he, giving us a bundle of soft threads to handle. 'It will take five or six days in winding off, though kept moving ten hours a day. Some are the produce of Persia; others of Canton, coarse, and in small slips. You see that some is of a yellowish colour; that is from Piedmont, but that from China is perfectly white.'

Having thrown the hank of raw silk back into the bale, he brings us to a halt next to one of the machines with a row of rotating wheels all covered in the silken yarn. 'The work passes through three different engines; this one winds the slips together.'

In observing the process, we have much ado to avoid fellows who are darting along beside the machine keenly watching the whirring wheels.

'As you see,' Bennett continues, 'The workman's care is to unite, by a knot, any thread that breaks. Also to take out the burrs and uneven parts, some of which are little bags, fabricated by the silk-worm, as a grave for itself. They generally moulder to a darkish dust but frequently they may be taken out alive.'

He leads us on towards the downward staircase, talking,

or rather shouting, all the while above the din. 'There are twenty six winding machines upon the top three storeys. But the twisting and doubling machines are situated upon the first two floors.'

'Pray, sir,' I shout in his ear as we descend, 'how are all these machines continually kept in motion?'

For answer, he leads us along one of the walkways of the first floor towards where a massive array of interlocking cogs, some near five foot in diameter, are in ponderous, creaking motion. He points out where the huge axle of the waterwheel enters the mill through a kind of navel hole in the wall.

The uproar of creaking and groaning is here so loud that he is obliged to draw our two heads into proximity with his own in order to be heard. 'All the machines are powered by the wheel. It is eighteen feet in diameter and seven feet wide and performs two revolutions every minute.'

He points to where a rotating square vertical shaft rises from the tangle of moving cogs. 'That drives a line shaft that runs the length of the mill and powers the spinning mills upon the first two floors. An extension of that vertical shaft reaches the top three floors to drive the winding machines.'

Exhausted for the moment by the effort of bellowing above the clamour, he motions us to follow him down to the ground floor.

Here are eight more clattering machines where the spooled silk filament from the upper floors is being spun into thread. Round bobbins whirr, drawing countless threads through numerous wheels and pulleys whilst men, a few women and numerous small children dash between them. Each man has oversight of some fifty or so whirling threads and it seems to be principally the business of the children, whose fingers are nimble, to tie the threads when they break, which they seem to do constantly.

As soon as one breaks, the spool of filament slows to a halt and a child darts forward.

Even as we watch, several spools fall idle, rotating slowly as the broken thread ravels out. Two hapless boys and a skinny girl scurry frantically along the line, trying to decide which thread to knot first. They rush and hesitate and get in each other's way, earning the wrath of the mill-hands who scramble clumsily to knot the threads themselves.

An overseer strides up and cuffs the boys, then berates the mill-hands. Once he moves on, ignoring their resentful glowers, the boys get double punishment from the chastised men whilst the girl cowers away from an expected blow.

I cannot help but think that when punishment is so often and so summarily inflicted, for a mechanical rather than human fault, it must breed bitterness. Perhaps it might be true, after all, that Robert Ross was just such a callous overseer that he brought retribution on himself, as the local magistrate so conveniently concluded?

Once we are back in the comparative quiet of Mr Bennett's office, though with the clash of the machines still ringing in my ears, I broach the subject of discipline. 'The treatment of the workers just now seemed somewhat harsh, sir. Does it not breed dislike of the supervisors?'

'I care not whether they be liked or not, Mr Hodges, as long as they be respected and feared. Time lost and waste made is money forfeited. Their job is to ensure that it does not happen. But if you balk at doing that, then this is no job for you, and I shall bid you good day.'

'Oh, come, Mr Bennett,' Hugh Bateman protests, 'Mr Hodges was merely expressing an opinion.'

'I do not expect opinions from my employees, sir, just hard work and obedience. I have entertained Mr Hodges as a favour to you, sir, but if he has no appetite for the job, I shall have little trouble in finding others who have.'

'Indeed, Mr Bennett, you misunderstand my husband,' says Agnes in a placatory tone. She takes my arm in hers, moving to stand close beside me. 'He is a diligent and trustworthy man and I dare hazard that it is more his unfamiliarity with the nature of the work than any disinclination towards it that makes him appear contrary. Is there, perhaps, one of your overseers who might lesson him in what the job requires?'

Bennett looks at her dubiously. 'You speak sense, ma'am,' says he somewhat reluctantly. 'Mayhap I have been somewhat hasty. A moment, if you please.'

He leaves the room and I hear him bellow out a name. Then, almost immediately, he returns with a tall, broad-shouldered fellow in tow.

'This is Ned Radford. He has been a supervisor here for the last four years. Ned, this is Mr Hodges who may be taking Ross's old job. I want you to tell him what his duties will be.'

Radford eyes me with a distrust that I seek to allay. 'My name's Seth,' I say holding out my hand. 'You can teach me the ropes, eh, Ned?'

Grudgingly he accepts a brief handshake. 'What do 'ee want to know, Mr Hodges?' he growls. A handshake is one thing, but obviously first names is a step too far.

'Everything you can tell me,' I reply earnestly. 'But, by your leave, not here or now. I have no doubt that I shall get used to the noise of the Mill in due time, but for the moment, my head is ringing. Might we meet later, after you have finished work?'

With a glance at Mr Bennett, he reluctantly agrees. 'Eight o'clock, by the wheel.'

Widow Ward

It being only just past 1-o'clock when we leave Lombe's Mill, Mr Bateman offers to make good on his promise to show us Exeter House where the Pretender stayed during his time in Derby.

A short walk along Full Street brings us almost to the Market place, on the corner of which stands Exeter House, a handsome, three storey brick building in the style of last century. Being situated on a corner, the entrance is approached across a triangular courtyard, set back from the street.

The place looks unoccupied to me, the interior shutters all closed and weeds sprouting freely amidst the gravel of the courtyard. Nevertheless, Mr Bateman raps confidently upon the door and after a few moments we hear bolts being drawn. It is opened by a tall, austere looking matron dressed all in black, whom I take to be the Widow Ward he told us of last night.

'Why, Mr Bateman, what an unexpected pleasure,' says she with a forced smile, but in a tone belying her words. 'How may I be of assistance?'

Bateman, unaffected by her coolness, is his usual enthusiastic self as he asks if she might show us round the house where the Pretender Prince so lately stayed.

She offers another smile which seems to mark a slight rise in temperature from chilly to tepid and invites us in. Clearly the opportunity of vicarious fame bestowed by an association with former, and possibly future, royalty is stronger than her reluctance.

'To be sure, ma'am, this is most civil of you,' says Agnes in her most ingratiating manner. 'It is not too great an imposition, I hope?'

'No imposition at all, ma'am,' replies Mrs Ward unconvincingly, according us another lukewarm smile.

She leads us up a wide staircase that ascends from the small hallway into a spacious oak-panelled chamber with a pleasant outlook across gardens which lead down to the river.

'This room was chosen by the Prince as his Presence Chamber,' she tells us, 'where he received deputations and where he met with his counsellors.'

'Is this where the decision was made to retreat back to Scotland?' asks Charlie.

Widow Ward purses her thin lips. 'It is where Lord George Murray and others persuaded his highness to that course of action. Much against his will, for I believe the Prince had no such thought, being keen to press on to London, despite all the odds.'

'It was by far the wisest decision,' Mr Bateman cuts in for our information. 'Whilst many were sympathetic to the rebels' cause, few were willing to commit themselves to it. Their officers tried to recruit volunteers - five shillings advance and five guineas when they should reach London – yet only three volunteered, and they were men of degraded life and sullied character. One scoundrel, James Sparks, a stocking-maker provided them with information upon the inhabitants of the town, advising who should be favoured and who oppressed.'

'A nasty piece of work,' adds Mrs Ward with an uncharacteristic burst of fervour. 'He led them to Squire Meynell's place at Bradley where they wreaked havoc, plundering his cellars and making free with his liquors. But the villain got his just deserts. The rebels abandoned him, drunk as an emperor, in the cellar, declaring he was not worth their regard. The last I heard, he's been hanged for thieving,' she concludes with satisfaction.

'I am sure the Prince would count men of that sort no great loss,' says Agnes. 'I have heard that many account him a fine and noble young gentleman.'

'Why, so he is, ma'am,' agrees Mrs Ward with far more warmth that she has displayed so far. 'And so were most of his companions, fine gentlemen all. The very epitome of politeness and good breeding. '

Now, her tongue loosened, she shows us into two rooms that adjoin the main chamber, one where the Prince slept, the other where he dined, and discourses at length upon the family history of the owners of Exeter House. A complicated catalogue of Bagnolds and Chambers in which I soon lose interest, with all its intricacies of heiresses marrying into rich families and the additions and renovations they made to the building.

All, it seems, to little purpose as the house is now shut up for most of the year. The latest heiress, having made a most providential marriage to the Earl of Exeter, spends most of her time as mistress of Burghley House, her noble husband's principal residence.

'Tell them of young Samuel,' prompts Bateman, interrupting the cloyingly deferential recital as she is inviting us to admire the table whereon the Prince dined. He turns to us, 'The Prince accorded Mrs Ward's son a singular honour, Mr Hodges – as Mrs Ward shall tell you.'

The lady, however, puts up a show of modest reluctance.

'Pray tell us, ma'am,' urges Agnes. 'What favour did he show your son?'

'Samuel is but thirteen, ma'am,' simpers Mrs Ward, 'yet the Prince appointed him his food taster whilst he was here.' She goes on rapidly, 'Of course, I could not have countenanced such an office, however prestigious, had I not personally supervised the preparation of all meals that the Prince and his court partook of. And the Prince was gracious enough to reward our services with this ring upon his departure.'

She holds out her hand to show us a magnificent gold ring set with diamonds, an impressively large cut stone in the centre, surrounded by a circle of ten smaller stones all of the first quality.

'That is indeed a most generous token of his thanks, ma'am,' I say, adding quickly, 'and I am sure, fully deserved.'

'And Samuel,' asks Charlie, 'what did he get?'

'The ring was by way of thanks to both of us,' says she somewhat huffily. 'Though he did receive a small token from one gentleman...'

She breaks off momentarily, as if having second thoughts, then rapidly changes the subject.

'...but that is of no moment. Now, if you would care to follow me, Mrs Hodges and gentlemen, I shall show you the gardens which her ladyship has spent much time improving and about which the Prince and his followers were most complimentary...'

As we come out of the house into the garden which slopes down to the very banks of the river and which is laid out in a series of formal parterres, I catch sight of a slim young lad riding a hobby-horse between the low cut hedges.

Allowing Bateman and Agnes to stroll ahead with Mrs Ward who is discoursing upon the planting and design, I whisper to Charlie to intercept him. 'Find out about the gentleman that she seems reluctant to talk of, and what the boy was rewarded for.'

Then I quickly rejoin them as Charlie saunters into the path of the galloping boy. Out of the corner of my eye, I see the encounter and note an exchange which lasts for several minutes.

After a further half hour of Mrs Ward's fulsome praise for her absent employers, it is only the first few drops of a rain-shower that bring our visit to a close.

And also herald a return of Mrs Ward's cool haughtiness. By the time we find ourselves once more upon the corner of the Market Place, I have the distinct impression that, however enjoyable the opportunity to laud her romantic visitor and her noble employers, the Widow feels that we have been unworthy of her condescension.

Far more interesting is what Charlie has to tell us once we have returned to Bateman's house and he has excused himself upon business.

'That lad's a cunning shaver,' says Charlie admiringly. 'He'll go far, you mark my words.'

'Did he tell you anything useful?' asks Agnes. 'Was he

more forthcoming than his mother about the man who rewarded him for his services – and what those services were?'

'Once I'd gained his confidence, yes. But I had more'n a bit o' mud to wade through afore I struck land, so to speak.'

'Aye, well spare us the mud,' say I impatiently, 'and give us the gist.'

'Accordin' to Samuel, it weren't one of the gentlemen wot stayed at the 'ouse, though 'e was there during the day. The lad couldn't tell me where 'e was billeted, though 'e thought it might've been somewhere close by. An' 'e thought 'e were an officer, cos of 'is uniform.'

'A Jacobite uniform?' I ask.

'Aye, 'e thought so, though somewhat stained and torn. In fact, the fellow asked one o' the maids if she could mend it for 'im. Which is 'ow 'e came to speak to Samuel, whilst 'e was a-waitin' for it to be done. A real smooth-boots 'e was, accordin' to Samuel, flirtin' and teasin' the maids.'

'And what did he want of Samuel?' asks Agnes.

'Aye, well that's when 'e became a bit close-lipped. Said 'is mother 'ad told 'im not to speak of it.'

'The man didn't ask 'im to do anything unnatural, did he?' enquires Agnes hesitantly.

'Oh no,' Charlie reassures her. 'Fact I asked 'im the very same thing, an' 'e just laughed. "No," 'e said, "tweren't me 'e

98

wanted. 'Twas a fellow at the mill - one o' the overseers that he thought 'e might know. Two of a kind, if you ask me, a-flirtin and a-carryin' on wi' women." Young Samuel may be only thirteen, but 'e's a sharp un.'

My heart leaps. 'Don't tell me - Robert Ross!'

'You've hit it! Anyway. 'e took 'im to the mill an' pointed out this 'ere Ross. An' for reward, the officer give 'im a silver buckle. Then a few days later, Ross copped it and Samuel's mother told 'im 'e'd better keep mum.'

'No wonder Mrs Ward was loth to say anything further. Or that she told her son to hold his tongue. Mayhap she, like Mr Bateman, suspected there was more to Robert Ross's death than met the eye.'

'Did Samuel tell you this man's name?' asks Agnes urgently.

'Says 'e never knew it,' replies Charlie with an apologetic grimace.

'Did he describe him, then?' I say.

'Not so's you'd know 'im from any one of a hundred,' he says with a shrug. 'Tallish, not fat, fair hair, perhaps reddish. Only thing 'e noticed was that one of 'is eyes seemed more closed-up than the other, like 'e 'ad a bit o' a squint.'

'Well, that's something at least,' I say. 'Did Samuel say if this man departed with the rebels?'

'Now there's the odd thing,' replies Charlie. 'Samuel said

as 'ow he, together with most of the town was roused by drums and pipes early on the Friday morning and went to see the rebel army marching out. Everyone thought they'd be going south towards London. An' so they did, to start with. But then they all about turns an' sets off north instead. 'E says the Prince didn't look too 'appy about that. There'd been a lot of raised voices, Samuel said, the night before in Exeter House, what'd kept him awake.'

'The Pretender's advisors persuading him that retreat was the only option. No wonder there were arguments, I can't imagine the Pretender was happy after having advanced so far,' observes Agnes.

'Mind you,' continues Charlie, 'the townspeople weren't that sad to see the back o' them. He told me of one gentleman who'd had six officers and forty lower ranks billeted on him. On the morning the rebels left, he was waving and huzzahing with the rest, but all the time muttering under his breath to the others he was standin' with, how "the bold and insolent fiends left a regiment or two of highland lice, several loads of their filthy excrements and other ejections of different colours scattered before my door, around my garden and all over my house!" Remembered it word for word, young Samuel had. Tell you, that lad'll go far!'

'Yes, well unfortunately with an occupying army that's

only to be expected. But what was this 'odd thing' you told us of?'

'Oh, yes,' says Charlie, returning to the point. 'Samuel says he looked out specially for the gentleman wot 'ad given 'im the silver buckle in order to wave to him. But 'e wasn't nowhere to be seen.'

'That really is odd,' I agree. Then a thought strikes me. 'Do we know exactly when Robert Ross was killed? No one has said whether it was actually *during* the rebel occupation, have they?'

Both my companions look blank as we all realise our ignorance on the matter.

'Mr Bateman will know. I'll ask him before I meet Ned Radford tonight.'

'Are we all going?' asks Charlie.

I shake my head. 'I think it better if I go alone. He may be less forthcoming if we are all there. If he has anything to tell about Robert Ross, there is more chance he will tell it to me if I am by myself.'

The Waterwheel

Dusk is already well advanced by the time I approach Lombe's Mill for my meeting with Ned Radford. The rain which started this afternoon at Exeter House has settled into a steady drizzle, bringing grey lowering clouds to add to the natural loss of light at the day's end.

The lane to the Mill is deserted, the mill-workers having gone home for the night. Yet I note with some surprise that the huge wheel is still creaking round, the water splashing against its paddles and swirling rapidly, crashing and foaming against the sides of the narrow mill-race that runs alongside the lane.

The white spume flecks the murky evening light with an eerie luminescence, for the vast bulk of the mill near blots out what little daylight remains.

I cannot think why Radford chose such a meeting place, except that the wheel might provide a landmark private enough at this time of night and yet recognisable to a stranger in town such as myself.

All the same, I cannot prevent a feeling of uneasiness as I draw nearer to the groaning, lumbering structure that towers like a huge juggernaut to near three times my height.

Words that my master, Mr Garrick, often spoke when he

was at his lowest ebb come unbidden. *As flies to wanton boys are we to the Gods. They crush us for their sport.*

At this moment, I feel as insignificant as an insect under this gargantuan monster, knowing that it could break my body as easily as a stick upon the tide.

It must be at least five minutes past eight – our appointed meeting time – and Radford is not here.

A tiny germ of foreboding flickers in my chest, bursting into full-flowering alarm as two figures emerge from the shadow of the Mill.

My hand goes automatically to the dagger I always carry concealed at my waist as they draw closer.

There is something menacing about the deliberation of their gait which tells me these are not just two mill-hands coming late from their work.

Nevertheless, as they come to a halt in front of me, I summon my courage to wish them good evening.

'And who are you to gie us good e'en?' growls one, thrusting his face close to mine.

'My name's Seth Hodges, friend,' I say, determined not to give ground, but tightening my hold upon the hilt of my dagger just in case. 'I am a stranger here...'

'Yeah, well strangers ain't welcome in this town, *friend*,' he sneers. 'There ain't nothin for 'ee 'ere. What're 'ee doin' 'ere at this time o'night?'

'Up to no good, I reckon,' butts in his companion with a derisive curl of his lip.

'I am here to meet someone,' I reply. 'A Mr Ned Radford, an overseer at the Mill.'

The first ruffian utters a scornful bark. 'Well, Radford ain't a'comin'. You'd best be on yer way, if you knows what's good for 'ee.'

'And if I don't?'

For answer, he grabs my arm and tries to wrench it up my back.

I draw out my dagger, but before I can use it, his companion has aimed a punch at my stomach that doubles me up in pain. My weapon skitters uselessly away.

The two of them haul me up and drag me, struggling, to the very edge of the mill-race. I feel the spray splashing against my face as they force me to my knees, holding me over the churning torrent.

'Want some o' that, do yer?' shouts one above the clamour. 'Want yer pate broken and yer bones smashed to kindlin' by the wheel, do yer?'

'Tell us what ye'r really 'ere for,' yells the other as they throw me to the ground. They follow up by launching heavy kicks. I desperately curl up and try to scramble way, but they pin me down by kneeling on my arms and legs.

I squirm helplessly under their weight. 'I told you,' I

gasp. 'I'm here to meet Mr Radford.'

'What for?' demands the one squatting on my legs. He raises himself slightly only to come down with his full weight, near breaking my shins, sending stabs of agonising pain shooting up my legs.

'A job,' I bellow as soon as I can catch my breath, 'an overseer's job.'

'No way,' snarls the one pinning down my arms. He manhandles me roughly to my feet. 'We ain't 'avin' no incomers.'

Together, they drag me back to edge of the mill race and I have no doubt that they will throw me in to be broken by the waterwheel, leaving my mangled body to be carried away in the river.

Faced with imminent death, I feel as if the world suddenly slows down and my senses dim. The creaking of the wheel and rushing of the torrent seem to recede into the distance as I concentrate all my efforts on fighting against my captors.

I feel their grip tighten and brace myself for the all too brief flight through the air and the plunge into cold water. But they have misjudged their throw. I fall half in, half out of the stream and am able to snatch precariously at the slimy brickwork edging the channel

The water flow is nowhere near as fierce as I expect, but

I have difficulty in keeping hold all the same. My fingers slip on slimy moss and lichen.

Frantically I look towards the vast looming shadow of the wheel and feel a sudden wondrous surge of hope. The sensation I had of the noise lessening proves to be no dream. The wheel really is slowing down.

Above me, I hear one of them curse. 'Fuck, Radford's shut the sluice! Let's get out of here!'

They launch one last desperate kick, loosening my scrabbling fingers and I feel the flow take me. I think I hear a distant shout. 'What in the devil's name are you villains at!'

Then the water closes over my head.

The dull thrumming of the smothering stream. The muted sound of running feet. The muffled pounding of boots.

Then strong hands grasping me and pulling me upwards to lie, gasping, upon solid earth once more.

'My God, Mr Hodges? Are you all right, sir?'

I manage to cough out an assurance that I am unharmed.

Ned Radford helps me to my feet.

'My apologies, Mr Hodges. I would have been here and might have averted this assault, only when I arrived, I found that the sluice was open and the wheel was in motion.' His words come out in a rush, apologetic yet angry. 'The flume should be diverted at night to prevent the machinery being overtaxed. I cannot understand how it came to be in full flow. Someone's head will roll for this!'

I am only half paying attention. My garments are soaking wet and my ribs beginning to ache from the blows of my assailants. 'Might we – go some – place more convenient...,' I suggest, stuttering from the violent shivering that has suddenly seized me.

Radford recollects himself. 'Of course, sir. Forgive me, my anger has made me thoughtless. Come, my house is not far.'

His house is, indeed, but a short distance away, but so hidden away in a maze of streets and alleys of closely packed cramped dwellings that I begin to see why he suggested we first meet at the waterwheel. I would never have found it on my own.

As soon as we enter the small parlour which seems to be the only room on the ground floor, he leads me to a wooden armchair and bids me sit. He throws another log upon a smouldering fire and stirs it into life with a metal poker.

'Would it trouble you, Mr Radford, if I were to remove my garments and lay them before the fire?' I ask.

'Not at all, sir,' he replies shortly. 'I have no wife to take offence, and it is of no account to me one way or the other how you are attired. For the sake of your modesty, however, I shall find you something.' He hurries over to a stairway at the side of the room, runs up it and reappears a moment later with a coarse blanket for me to wrap about myself.

Awkwardly, stiff from the beating I have suffered, I start to undress, whilst he busies himself pouring liquid into two tankards which he then places on the hearth and warms in turn by plunging the hot poker into them.

Once I am settled, my body swathed in the blanket and my discarded clothes steaming in front of the fire, he hands me one of the mugs. I take a sip and find it to be a kind of spicy punch which is pleasantly warming.

He sits opposite me at the other side of the hearth and asks that I tell him what happened. His manner throughout all the previous actions has been dutiful and efficient, but I detect no trace of friendliness in them. Nor, in his request for information, any trace of sympathetic interest.

I give him a bald account of the attack to which he listens attentively, nodding grimly from time to time.

When I have finished, he says, 'I cannot say I am surprised, Mr Hodges. Feeling against strangers runs high in this town and I admit that I, to an extent, share such sentiments – as, perhaps, you were aware this morning at the mill?'

'I do not blame you,' I tell him. 'Mr Bennett was somewhat peremptory in his introductions and I quite see how you must feel about the possibility of having someone totally unknown thrust upon you in such circumstances. I, too, was not easy with the situation.'

'It seems we understand each other, then,' says he bluntly, 'so I'll be straight with you. I don't like the idea of the guv'nor bringing in a complete stranger who's not from around here and has no previous experience of the work. But I've been given an order that I'm to explain the work to you and answer any questions, so 'tis my duty to put aside any personal feelings and do what is required of me.'

'You are an honest man, sir. I appreciate that,' I say truthfully. 'And I shall be as candid with you, if I may?'

'Go ahead, sir. I welcome frankness.'

'From what I saw at the Silk Mill this morning, I am not sure of my suitability for the job. The organisation of the work and the way the employees are treated are both alien to me. I might, under necessity, eventually come to tolerate such conditions but I cannot see myself ever being totally at ease perpetuating such a system of relentless harshness.'

'Aye,' replies Radford gruffly, 'that's finely spoke, Mr Hodges, but fine words butter no parsnips and when it comes to a choice between being high-minded or starving, there's usually only one winner. Your clothes, though shabby, tell me you've fallen on hard times. Perhaps you're not yet desperate enough, but you'll soon learn that beggars have not the luxury of choice.'

I could take offence at his tone, were I genuinely in the situation he describes. As it is, my only reaction is one of sympathy. I suspect Ned Radford is a decent man forced by circumstance into a life not wholly of his choosing.

'You may be right, Mr Radford. But tonight's events have done much to bring home the reality of my situation. I am all too aware that things might have ended differently but for your timely intervention. My distaste for conditions in the Mill is one thing. But such violent antagonism as I have experienced tonight - that is another matter entirely. How could I perform my duties knowing that those under my charge hated me so much?'

His look clouds. 'You think those villains were from the Mill? That is a serious accusation, sir,' he says with barely suppressed anger. 'What proof have you that the men who attacked you were Lombe's Mill men?'

I do want to antagonise him. 'None...' I begin, but he cuts me off.

'Have you names? Can you describe them?' he demands indignantly. 'If you can identify them, you may be assured that I shall find them out and see that they receive appropriate punishment.'

I hold up a conciliatory hand. 'Pray do not be offended, Mr Radford. I make no accusations. It may be just unfortunate coincidence that I encountered these two ruffians at the very time and place you suggested we meet...'

An angry glint appears in his eye. 'You are not suggesting that I had aught to do with it, I trust?'

I shake my head. 'By no means, sir. Your rescue and subsequent conduct are most eloquent witnesses to the contrary. I owe you my life.'

'And you would do well not to forget that, Mr Hodges, before you begin making accusations,' he growls, slightly propitiated. Then, in a calmer tone, 'But what grounds have you for thinking the encounter was no mere coincidence, sir?'

'Only this, Mr Radford - as the villains fled they mentioned your name...'

'My name!' he exclaims in genuine surprise.

'...saying you must have shut the sluice. What is the sluice?'

'The sluice-gate is a wooden shutter which can be raised or lowered to control the amount of water diverted from the river into the mill-race. It is raised each morning and shut down each evening, as there is no need for the machines to be working at night. That's why I was delayed. When I found it open, I had to shut it down or lord knows what damage might have been done.'

'I think the damage was intended to myself,' I say. 'I suspect they deliberately opened the sluice-gate to divert you. Which suggests to me that they knew about our meeting.'

'And also suggests they know the Mill routine and that I would look to it,' says he gloomily. He looks troubled. 'It grieves me to say so, but you could be right, Mr Hodges, they might be men from the mill. They must have overheard talk of our meeting. You think they intended murder from the outset?'

'I do not doubt it. Another reason, perhaps the prime one, for opening the sluice would be to create a torrent fast enough to ensure I drowned, or was broken upon the mill wheel.' I pause to let him come to terms with a truth so unpalatable before broaching my real justification for our meeting. 'And there is precedent, is there not? My predecessor died at the hands of disgruntled workers, so I was told?'

Radford looks up in bewilderment. 'Ross? No, Mr Hodges, you are misinformed.'

'But the official version …'

'Is a pack of lies,' says he forcefully. 'But one does not argue with the likes of Sir Richard Everard. As the local Justice, his word is, literally, the law. And he had other reasons.'

'Other reasons, Mr Radford?'

Suddenly, he looks discomfited. 'Ross was no angel, Mr

Hodges. He was not a bad man, but he had his weaknesses. 'Twas rumoured he and Sir Richard's daughter... I don't need to go into details, I presume?'

Is this yet another suspect I must add to the list of Ross's possible killers?

'You think Sir Richard Everard may have had something to do with his death?' I ask. 'Because Ross had sullied his daughter's good name.'

Radford gives a bark of a laugh. 'He sullied more than her name! But Everard is a coward as well as a bully. He has not the balls to do aught himself. So, instead, he fabricated this calumny against the mill-workers.' He shakes his head as if to rid it of the thought, then looks directly at me. 'But I can assure you, Mr Hodges, that the men had no grudge against Robert Ross. He was not killed by anyone from Lombe's Mill. It is my belief that he was killed by a rebel soldier.'

'But Mr Hugh Bateman told me only this afternoon that Ross died at least three days after the rebel forces had quit the town?'

'Aye, the rebel forces left, but this soldier did not go with them. He was here, though not in uniform, after the Prince's army left. I saw him with my own eyes.'

'Really, Mr Radford, you intrigue me.'

'Yes, sir. I first saw him, in uniform, with Mrs Ward's

young lad, Samuel. A day or two after the rebel army arrived, the boy stopped me outside the mill and asked where he might find Robert Ross as he had a gentleman who was desirous of renewing his acquaintance. The lad pointed out a Jacobite officer waiting at the end of the lane. I thought nothing of it at the time. Then I saw the same man again a few days later, but not in uniform this time. He was in conversation with Ross. They seemed amicable enough. But the next day, Robert Ross was found dead.'

'You did not think to tell anyone?'

'I spent a whole day scouring the town for sight of the man with the intention of bringing him before the authorities. But he had vanished.'

'You could still have told someone.'

'Told them what, Mr Hodges? That I'd seen a soldier who was not a soldier speaking to a man several hours before he died? And that the same non-soldier had now disappeared off the face of the earth? No, Mr Hodges, no one listens to folk like us. And in face of war and rebellion, what is one more death? I grieved for Robert Ross as a colleague but, in the absence of any close family to grieve for him, I did not see why a trumped-up explanation of his death should not stand as well as an unprovable real one.'

On the Road Again

By the time I leave Ned Radford, we are on polite, if not exactly amicable, terms. In large part, this is due to my telling him I have decided to move on from Derby and that consequently I shall not be seeking employment at the Mill.

He makes no attempt to hide his satisfaction. 'It is for the best, Mr Hodges. You know my views – you're not suited to the work and you'd find the men resentful. I doubt Mr Bennett will shed any tears. He only agreed to see you because he did not wish to offend Mr Bateman, who is well respected in the town. You have made the right decision.'

I permit myself a smile. 'Blunt as ever, Mr Radford.'

'It is my nature, Mr Hodges. Now, as your garments are sufficiently dry, there is little purpose in prolonging our acquaintanceship. I shall, for my own peace of mind, accompany you part way back to Mr Bateman's house.'

'Really, there is no necessity...'

'I will brook no argument, sir. You are all too well aware of how some in this town treat a stranger walking alone at night. I will not have you miscarry again.'

Thus commanded, I demur no further and, after having donned my clothes, we step out into the dark street. So dark is it that I immediately see the reason of his insistence. On my own I should be lost within minutes!

'Rest assured, Mr Hodges,' he says as we negotiate the confusion of alleyways, 'I shall make sure I find the culprits.'

'It will prove a fruitless task,' I reply. 'They revealed no names and in the dark I could not swear to describe them with any accuracy. Apart from a soaking and a few bruises, I am unharmed. Pray do not pursue them on my account.'

'It is not on your account, sir,' he retorts scornfully. 'It is for the Mill. You and your family will be gone tomorrow, but Lombe's Mill will still be here. Their apprehension will benefit you not a jot, but opening that sluice gate was an action fraught with danger. I will not have men under my charge who play fast and loose in such a reckless manner.'

Having brought me safely to the Market Square, whence I assure him I can find my way the last few yards to Bateman's house unaided, he bids me goodnight.

'I wish you a safe journey, Mr Hodges, and luck with finding employment. But you will not take it amiss if I also refrain from saying that I hope I may see you again.'

And with that, he turns on his heel and disappears into the night.

Next morning, my ribs and chest are black with bruises and my shoulders are stiff from being wrenched by last night's assailants.

Agnes immediately goes in search of Hannah, Mr Bateman's housekeeper, to ask if she has any arnica in the house. The lady herself appears a few moments later with a pot of salve and a raw onion sliced in half.

'Onion?' I query with a sense of trepidation.

I remember all too clearly the lingering stench of one of Mrs Wiggins' patent remedies that I used once to treat saddle-sores. It caused wrinkled noses and expressions of disgust from all my near acquaintance for the best part of a week.

Now I can see a similar expression on Agnes's face as Hannah explains. 'A sovereign remedy, Mr Hodges, for drawing the blood to the surface and expelling toxic humours. Pray undo your shirt, Mr Hodges,' she says in a manner that brooks no argument.

I look to Agnes for rescue, but she only shrugs, leaving me no recourse but to submit to Hannah's brisk ministrations. These consist in clasping a half onion in each hand and vigorously rubbing the cut side in circular motions all over the bruised areas. By the time she has done, my eyes are running. Not just from the discomfort of the rubbing, but from the pungent smell which the warmth of my chest has converted into an all enveloping vapour.

Hannah stands back, dropping the two battered onion

halves into her apron pocket. She hands the pot of salve to Agnes. 'Give the juice a minute or two to dry, Mrs Hodges, then apply this salve to the affected areas. It is pure essence of arnica mixed with beeswax, very efficacious.'

She departs, allowing us privacy for what is a more intimate, gentle procedure than her vigorous onion rubbing.

'Are we really to leave today?' asks Agnes, once the housekeeper is gone.

'Yes,' I reply. 'There is little point in keeping up the pretence of looking for work any longer. And I think we have learned all that we are likely to about Robert Ross's death. Besides which, our presence here is earning us enemies. Ow!' I exclaim as she presses one bruise just a little too hard.

'Sorry, my dear,' she says, as her cool fingers continue more gently to stroke my warm, tender flesh. 'It is to be hoped that Charlie does not burst in at this point.'

'No fear of that,' I reply. 'He's seeing to Rosinante, readying her for departure.'

I reach out and stroke her forearm affectionately. 'He'll be gone for a good half hour yet,' I say with an endearing smile.

True to form, Charlie doesn't return for some time.

When he does, Agnes and I are in the parlour with Hugh

Bateman and he is expressing his disappointment at our imminent departure and his apologies that I have been so ill used.

'Though, regrettably, I cannot say I am surprised,' he says disconsolately. 'Since the Pretender descended upon us, it has brought out the worst in people, I'm afraid. To those who pine for a return to the past, he personified all their hopes that a golden age might return. But to those who value stability, he represented the spectre of the civil and religious strife that blighted us for so many centuries before this. Animosities which people thought long gone have resurfaced, setting even families at war with each other.'

'Aye, many may be dissatisfied with their present lot,' I agree contemplatively, 'but the grass is not always greener on the other side. And, as we have all too painful reason to know, you never appreciate what you have until it is gone.'

'Indeed so, Mr Hodges,' nods Hugh Bateman enthusiastically. 'I thank the Lord I am a sanguine sort of fellow. I believe we shall eventually see an end of this unpleasantness. Pragmatism and reason must, in time, prevail over hostile factionalism. If we cannot believe that good will inevitably conquer evil, then I fear we are lost,' he ends with a sad smile. Then, clapping his hands together, 'But here we are be-miring ourselves in melancholy philosophy when you are eager to be off! Have you all that is needful for your journey?'

'The cart is packed,' says Charlie, 'and Rosinante fed and watered.'

'And I have had Hannah put up some victuals to see you on your way,' beams our host, ringing the bell. 'They will, I think, prove more palatable than her physic,' he laughs, wrinkling his nose. Then more seriously. 'I cannot apologise enough for those brutes who attacked you, Mr Hodges, and I implore you not to think badly of our town on their account. It is, unfortunately, the times which bring out the worst in people.'

'Rest assured, Mr Bateman,' says Agnes, our abiding memory of Derby shall be your generosity, not the animosity of any of its other inhabitants.'

An hour later, with the May sunshine bright above us, we are jogging gently out of town along Fryers Gate. Beyond the dwellings that line the road lies open pastureland dotted with trees through which meandering brooks make their way to the river.

'So,' says Charlie when the last of the houses is well behind us, 'are we any the wiser about Robert Ross's death?'

'I think we are, ' I reply. 'One thing we can be sure of: the official version put out by the town Justice, Sir Richard Everard does not hold water. Whether or not Everard had his own grudge against Ross for debauching his daughter or not, Ned Radford believes he would not have the courage to carry it through.'

'Which is why he put about the story about workmen with a grudge being the culprits, which no one believes, including Mr Bateman,' says Charlie. 'And if anyone knows what goes on in that town, he does. Whether or not he knows as much about what goes on inside the Silk Mill's another matter.'

'He may not, but Ned Radford does, and he called the official version a pack of lies.'

'Yes, but he would say that,' objects Agnes. 'His loyalty is to the mill. He doesn't believe the men who attacked you could be mill-workers.'

'I'm not so sure,' I reply. 'Radford is brusque, but he is honest. I believed him when he said he'd find out who was responsible. He won't like doing it, but he *will* do it – not so much for the sake of the mill's reputation, which is his excuse, but for his own sense of justice. I'm sure he doesn't like the way people are at odds with each other any more than Hugh Bateman does.'

'From what I saw of him at the mill, he wasn't too friendly himself,' says Charlie dismissively. 'Are you absolutely sure *he* didn't put 'em up to it?'

'I must admit the thought crossed my mind. But what

would be the point of rescuing me, if that was the case?'

'What about Thomas Bennett, the manager?' suggests Agnes. 'He knew about the time and place of your meeting.'

'I wouldn't put it past him,' I say, considering the idea. 'It was clear he didn't want to give me the job. And Ned Radford admitted as much. It was only because Bennett wanted to keep on good terms with Hugh Bateman, that he agreed to see us in the first place. Much easier, then, to remove the problem by staging an 'accident' than to directly refuse to employ me. That way he doesn't fall out with Bateman – and he avoids stirring up further the current animosity towards strangers.'

'Yeah, well,' says Charlie smugly, 'perhaps it'll teach you to let me come with you next time. You're not safe to be let out on yer own!'

'I don't think you'd have been of much help against two ruffians like that,' says Agnes.

Charlie bridles. 'I can hold my own in a scuffle, miss, don't you worry! An' it's not like I wasn't no help in other ways, too. 'Oo was it 'oo got young Samuel to tell me 'bout the cove wot most likely killed Robert Ross?'

'Calm down, testy-britches!' I grin. 'Yes, that information was very useful. And Ned Radford confirmed it. You're right, Charlie. He is our most likely suspect. The man who might have been with the rebel army – he wore an officer's uniform at any rate – but didn't leave when they left, because Radford saw him, out of uniform, talking to Ross on the day before he died.'

'The trouble is,' says Agnes, 'that, according to Ned Radford he disappeared without trace immediately after the murder.'

'Probably to go down south and see off that cove in London,' adds Charlie.

'Very likely,' I agree. 'We must get word to Sir William to tell him what we've found out, and to inquire if a man with a squint or a lazy eye was observed at the time of that murder.'

The road which takes us towards Ashbourne is pleasant enough this fine May day, but it still bears marks of the armies which marched this way near four months ago.

In the neighbouring farmland, we see many a fence still broken down and several outbuildings, sometimes the farmhouses themselves, in a state of dereliction or blackened by fire. Even now, three months since the last troops passed through, carts and farm implements lie abandoned in the fields, wheelless and broken.

And, as we trundle slowly through woodland, the pathside trees give ample evidence of the armies' passage. Branches broken and shattered, strewn haphazardly in the undergrowth or hanging crookedly, the splintered fissures only just starting to lose their raw whiteness.

Despite this, green shoots are beginning to show, and the woodland birds are in full song as if the affairs of warring men and the carnage that has already cost so many lives, are of no account in the vast scheme of things.

The physical marks of conflict may be starting to fade, but less material scars in the minds of people are not so easily erased – as we are soon to discover.

Reluctant Guests

We have been journeying a little over three hours and the warm afternoon, together with the steady plodding of Rosinante and the companionable creaking of the cart, has made us drowsy.

We are ambling through a wood, the trees thick around us, shafts of brightness from the late afternoon sun piercing the gloom, when the sudden appearance of several rough-looking fellows shakes us out of our lethargy. They emerge from the trees a dozen yards ahead of us and stand, blocking the path. Only two or three at first, but by the time I draw Rosinante to a halt, their number has swelled to about fifteen.

They surround our cart, one taking hold of Rosinante's halter to prevent her moving further. Far from taking fright, however, the fickle jade allows the fellow to stroke her, even going so far as to butt him affectionately as he scratches her muzzle.

Most of them are unkempt, their hair long and matted, their faces weather-beaten, clad in a nondescript variety of garbs.

For a moment, no-one speaks. They stare menacingly at us and we stare back, trying not to be intimidated, silently assessing the danger.

It is Agnes who breaks the silence. 'God give you good day, friends,' she says in a firm good-natured voice, which shows no trace of the trepidation she must be feeling.

A tall, thick set fellow steps forward. The rest seem to accept him as their leader.

'A good day for some, aye.'

I detect the trace of a Scottish accent which he is trying to hide. Are these stragglers left behind by the retreating rebel forces?

'Where are ye bound, and where d'ye come from?' he continues.

'We come from Derby, friend, and are headed for the town of Ashbourne,' I tell him. 'Have we far to go?'

He ignores my question, countering with one of his own. 'And your purpose?'

'To go on to Manchester to look for work.'

'You're a deal out o' your way, to judge by your accent,' says he. 'Southerners are ye?'

'We have lived in London, yes. But I am a Yorkshiremen by birth. And you, sir?'

'None o' your business. What's in your cart?'

'The poor remains of our home,' replies Agnes with affecting sadness. 'Soldiers ransacked our farm and left us destitute. Alas, we are just three more of the victims of the late troubles. Which is why we are travelling in search of work.'

There is a low muttering from some of the ruffians around us, but whether of sympathy or not, I cannot tell.

Their leader silences them with a warning glance.

'Get down from the cart,' he orders us. 'Don't try to resist, or it will be the worse for you. You see you are outnumbered.'

We have no option but to obey and are immediately surrounded by half a dozen of them. In such close proximity, it is clear that they have lived rough for some time. They stink. Agnes recoils, huddling against me. I put my arm around her shoulder.

The leader singles out two men. 'Caleb, Dickon – search the cart.'

'Don't know what you think you'll find,' says Charlie, sullenly. 'We ain't got nothing.'

'Hold your peace, boy!' says the leader, half raising his fist.

One of the ruffians behind the leader murmurs, just loud enough for us to hear, 'Why not just kill 'em, Callum? Their cart'll come in useful.'

'Shut it, Jamie. I decide what happens here, and there'll be no more killing.'

The two men assigned to search emerge from under the

canvas. 'Nothin' here, Callum, 'cept a few pots and pans. They're tellin' the truth.'

Callum grunts, then tells the man holding Rosinante's head to lead the horse on into the forest. He nods to two of the men beside us. One grabs my arm, the other Charlie's and urges us forward.

'Where are you taking us?' I protest.

He gives a growling laugh. 'You're going to be our guests for a while. No objection to that, have you?'

They lead us deep into the forest. Our captors are sure-footed, moving fast and easily through the trees, though there is no real pathway that I can discern.

Soon we arrive at a clearing where bracken, laced among the branches of several trees forms a series of makeshift shelters in front of a steep slope or cliff. By now the sun is beginning to set, but by its waning light I can make out several darker openings under this leafy portico.

A campfire burns in the centre of the clearing, tended by two wild-haired women who look up in curiosity at our arrival.

Our captors manhandle us roughly into one of the dark openings in the hill side and order us to sit on the ground and not move. One of them disappears outside leaving his companion on guard at the entrance.

In the gloom within, my eyes gradually adjust and I can

see that we are in a sort of huge rabbit burrow hollowed out of the hillside. Thick tree roots, like pillars in a church, support a roof which is a tangled tracery of tendrils a couple of feet above our heads. At the back, just visible in the gloom between the knotty stems, is a pile of weapons. Billhooks, bayonets and one or two ancient-looking muskets together with sundry leather powder flasks and bandoliers.

I also catch a glimpse of rolled up bundles of chequered cloth, the plaid worn by rebel soldiers.

So it is as I thought. This must be a bunch of renegades, either deserters from the Pretender's army during his hasty retreat, or fugitives from the pursuing English forces. In either case, their lives are forfeit.

As ours may be. Desperate men are dangerous

I convey as much of this as I can in low whispers to Agnes and Charlie before our sentry notices and orders us to keep quiet.

It is, I suppose, a hopeful sign that our captors have not thought it necessary to truss us up like prisoners. But even so, in the ensuing enforced silence, I have to dissuade Charlie with frowns and a shake of my head from creeping through the maze of twisted roots, taking up one of the weapons and setting upon our guard. An intention which he has conveyed with many eager nods, winks and raising of eyebrows.

To explain to him that, even if he overcame the guard, there are twenty more rebels out there who won't think twice about killing us, is beyond my powers of gesture and facial expression, so he lapses into a disappointed sulk.

We have been sitting in silence for above an hour when a fellow arrives and orders us to follow him. He and our guard conduct us out into the clearing.

Night has fallen, and the rebels are gathered around a blazing campfire upon which an iron cauldron stands. One of the women is ladling broth from it into wooden bowls.

Callum, the undoubted leader of the group, beckons us to sit near him. Bowls of steaming soup are thrust into our hands. It is thick with barley and oatmeal and contains lumps of some kind of meat, rabbit I guess. But it smells good in the cool night air and, in the absence of spoons, I half drink, half scoop it with my fingers and find it palatable enough to slake my hunger.

'You are fortunate, friend,' says Callum, gruffly. 'We have been debating what to do with ye and we have decided to let ye live.'

I notice that he is no longer trying to disguise his Scottish accent.

'No' that there weren't strong voices to the contrairy,' he continues, 'but there's been killin' enough a'ready wi'out us adding to it. Ye shall hae justice though we hae none.'

'That is noble of you, sir,' I reply gratefully. 'We are both casualties of this recent conflict, I think?'

'The soldiers who evicted you from your home,' says he suspiciously, 'which side were they on?'

I choose my words with care. 'Those loyal to his Hanoverian Majesty. They accused us of having Jacobite sympathies.' Then, before he can ask if there was substance in the accusation, 'By my guess, you are soldiers of the Prince's army, are you not? How comes it that you are still in these parts so long after he retreated from Derby?'

Again, he gives me a suspicious look. 'You're mighty well informed, sir. How do ye know about the Prince's retreat?'

'We tarried some days in Derby. It was the talk of the town – his reluctance to turn back, the strong counsels of his generals to persuade him to do so, the speed of their departure.'

'Aye, 'twas that speed undid us!' he exclaims angrily. 'So secret were the plans that we foot-soldiers knew naught until the army was well on the move. At first we were ordered to march south, but we were no mair than a mile out of town than the order was gi'en to turn around and go back at the double the way we'd come.'Twas aw rabble and confusion!'

And the weather cannot have helped,' I say. 'It was the depths of winter, was it not?'

'The sixth of December, and snow still thick on the ground, the wind raw and blawin with squalls of rain like grapeshot in our faces. Impossible to march a'togither. The whole army became scattered through the woods and hills. Our small group lost our bearings and by nighttime discovered we were still no more than two miles from Derby.'

'Couldn't you make up the time the next day?' asks Charlie.

'D'ye think we didna try? But word was that Marshal Wade's forces were a'coming from the east to cut us off. We had a skirmish wi' an advance party and lost a many, and others wounded. So we went into hiding here until the English troops moved on, intendin' to go north as soon as we could.'

'Yet you are still here?'

'Caleb, tell them what passed,' says Callum, summoning one of the two men who searched our cart earlier.

Caleb is a dark, broad-shouldered fellow with brooding eyes and hardly has he uttered a dozen words than I realise he is not a Scot like most of this gang. He has the broad, flat vowels of a North Englishman, but not the growling lilt of the Highlanders. 'I weren't wi' these at the start. I managed to stay wi' the retreat as far as Macclesfield. By which time, beset by enemy raids and despairin' o' the Prince's failing fortunes a fair number of us lost hope and began to think on savin' our own skins.'

'You deserted?' says Agnes with no hint of either reproach or approval.

'Aye, to my shame. And it cost me dear. I became a fugitive, a man without a cause, reviled by friend and foe alike. Then, in Ashbourne, I chanced to see one of my former comrades executed. Condemned and hanged within the hour, 'e was. Word is the Duke of Cumberland himself ordered 'is troops not waste time trying rebel stragglers, but to leave them to the mercy of local watchmen.'

I can see that he is deeply affected by recounting his tale, despairing at a world where justice and humanity now seemingly count for naught.

Callum pats him on the back. 'Caleb here fell in with us by chance and his news persuaded us to lie low here in the forest till the time comes when we may all take our chance and go our separate ways.'

'We have seen no troops on our way here,' says Agnes.

'Nay, they're all up in Scotland now. Tales tel o' a great battle near Inverness at a place called Culloden. It's said that Cumberland's forces have beaten Prince Charles and that he's fled, telling a' those who've risked so much for his cause that they must now shift for themselves,' says Callum disconsolately. 'So much for all oor hopes and fine ideals!'

'Aye,' says Caleb, 'there'll be those who'll make sure Charles Stuart gets safe passage to France, while the rest of us who put such faith in him and gave him our loyalty get hunted down to die like dogs.'

There are murmurs of assent from the others gathered round the fire. Their faces suspended in the darkness, lit by the ruddy glow of the flames, every one a mask of despair and thwarted hope.

Of a sudden I see not a gang of threatening brigands, but a group of frightened, disillusioned men. We are as much a danger to them as they to us. Their treatment of us is born more of fear than menace.

'I myself have seen service last year in Europe,' I tell them. 'And one thing I have learned is that we common men are naught but pawns in rich men's games. A nobleman's death will make a stir in the world, but the slaughter of hundreds like us will cause hardly a ripple.'

'Fine words, my friend,' says Callum with just a hint of scorn. 'And said to save your hides, by persuading me to let you go, I do not doubt. But you and us - we're not the same. How do I know you'll not inform on us as soon as you get chance?'

'You do not,' I reply frankly. 'All I can give you is my word as an ex-soldier like yourself – and that of my wife and brother. Our only purpose is to journey on to

Manchester in search of work. My one loyalty is now to my family and its survival. My only animosity is to those who made this journey of ours necessary by depriving us of our home and livelihood.'

'Seth speaks for all three of us, sir,' says Agnes. 'If you choose to let us go on our way, we give you our promise that we shall say no word to anyone about your presence here. We, too, are strangers in these parts and, in these present times, as much subject to suspicion as yourselves.'

'Aye, but your voices dinnae condemn ye as soon as ye open your mouths,' retorts Callum.

'Nor does mine,' puts in Caleb. 'Let me stand as their surety, Callum. So be they let me travel with them to Manchester, I'll see they don't blab. How say you?'

For answer, Callum looks at me, 'Well, what say you, Hodges? Will you accept Caleb here as your travelling companion?'

My first reaction is to refuse. The last thing we want with us is a renegade rebel soldier. Not only will he be acting as our guard, but he might also be recognised and jeopardise our mission.

But then Agnes speaks up. 'I see no objection to that, Caleb. You are, by your accent, from around these parts?'

'From near Preston, north of Manchester.'

'You know the area, then?'

He shrugs assent. 'I know my village and the places I've seen since I've been in the Prince's army.'

Agnes turns to me. 'What say you, Seth?' There is an intensity in her gaze which urges me to agree.

'But if anyone should recognise him...?' I hesitate.

'A haircut, a shave, a broad hat...?' she says lightly. 'There are ways enough to disguise a man.'

'Well...,' I say hesitantly.

Callum gives a scornful laugh. 'I see you expect us to trust you, but have difficulty in returning the favour, sir! Come, let us have an end tae this. Either you leave here tomorrow morning and Caleb goes with you – or I yield to the advice o' my men who'd have ye stay wi' three shallow graves for your beds. 'Tis your choice.'

Faced with a a decision between two evils, I choose the lesser. Reluctantly I agree to accept Caleb as our travelling companion.

The Road North

The wariness with which we were treated on the road to Derby becomes outright hostility as we push further north.

Whilst it was only rumours that progressed further south than Derby - fearful stories and exaggerated accounts of wild Highlanders ransacking houses, raping women and eating children - these northbound roads we are now travelling have actually been trodden by the rebel army. First during its triumphant advance and later in its pell-mell retreat, with government troops following hotfoot after.

Spring is starting to erase some of the physical traces of their passage, but in people's hearts – whichever side they supported – memories are still bitter. Every stranger, as we find to our cost, is now seen as an enemy.

In Ashbourne we find no place to stop. As soon as our cart draws to a halt we are accosted by a surly bunch of men who order us to move on.

'There's naught for the likes o' you here,' growls a scowling woman who seems to be their spokesman, 'be on your way!'

In vain we plead that we only want to buy provisions at the market but the more we try to reason, the more aggressive they become. A couple of young men produce cudgels and set their jaws ready for a fray.

We are within sight of the market stalls. I look at Caleb and we decide to chance it, hoping that if we show we mean no trouble, this small rabble won't provoke any either. Telling Charlie drive the cart slowly onwards, we help Agnes down from the cart and join her, acting as bodyguards, as she walks to the nearest stall.

The sight of two strapping young men acts as a slight deterrent. The men with cudgels keep close, but the older woman stays them from any further action as Agnes proceeds to haggle over a withered selection of vegetables and scraggy meat.

We are only at the stall for a few minutes, but during that time, we attract yet more notice. By the time Agnes agrees a sum well over the odds for the few miserable viands, the crowd has increased, and their mood is menacing.

The bargain struck, we stride hurriedly after the cart which Charlie is pluckily keeping to a slow plod, the crowd sullenly parting to allow us through. We clamber up and Charlie encourages Rosinante into sedate trot amidst an escort of unfriendly townsfolk, the last of whom do not leave us until we are well past the town boundary.

'It is lucky 'twas midday,' says Caleb later as, a few hours later, we draw the cart onto a patch of ground in a woodland clearing. 'Had it been now, at evening, we'd as like ended up in a ditch with our heads stove in, such ill-will has the recent conflict caused.'

Our afternoon's journey has taken us through largely deserted countryside and we have all been unusually silent, downcast by our hostile reception in Ashbourne. I have been quietly reflecting upon my recent march across Flanders, when I myself was a member of an advancing army, remembering the effect we had upon the local populace.

'It is understandable,' I say, helping Agnes down from the cart. 'To have an army march through, or worse stop in a town is like being hit by a hurricane. The men to be housed, the horses stabled and all to be clothed and fed. A poor villager may lose a year's provisions within an hour. I have seen it with my own eyes.'

'And I,' says Caleb. He helps Charlie remove Rosinante's halter. 'Yet I have also seen folk give up their beds and all willingly. 'Twas so at first, when we were marching south. There were many in this area who welcomed us. Greeted us with gifts and huzzahs.' His face clouds. 'And only three months later the very same people threw stones and spat at us as we were forced to retrace our steps.'

Agnes is preparing the vegetables for the pot. 'What caused such an about-turn?' she asks.

'Disappointment. The loss of hope,' says Caleb morosely. 'I remember when I first saw the Prince in the midst of his army. Like a Trojan Hero he was, drawing admiration and love from all who beheld him. I was drinking with some friends in a public house when there was a commotion out on the highroad. We all piled out to see the rebel army passing by, with the Prince at its head. Then there was an officer came by, distributing a pamphlet that spoke of how the people, under the tyranny and oppression of the usurping Hanoverians, were like oxen yoked down to the plough. The Prince, it said, was here to free them, to help them shake off that yoke which had too long galled the necks of free-born Englishmen!'

'And you believed it?'

'I was in my cups,' he says with a wry grimace. 'My friends and me, we were all for it and in the following days went about spreading the word. But alas, despite all our exhortations, few consented to join us. Throughout all the march through Lancashire we garnered but a couple of hundred, which the Prince agreed to call the Manchester Regiment. Last I heard, they've been left to guard Carlisle while the Prince hides out in Scotland.' His voice is full of scorn and bitterness. 'Renegade Englishmen abandoned to face the English army – they'll all be slaughtered for sure!'

* * *

During the next few days we get to know Caleb better. Born in the village of Salmesbury near Preston, he is the second son of a non-juror clergyman.

'What's a non-juror?' asks Charlie. 'A Roman Catholic? The Pretender's followers are mostly Papists, ain't they?'

'I'm no Papist,' says Caleb firmly. 'My folks are Protestants through and through, like a lot of the Scotsmen who support the Prince. Can't say as how I understand it all, but my dad told me that it all comes from when the old Stuart King, James II was sent packing. Lots of churchmen refused to swear allegiance to King William, even though his wife was a Stuart. And, when Queen Anne died childless, they were even more adamant they wouldn't swear allegiance to the Hanoverian usurper, George I, whilst the 'true' King, James II's son, is still alive.'

'That's the Pretender's father?' Charlie interrupts.

'That's right,' says Caleb. 'The one in exile in Rome who styles himself James III.'

'So although *he's* a Catholic, not all his followers are Catholics?' says Charlie with a puzzled frown.

'Things are rarely simple, Charlie,' I explain, 'despite Mr Fielding's imagined nightmare of Popish priests burning Protestants on the streets of London! Jacobites aren't only Scotsmen. Nor are all Scots Jacobites. Like Caleb here, there's men of different nationalities and religions.'

The tedium of our daily jog through the countryside is, to some extent, dispelled by these discussions. Yet, even as I come to know and like Caleb, he brings to mind others whom I have accounted my friends: Finn Kelly from my time in Dublin and Ben Woodrow from my long march through Flanders. Finn, whose love for his country and the injustice meted out to the Irish, and Ben, whose abhorrence of all kinds of tyranny, persuaded them both into desperate acts. And I reflect how easy it is for passionately held views to turn to violence.

Caleb occasionally shows flashes of that same ardour I saw in them, but it is tempered by disillusion.

I feel sad for his shattered dreams and deplore the simmering animosities this rebellion has brought to the boil in people. Yet I cannot help but feel that the Jacobite army is more a collection of disaffected individuals, like Finn Kelly and Ben Woodrow, than a united fighting force.

The story Caleb tells us the second day of our journey only serves to underline the sense of intrepid individuals engaged in a reckless enterprise.

'Soon as I heard the Jacobite army was on its way to Manchester last Autumn, I set out to see it. I walked for two days, arriving in the city on the morning of November 28th. The place was near deserted, none o' the crowds I'd expected. Seems that most of the people had left. And the town militia had been stood down the day before, fearin' the town couldn't be defended.'

'Mr Bateman said something very similar happened in Derby,' says Agnes.

'Aye, and in all towns the Prince visited on his march into England. 'Twas that, perhaps, which gave him hope, for with so many quitting the town, there was only the poor who had nowhere to flee to, and those sympathetic to his cause left in town,' says Caleb with regret.

'Was it the cavalry who arrived first, like at Derby?' asks Charlie.

Caleb laughs, ruefully. 'Nothing so grand, lad. 'Twas but two fellows in highland dress arrived about three in the afternoon, followed by a wild-haired doxy beating a drum. No one took much notice of them at first until the sergeant started shouting, inviting people to join up for "the yellow-haired laddie". '

Caleb laughs as he remembers. 'He was a real character. Name o' Tom Dickson. Like the friend I saw executed in Ashbourne, he was one o' many who'd deserted from the British army and joined the Jacobites at Prestonpans. After checkin' there was no army following, some locals surrounded him, thinkin' to take him prisoner. But he swung his blunderbuss around, roarin' like a lion and promisin' that if anyone dared to attack him or his girlfriend, he'd blow their bloody brains out.'

'And did he get any recruits?' I ask.

'An hundred and eighty that same afternoon,' replies Caleb with pride. 'There be plenty of Jacobites in Manchester and they soon stepped forward, causin' those who would make trouble to slink away with their tails between their legs. And that's how the Manchester Regiment came into being.'

He lapses into a sad silence, perhaps recalling what he told us back in the forest near Ashbourne, that most of those brave fellows are now probably dead or imprisoned after being left by the Pretender with the doomed task of defending Carlisle.

By the time we are approaching Manchester, his role to guard against us informing on Callum and his band of fugitives near Ashbourne is all but forgotten.

We have encountered no English troops on our way. Nevertheless, for his own safety, in case he should be recognised, Agnes has cropped most of his hair and tied the rest into a pony tail. In this respect, though not in facial features, he and Charlie and I might be taken for brothers. But as his accent is so removed from ours, we concoct the fiction that he is a cousin, joined with us to look for work.

So far, we have provided him with a secure passage almost back to his home village. In return, his local accent has occasionally eased our progress where we would otherwise have been regarded with suspicion.

As we draw nearer to Manchester, however, Agnes intends that he shall be of even more use. The night after she argued for him to be included on our journey, she confided her purpose to me.

'He was with the Jacobite army in Manchester when David Ross was killed. Perhaps he knows something of the circumstances. At the very least he is familiar with the territory.'

Just over a week after leaving Derby, we reach Manchester.

Gradually, open countryside gives way to cultivated fields and gardens. Over to our left as we amble slowly along the road is a large lake or pool which Caleb informs us is called Daubholes and was the place where scolds and lewd women were ducked in the last century.

'Six stools there were at one time for dipping them,' says Caleb, much to Agnes's disgust.

The road along which we are travelling is, Caleb tells us, called Market Street Lane, and it is a busy highway indeed. For several miles there has been a constant traffic of wagons and strings of pack-horses, those overtaking us largely empty, those headed in the opposite direction loaded high with bulging bales of cloth.

The town is a prosperous-looking place, with many fine, recently constructed stone or brick-built houses, though those in the area round the big church are older, built of timber and plaster.

Caleb directs us past the church down towards the river.

'There'll be space enough to leave the cart on Parsonage Croft,' he says.

This turns out to be an expanse of scrubland on the riverbank between houses upon one side and open fields on the other, crossed by diagonal paths.

We draw the cart into a corner well-removed from the houses, not wanting to attract either curiosity or the ire of the townsfolk.

Manchester

Manchester is bigger than Derby and more friendly.

'We're down to earth folk round 'ere,' says Caleb as we walk along Deansgate into town next morning. He is dressed in a loose fustian jerkin and coarse woollen britches with his hat pulled well down on his brow. 'We tek what comes and mek the best o' it. I think the Prince chose to march through here because Manchester's allus bin well inclined to his cause. See that square over there? St James's, a Jacobite name. The uprising was as like to 'ave started 'ere as in any town in England.'

I am looking about me at all the fine town houses. 'But the response wasn't what he hoped?' I say.

'Sadly not,' he sighs, following the direction of my gaze. 'As you see, 'tis also a prosperous town – all those carts and 'orses laden wi' bales on our way in yesterday, you recall them? And the barges that have passed along the Irwell, next to where we've left the cart? That's all cloth, made here and bound for Liverpool and London.'

'Yet I didn't see any mills along the river, like those at Derby,' says Agnes, puzzled.

'No need for big mills,' he replies with a touch of pride. 'There's plenty o' fair-sized workshops in the town with a dozen Dutch looms apiece, as well as countless farmer's wives wi' broadlooms in all the villages around. There's a many o' my old schoolmates is weavin'-hands still, them as declined to join us.' The note of sad bitterness returns. 'I railed at them at the time, but I understand 'em now. 'Tis all very well 'aving romantic notions of restoring the true King, an' listenin' to preachers spoutin' about it's only God what chooses 'em, but it can't be denied that even the lowliest of us 'as done all right under the Hanoverian Georges. We ain't rich by no means, but we ain't 'avin to beg neither. Even humble folks know which side their bread's buttered, as they say. Even though them in London probably 'as no idea that Manchester exists, let alone where it is, I'll lay they'd soon sit up and tek notice of us if money from the cloth trade dried up.'

'Is that why you enlisted?' Agnes asks him. 'Because London pays no heed to folk in the north?'

'Partly, but it also had a lot to do with mi' dad. 'Im and Bishop Deacon at the Collegiate Church.'

'Is that the building we can see over there?' asks Agnes, pointing towards a four-square pinnacled tower rising above the roofs a little further along the river.

'It is,' Caleb confirms. 'And Dr Deacon is probably one o' the last non-juring Bishops in the country. All three of 'is sons joined the Prince's cause, God rest 'em.'

148

'They're all dead?' inquires Agnes with sympathy.

'I 'eard Robert died in prison. His two brothers, Tom and Charlie, are captured and are like to be hanged or transported. Good lads all three.'

'How sad for their father,' says Agnes sadly.

'Huh, I shouldn't waste your pity upon such as him,' snorts Caleb. 'As stiff-necked an old Puritan as you'd never wish to meet! When not preaching sermons favouring the Jacobite cause, he's forever railing against the evils of drink. There was one such sermon he preached just about the time the Prince was here, rejoicing in the death of a wine merchant in the town – I can't ever recall hearing such an un-Christian tirade! Fortunately the man's family were not there to hear it as they attended the Presbyterian Church, St Ann's, in the new town. In fact, that's the poor fellow's shop there.'

We have come into the older part of town, near to the big church we noticed earlier, where the houses are smaller, though they might have been accounted grand a hundred years or so ago when they were built, with whitewashed walls and overhanging beams. A little distance away, but still in the shadow of the church is a thriving Market Place.

The building Caleb is pointing out is at the corner of a street with the unappealing title of Hanging Ditch. A wooden sign in the shape of a wine bottle swings from a metal bracket above the doorway: *Feilden and Ross, Importers and Purveyors of Quality Wines.*

I glance at Agnes and see that she, too, has recognised the significance.

'So which partner was it that died,' I ask disingenuously, 'Mr Feilden or Mr Ross? He'd be an old man, I suppose?'

'It was Ross and he weren't that old. Around thirty-five, I'd say.'

'Oh, that's sad,' says Agnes, 'when one so young is taken. Did he have a wife and children?'

'A wife and a child, I heard, I don't know whether 'twas a boy or girl. But they'll be well taken care of I have no doubt, for Mr Feilden, his partner, was also his father-in-law.'

'A sudden death, was it – or had he been ill?'

'An apoplectic fit, so 'tis said, right here in the street. Though tongues wagged at the time, saying he must have been poisoned, for he'd never ailed a day in his life.'

'You seem to know a lot about it, Caleb,' says Agnes, 'considering you were only in Manchester a few days.'

Caleb laughs, 'Aye, four days. But gossip travels fast, especially when you've got a tattler the likes of Beppy Byrom! A proper Miss Flibbertigibbet!'

'An acquaintance of yours?'

'And of most of the fashionable young bucks around

town! Pray, don't misunderstand me, Mrs Hodges. I do not mean to besmirch her honour. I knew Beppy from long before the Prince came on the scene. I may have lived out of town, but my friends and I came into town on high days and holidays. And there was never a levee, ball or assembly at which she was not present. I doubt she'd know me from Adam. But everyone knows her.'

'She sounds like a spruce giggler,' observes Charlie rudely.

'A gossip, certainly,' says Caleb. 'But where Ross's death is concerned she had the story first hand. Her father and Mr Feilden are two of the town's notables, so she and the dead man's wife were friends.'

We are now in the midst of the market which, unlike the poor affair at Ashbourne, is as crowded and bustling as any I have known in London. Stallholders are shouting their wares, pedlars and hucksters touting their ribbons and trinkets. In the centre of the square is a clearing around a stone cross where a juggler is performing with wooden clubs, tossing them high into the air and catching them, accompanied by squeals and gasps from a small crowd of onlookers.

We join them, watching in delight as he switches to throwing two at a time, then adds several brightly coloured wooden balls into the mix.

It is as I am watching his display that I feel a tug at my sleeve. I look round to see a ragged youngster at my elbow. I make to push him away, thinking him but a beggar, but he clings on.

'You the man wi' the 'orse and cart on Pars'nage Croft?' he asks. 'Name o' 'Odges?'

Immediately I am on my guard. 'And if I am?'

He rummages in his tattered jerkin and produces a crumpled piece of paper which he holds out with a grubby hand. 'Gen'man told us ter gi' this to yer,' he says. His mouth twists and his eye sparkles with crafty expectation. ' 'E give me sixpence...'

'Then you're well paid,' I tell him, twitching the note from his greasy fingers. 'Now be off with you. I've no coin to pay you more.'

'Bloody skinflint!' I hear him mutter as he slopes off into the crowd.

I unfold the note and read it. The message is short and to the point. But it seems to make no sense.

3 o'clock this afternoon. The Angel.

Charlie and Caleb, engrossed in the juggler's performance, have noticed nothing, but Agnes is looking at me curiously. I hand her the note and see her look of worried puzzlement.

'Who or what is the *Angel*?' she whispers.

152

'I have no idea,' I whisper back. Then, in my normal tone, 'Caleb, does the *Angel* mean anything to you?'

'It means good company and good beer. I used to go there before.... but I wouldn't dare show my face there now. Not till the recent troubles are well forgotten.'

'It's a public house, then?'

'Aye, down by the Shambles. That and the Bull's Head are the two best taverns in town. But they're not for the likes of us. They're for respectable gentlemen and upright citizens, not poor fugitives like ourselves.'

The juggler concludes his act with an elaborate bow to a ripple of applause. He skips around the audience, shaking his cap for appreciative donations but we walk on before he has chance to accost us. I think Caleb is about to ask what my interest in the Angel may be when Agnes distracts his attention.

'What is that place?' she asks, pointing to an imposing, many arched building on the south side of the Market Place where many well dressed men are going in and out.

'That? That's the Exchange, built for the cotton trade by Sir Oswald Moseley of Ancoats Hall. I remember seeing it being built one time when my dad brought me to hear a sermon at the Collegiate Church. I was about seven at the time.'

'What's the place next to it, with all the pipes?' asks

Charlie.

'That's the Conduit,' Caleb tells him. 'Water from the spring in Fountain Street is piped along Market Street to form a central supply of fresh water for the townsfolk.'

'Blimey,' says Charlie, ' we could do wi' some o' them in Lon...'

'Lunnington - the nearest town to where our farm was,' I interrupt him, then quickly change the subject, 'But what's that delicious smell?'

From somewhere amongst the market throng, we are assailed by the savoury aroma of cooking. Unable to resist, Agnes strides in true farmer's wife fashion over to a stall selling warm meat pies.

The others follow, but my eye has been attracted elsewhere. As our attention was on the Exchange and the Conduit, I had the impression that one of the well-dressed men at that side of the square was looking in our direction.

Now, whilst the others are at the pie stall, I search for him amongst the milling bodies. But if there was anyone watching us, he is now gone.

The others return, Agnes carrying a wrapped parcel. 'Come,' she says, 'let's return to our cart. This will not stay hot for long.'

Hurrying back to Parsonage Croft, I have the uncanny sensation that we are being followed.

The Angel

We have just finished the pie and are wiping our greasy fingers on hunks of bread washed down with small beer, when Caleb asks if, having arrived in Manchester, do we mind if he now goes his own way.

'I have fulfilled my promise to Callum and my erstwhile comrades back at Ashbourne to ensure that you would not inform on them...'

'I never had any intention of doing so,' I interrupt him. 'None of us had. What good would be served by adding to the woes of already desperate men? When I gave Callum my word, I meant it.'

'Aye,' answers Caleb, 'I see that now, and these last few days have given me more than enough proof of your good faith. But an unfortunate consequence of this troubled time is that it leads us to mistrust even the best of men. I am sure that by now Callum and the others will have disbanded and gone their separate ways, so my role has no further purpose.' He pauses, eyes cast down. 'Moreover, our journey has, I think, been of mutual benefit. I own I have been most grateful for your company these last few days...'

'And we for yours,' smiles Agnes. 'We have become friends, I think.'

'You are kind to say so, Mrs Hodges,' replies Caleb, 'but now we are in Manchester, I fear I may prove a perilous friend to have. There is more chance I may be recognised here. If that happens it might drag you all into danger, and I would not have that on my conscience. Already this morning, even though we have taken pains to disguise my former self, I have noticed one or two people looking askance at me. It can only be a matter of time before someone identifies me as the firebrand who promoted the Pretender's cause a few months back.' He looks up, his eyes sorrowful. 'Though it pains me to say it, I think it is safer that we part.'

'What will you do?' asks Agnes.

'I'll make my way back to Salmesbury, if I can. There I may lie low. There will be some in the village who'll censure me for my recent actions but we stick together, we village folk, and in time old wounds will heal.'

'We shall miss you,' I tell him as I clasp his hand in farewell. 'We pray you may stay safe.'

Then, having received similar good wishes from Agnes and Charlie, he pulls his hat over his eyes and, with one last backward wave, strides away along the river bank.

The Angel has an imposing twin gabled frontage freshly whitewashed, with exposed beams in the old style. It stands twenty yards or so from the Market Square, almost on the corner of The Shambles, a narrow, cobbled lane with a channel running down the centre towards the river.

Butchers still ply their trade here and the channel, aided by occasional pails of water, still runs red with offal, though now in a brick-lined channel covered by a metal grating rather than the shallow runnel it must have been in former times, slopping over people's shoes and spattering their hose. Like the Conduit, this small improvement is another example of this northern town's civic pride which puts parts of London to shame, where many noisome streets still stink with rotting excrement and rubbish.

A six-foot high whitewashed wall projects some four feet or so from the inn, as if to shield its patrons from any offence caused by the neighbouring meat-traders. A liveried doorman stands, haughty and erect, next to the entrance.

Conscious suddenly of our shabby appearance, and recalling our late companion's comment that The Angel is 'not for the likes of us' I approach him, cap in hand, and show him the note.

He takes it, holding it disdainfully between the finger and thumb of his gloved hand as if it were one of the floating pieces of offal in the nearby channel. Summoned by an imperious wave, a junior footman emerges, is given the note and disappears inside once more, leaving us standing awkwardly in the road. The doorman stares straight ahead, ignoring us completely.

Several minutes elapse before the footman reappears. He beckons me to come forward.

'Are you Seth Hodges? he asks and, receiving my confirmatory nod, says, 'Just you. The others must wait outside.'

I glance briefly at Agnes and Charlie and see they are uneasy. 'All will be well,' I assure them, though my own heart, too, is beating with trepidation. Then I follow the footman into the inn.

The Angel is as impressive inside as out, its old wooden panelling painted in the most fashionable hue of sage green, a Turkey carpet upon the tiled floor.

The footman leads me silently into a small side room where a familiar thin figure clad in black awaits me, standing erect, hands behind his back like a schoolmaster about to admonish an unruly pupil.

'Master Archer,' says Nathaniel Grey, surveying me disdainfully from head to toe, 'and looking so down at heel I'm surprised they let you in.'

He offers no handshake in greeting, but I expect no less from this condescending lieutenant of Sir William Hervey who seems to dislike me for some reason I have never been able to ascertain.

'Mr Grey,' I reply with a civil nod. 'As you are pleased to observe, I am clearly playing, with some degree of success it would appear, the role that Sir William gave me.'

He gives a sneering tut of annoyance at my turning his insult into a compliment.

'I did not expect to see you,' I continue. 'Indeed, I did not know what to expect, your note was so brief and baffling.'

'It does not do in our business to commit too much to paper, as you should know, Master Archer,' he replies smugly. 'And that is the reason I am here.'

'Sir William is not with you?'

'I am surprised you need to ask,' says he disparagingly. 'Did he not tell you at the outset that this whole affair must be conducted in a manner which must give no indication of his involvement?'

'He did, which is the reason Miss Mayer, Master Stubbs and I were obliged to adopt our present disguise as a dispossessed farming family.'

'Yes, yes,' says he tetchily, 'I am aware of that. The question is, has your disguise enabled you to discover anything of use?'

'I believe it has, sir. And I have already drafted a summary of my findings which I intended to post to Sir William this very day.'

'Well, I shall save you the bother, Master Archer, for

you may now report them directly to me, if you would be so good. Pray be concise,' he sighs.

'Very well, Mr Grey.' And I proceed to tell him what we have found out at Derby and since our arrival in Manchester. 'It was put about, as a matter of political expedience by Sir Richard Everard, the local Justice, that Robert Ross was murdered by disaffected workers at the Silk Mill where he was an overseer. No-one in the town is convinced by that. There was no evidence that he was disliked. I got the impression he was strict but fair in his duties.'

'Impressions are not facts, Master Archer.'

'I agree, Mr Grey, but I base them upon first hand testimonies. Not only of the manager of the mill, Mr Thomas Bennett, but also of Mr Ned Radford, one of Ross's fellow supervisors. Neither believes any of the mill employees were involved. Both are men of direct and forthright opinions and had no reason to lie.'

'Fair enough. But if it was not a worker who killed him, why would the Justice say it was?'

'There are two reasons. First, it was, as I said, politically expedient.'

He does not say anything, but his dubious expression is enough to demand an explanation.

I refuse to let it irk me and continue calmly, 'The murder

took place within days of the Jacobite occupation of the town. Everard was out of town whilst the Pretender's forces were there and, when he returned after their departure, the political situation was still uncertain. He might not have considered it wise to accuse a soldier in the service of one who might shortly be the ruling power in the land, for fear of future reprisals.'

'A moot point. And the other reason?'

'Ross had the reputation of a seducer of women, one of whom was Everard's own daughter.'

'Are you suggesting that Everard himself had a hand in his murder?'

'It is a possibility, though I do not think it likely – from what I heard of Sir Richard, he is a bully but also a coward. He would be too chary of his own reputation to risk being associated with such a deed. Besides, thanks to Master Stubbs, we discovered a more credible suspect. Someone posing as a soldier whilst the Jacobite army was in residence, but who was still in town, though no longer in uniform, for several days after the rebel army had gone. And Ross was not killed until after those forces had vacated the town.'

'Do you have a name for this man?'

'Unfortunately not. Only the merest of descriptions. That he was of an amiable, even flirtatious nature, and that he had a slight squint, what is sometimes called a lazy eye. I wonder, Mr Grey, if you might ask Sir William to inquire if anyone concerned with the murder of Mr Alexander Ross in London recalls such a person? If this is, indeed, our man, he would have had ample time after killing Robert Ross in Derby, to travel to London in order to kill Alexander Ross.'

'*If* he is our man,' replies Grey with a sceptical curl of his lip. 'Have you heard of such a fellow associated with the murder of Mr David Ross here in Manchester?'

'We only arrived yesterday afternoon, sir.'

'So you haven't yet discovered anything,' says Grey dismissively.

'On the contrary, Mr Grey, I have discovered that he was probably poisoned. Also that he was quite well connected in the town, being a wine merchant in partnership with his father-in-law, a Mr Feilden who, in turn, is one of the leading citizens and is acquainted with a Mr Byrom whose daughter, Beppy, is a known gossip. It is my intention to contrive a meeting with Miss Byrom – though how it may be managed I do not as yet know. It is unlikely that a young lady of quality would have dealings with folk such as we appear to be.'

Grey has listened sourly, piqued, no doubt, by hearing that I have discovered much in so short a time. But hearing of my dilemma, he says, with an air of bestowing a favour,

'What I have to tell you may perhaps be of some advantage, then, Master Archer.'

'You have further orders from Sir William?'

'I have.' He pauses, lingering out the moment with infuriating self-satisfaction.

'And they are...?' I prompt him as the silence lengthens.

Gratified to have stirred my impatience, he continues briskly. 'Events have moved on since you were given your instructions, Master Archer. You are no longer to regard the Ross murders as your first priority.'

'Sir William wants me to cease my enquiries?' I say, shocked and somewhat disappointed.

'No, you are still to find out what you can before you embark on your new task. But your imposture as the Hodges family will no longer be convenient. In order to carry out your new task, you must go up in the world.'

I am taken aback. 'How are we to manage that? We have only the clothes we stand up in...?'

He gives me a pitying smile. '*You* are not expected to manage it, Archer. Sir William and I shall, of course, provide the means.'

He reaches inside his waistcoat and produces a leather wallet which he places on the table. I contain my irritation at his patronising attitude.

'After weeks on the road, I don't suppose any of you are

particularly clean,' says he superciliously, 'and I do not suppose this wretched town boasts anything as civilised as a bath-house...'

'There is clean water to be had, sir,' I say, recalling the Conduit in the Market Square.

He shrugs. 'In that case, you, Miss Mayer and the Stubbs boy must make yourselves as presentable as you can. Then tomorrow morning you will seek out a reputable tailor's shop – or a dress shop in the lady's case – and purchase such items as may befit a well-to-do family. Nothing too showy, mind. You should not regard these funds...,' he taps the leathern wallet, '...as limitless Once attired, you will return here where I have booked rooms for you under the name of Mr and Mrs Lindsay and their brother.'

'For how many nights?' I ask. 'You said Sir William still wants us to find what we can about David Ross's death before we embark on whatever new task he has assigned us.'

'Two days at most,' he replies. 'I have arranged horses for you all to continue your journey at the end of that time.'

'To *continue* our journey?' I say in surprise. 'We are not returning to London?'

'No, Master Archer. You are going to Scotland.'

'To report to Mr Forbes what we have found about the mysterious deaths of his relatives? Surely Sir William will want to do that in person?'

' Indeed he will, Master Archer. And I have no doubt he will do so when all is known. In the meantime, he is issuing you with fresh instructions.'

'Fresh instructions?'

'As you may have heard, Master Archer - for I suppose even on the road news must have reached you – the rebel forces have recently been routed at Culloden. The Duke of Cumberland is now zealously pursuing the remnants of the rebel army. A little too zealously in Sir William's view. His Grace is so intent on retribution that the streets of Inverness are already lined with fully-laden gibbets. His main quarry, as you may imagine, is young Charles Stuart himself, and many believe he will not rest until he sees him on the scaffold like his unfortunate forbear, Charles I. That, Sir William believes, would be nothing short of disaster. It would create a martyr and cause such alienation of the Scots that they would rise up in even greater numbers. The very future of the Union would be in doubt. Everything that has been achieved since the Kingdoms of Scotland and England were united is in danger of being set at naught.' He pauses to let the enormity of the possibility to sink in.

'A serious situation indeed,' I agree, 'but what bearing has this upon the fresh instructions you bring me from Sir William?'

'At the moment, no-one knows exactly where the Young

Pretender is,' says Grey. Then with pursed mouth and a sceptical upturn of his brow, he sighs. 'For some reason beyond my understanding, Sir William holds a high opinion of you, Master Archer, and believes you capable of the task he is now setting you : to find the Young Pretender, Charles Edward Stuart, before the Duke of Cumberland does and then to ensure that he safely makes his escape to the Continent.'

Manchester Society

My head is still reeling when I walk unsteadily out of the Angel several minutes later.

Agnes and Charlie hurry forward, relieved at my safe return, but alarmed to see me so dumbfounded.

'Whatever is the matter?' asks Agnes in distress. 'What has happened? Who was in there?'

I hold up my hand and shake my head, waving aside her questions until I can gather my thoughts. Wordlessly, I beckon them to follow me and it is not until we have almost reached Parsonage Croft where our cart stands with Rosinante listlessly grazing beside it that I am able to find any coherent words of explanation.

'Hervey is sending us into the jaws of danger,' I tell them when I have recounted all the details of my meeting with Grey and the enormity of the task that Hervey has set us. 'Everyone will be our enemy. The Prince's friends will not trust us and, if we fall into the Duke's hands, we shall be accused of treason. We shall be lucky to come out of this alive,' I say despairingly.

Then, turning to address Charlie, 'Agnes and myself have no choice in the matter, we are Hervey's agents. But you are not his creature, Charlie, he has no hold over you.

You do not have to come with us if you do not want to.'

'You try stopping me,' he retorts belligerently. 'I've come this far, haven't I? And I didn't do it for Hervey, I did it because you need lookin' after. So no half measures now, mate, it's the whole hog or none!' Then an expression of dismay clouds his face. 'But, if we're to be all the crack and become spruce fellows, what's goin' to happen to poor Rosie?'

'Grey says he will arrange for Rosinante and the cart to be collected,' I reassure him. 'There's plenty of tradesmen or husbandmen who've had things taken during the recent conflict and who'll be glad of them. And once we've finished our business here in Manchester, there'll be horses provided for our onward journey. Mounts suitable for our improved status.'

'Yeah, well as long as Rosie goes to a good home.' Then his face cracks into a grin. 'And I'll be gettin' a horse o' mi own, you say? And be a-ridin' fine as any gennelman? Well rattle my bones, what would Susan and Mrs Wiggins say!'

The mention of Susan and Mrs Wiggins brings a momentary pang of longing for what I have left behind. My house in Soho Square that I may now never live in. The friends that I may never see again. An untroubled life which I have sacrificed for a perilous journey with an uncertain end.

But I brush such regrets aside. I have chosen this path and it is fruitless to dwell on the past. I have Agnes and Charlie to think of now and while we are still in Manchester there is an investigation to pursue. Having come so far in the quest to find the killer, I am loth to leave it unresolved, however imperative my new task may be.

And, in the meantime, there are clothes to be bought and new identities to assume.

The next day, in the forenoon, we present ourselves at the Angel as Mr and Mrs William Lindsay, together with their younger brother, Charles.

The same doorman who looked down his nose at humble, dishevelled Seth Hodges and his down at heel family only twenty four hours ago, now bows and scrapes with due deference, showing no sign of recognition.

The footman who conducted me into Nathaniel Grey's presence yesterday affords me a curious look, perhaps puzzled by some memory he cannot place, but once again the power of fine clothes and neat perruques carries the day.

First thing this morning, having obtained jugs of clean water from the Conduit, we banished the grime and sweat of the last few weeks and an hour later, clean and sweeter-smelling, entered into negotiations with several local shopkeepers to purchase all necessary accoutrements for a gentleman and his family upon their travels.

If the tradesmen harboured any doubts about such initially shabby persons entering their shops, they were soon won round by the welcome chink of coins and when we walk out, we are as elegant a trio as any to be seen in the fashionable haunts of London.

The bag containing our former garments, Agnes graciously donates to a woman selling old clothes and rags from a market stall and is immensely cheered to be referred to as 'milady' for her generosity.

As soon as we are shown to our rooms in the Angel, Agnes, quite confident now in her newly regained status, enquires if there are any events in town which may be of interest to persons of quality.

'I believe Mr Dickenson is holding a garden concert at his house this evening,' says the landlord.

'Mr Dickenson?'

'One of our leading citizens. 'Twas at his house the Prince – or, saving your honour, the *Pretender* – lodged whilst he was here. It is one of the finest houses in town, on Market Stead Street. Indeed, since the Pri- er - Pretender was here, it is known locally as 'the Palace"

'And may anyone go to this concert?'

'Only persons of quality such as yourself, Ma'am. I have no doubt you would be very welcome. Everyone of consequence in the town will be there.'

'The Palace' proves to be a fine, freestanding house built of stone, set back from the street and surrounded by formal gardens.

The evening is warm, but with a slight chill, for the sun has only just set as the days lengthen with the onset of summer. Charlie and I wear light, embroidered summer coats and Agnes a fashionable silken shawl around her shoulders.

From the rear of the building come the strains of a slightly strident string quartet as we approach along Market Stead Street.

'Not the most accomplished of musicians,' murmurs Agnes with a grimace.

'Certainly not up to the standard of those in Vauxhall Gardens,' I say, remembering the occasion there a year ago when I was in pursuit of a supposed kidnapper.

'Sounds like a sack of cats being strangled,' observes Charlie scathingly as the group launches into a desperately lively but uncoordinated jig.

A footman enquires our names as we pass through the wrought-iron gates and announces them loudly as we pass through into the forecourt.

A stocky gentleman approaches us. 'Mr Lindsay? I do

not believe I have had the pleasure...?'

'My wife and I are newly arrived in town, sir,' I reply with a formal bow. 'We were informed that tonight's occasion would be an opportunity to become acquainted with the quality of the town. You must be Mr Dickenson? May I introduce my wife, Agnes, and my brother, Charles?'

Dickenson takes our hands in turn as Agnes curtsies and Charlie bobs his head in acknowledgement.

'I am told you had the honour of entertaining the Pretender here during his recent stay?' I ask politely.

'Indeed, Mr Lindsay, he was accommodated here. His men ordered my house for his lodging after viewing several others which, for some reason, they did not like so well.'

His reply is cautious as is only to be expected. And he deftly changes the subject as a matronly lady joins us.

'This is my wife, Isobel.' Another round of introductions follows, then Mrs Dickenson says, 'Are you in trade yourself, Mr Lindsay, or a man of independent means?'

'I have recently had a small family inheritance, ma'am,' I reply, with a smattering of truth, 'which has enabled me to travel. But before then I was engaged in the wine trade. I worked with the Garricks in Lichfield.'

'Oohh!' she coos, 'not the family of Mr David Garrick, the famous actor?'

'The very same, ma'am. I am acquainted with that

gentleman – though he has little to do with the business now.'

Dickenson, who clearly does not share his wife's predilection for the theatre, takes my arm. 'Come, Mr Lindsay, let us leave the ladies to indulge in such taradiddle. I can see that talk of such theatrical stuff is not to your taste. I shall introduce you to Josh Feilden, our local wine-merchant. I'm sure you will have much in common. And you, young man,' he continues with a broad wink at Charlie, 'I shall put you in the way of some of our younger ladies whose company I dare say you'll find much more congenial.'

He leads us indoors where several middle-aged men are enjoying the benefit of Mr Dickenson's cellar and tobacco jar. Most are ruddy-faced and round bellied with good living.

But Mr Feilden, to whom Dickenson introduces us, has a more ascetic look and is neither smoking nor drinking as much as the others. He is in company with two others.

The first, tall and slim and, I judge, somewhere between fifty and sixty is introduced as Mr John Byrom. A man of pleasing, though not exactly handsome, features, he has a courteous and benevolent air and a permanent look of amusement, but his eyes are sharp and his gaze penetrating.

The other, spare and bony, his gestures as awkward as a string puppet, is Mr Peter Croxton. The downward curve of lip speaks of a critical nature and turns every smile into a sneer.

Dickenson leaves me in their company as he escorts Charlie out into the garden.

For some minutes the conversation between the four of us is polite but awkward as is the way with strangers thrown together. But gradually I learn that all three, in common with many other Manchester businessmen had a somewhat ambivalent attitude towards their late visitor. Whilst behaving civilly, they remained lukewarm in their welcome.

'Indeed,' Byrom boasts, with a characteristic sardonic twinkle in his eye, 'I composed an ironic toast intended to allay the violence of partisanship. It goes as follows:

God bless the King, I mean the Faith's Defender
God bless – no harm in blessing – the Pretender;
But who Pretender is, or who is King,
God bless us all – that's quite another thing!'

I laugh dutifully whilst his two companions smile indulgently.

'Always sitting on the fence, eh, John?' says Croxton.

'A fence is a convenient place to be,' replies Byrom, unabashed. 'One has a good view to each side. Don't you agree, Mr Lindsay?'

'I suppose so, sir. And neither landowner may accuse you of trespassing on his land.'

'Nor of favouring his neighbour, if you take my meaning,' says Byrom with a deliberate wink.

'Not like that young lass of yours, eh Johnny?' says Croxton pointedly.

'My Beppy?' Byrom hoots. 'Why, my Beppy, was only struck by the romance of him and his good looks. She's naught but a silly scatterbrain. Why, he's only been gone three months and already she's forgotten him. She'll be cock-a-hoop for some new wonder before summer's out, you'll see.'

And, sure enough, no sooner has her name been mentioned than what I assume to be the young lady herself appears like a whirlwind through the door that leads into the garden. And she has Charlie in tow.

'Papa! Papa!' she cries, then flings her hand up to cover her face. 'Faugh! What a reek of tobacco! I am near choked to death with it!'

She grabs her father's sleeve and pulls at it. 'Come outside, papa, where we can breathe. And you, Charlie's brother, you must come, too!'

I get up and follow as she bustles them both out into the garden where, seeing Mrs Dickenson, Agnes and another lady chatting together in an arbour, she makes straight for them, hauling both her captives along with her. From the look of indulgent affection on her face as the party bears down on them, I take the third lady to be Mrs Byrom.

'Mama! Papa!' I hear Beppy gabble excitedly as I draw closer. 'You'll never guess who Charlie and his brother know. David Garrick! They've not only seen him act – they've actually talked to him!'

'Yes, my dear,' says Mrs Byrom calmly, 'I know. Your Aunt Isobel and I have these past twenty minutes been talking to Mrs Lindsay about the very same person. But if you would have first-hand information, it is Mr Lindsay, Charles's brother to whom you should speak. It is he who is most closely acquainted with Mr Garrick. Is that not so, Mr Lindsay?'

'I do know the gentleman, yes,' I say.

'Why, how fascinating!' squeals Beppy. 'Stuck here in the north, we have so little by way of refined entertainment. All we know of fashion is what we read in the London journals. Come, Mr Lindsay,' she says, taking my arm, 'let us take a turn around the garden while you tell me all about him.'

'For shame, Beppy,' scolds her mother, 'where are your manners, to monopolise Mr Lindsay thus? He may not want to talk about Mr Garrick.'

'Oh, I do not mind,' I reply cheerfully, 'as long as Miss Byrom is willing to return the favour by telling me of life here in Manchester.'

Mrs Byrom smiles graciously whilst her husband tuts and raises his eyebrows. 'That may take some time where my daughter is concerned,' says he satirically. 'I hope you like gossip, Mr Lindsay!'

He turns to engage Charlie in conversation and I exchange a last glance with Agnes, silently warning her to ensure Charlie's discretion. Then Beppy Byrom carries me off among the close-clipped box hedging.

For the first ten minutes, I submit to her eager questioning about my master's voice and manner, his appearance and character and how wonderful it must be to see him act. I try to satisfy every whim of her awestruck and wide- eyed curiosity.

And then, as she hangs upon my arm, gazing up at me as if I, too, am touched with splendour from my association with the idol of her imagination, I say, 'As a matter of fact, Mr Garrick has not been well of late. The pressures of work and the uncertainty of the recent rebellion. Do you know, he even considered enlisting to help repel the expected invasion?'

She stops with such abruptness that we almost collide with a couple strolling behind us. Polite apologies offered, they move on as Beppy pulls me down onto a nearby bench.

Her adoration has been severely tested 'He really did that?' Her brow furrows with disappointment. 'He would have fought against that brave young man?'

'His friends dissuaded from so doing,' I reply neutrally. 'But perhaps the rumours and fears of London were without foundation. You had first-hand experience here in Manchester, I believe?'

'Oh, there were rumours here too, before the Prince's arrival,' she says with a return of her breathless enthusiasm, though now with a hint of scorn. 'All the Presbyterians from Saint Ann's were sending everything of value away, wives, children and all for fear of the rebels.' Then she giggles, 'But as for me, I went straight out and bought a blue and white gown from Mr Starkey, gave twelve shillings for it!'

Clearly she had heard of the blue bonnets and white cockades worn by the Pretender's men.

She goes on to tell me that she herself witnessed the arrival in town of Sergeant Dickson, his doxy and their drummer, confirming the account that Caleb gave us several days ago.

'And by eight-o'clock that night at least eighty men had enlisted,' she says joyfully. 'Later, Papa and I went to the Market Cross to see Lord Pitsligo's men arrive. 'Twas a very fine, moonlight night but the streets were exceeding quiet, there was hardly one person to be seen or heard.'

I ask her if she saw the Pretender himself during his stay, though I take care to call him 'the Prince' in view of her evident sympathies.

'Oh yes,' she cries eagerly. 'The day of his arrival, I and several other ladies were up till two in the morning sewing white crosses for the Highlanders to wear, for 'twas St Andrew's Day the day after, the 30th of November, and St Andrew is their national saint, you know, and his sign is a white saltire, or cross, which they wear with pride on their dress.' She pauses momentarily for breath. 'Then, after finishing our cross-making, I put on my white dress and an officer called on us to go see the Prince.' Here her voice is hushed with awe at the memory. 'So we went to Mr Fletcher's and saw him get a'horseback. Such a noble sight it was, I would not have missed it for a deal of money!'

'They say the Prince is a handsome young man?' I manage to interpolate.

'Oh, yes,' her eyes light up, 'so handsome! By the time we got there, his horse had stood an hour in the courtyard without stirring. But as soon as the Prince got on, he began a-dancing and a-capering, so proud he was of his burden. Then, when he rode out, there was so much joy and shouting – scarce anyone could dispute he was a true King! And when he had rode through the town, the same officer who had called for us to go and see the Prince escorted us home and told us that if we walked here to Mr Dickenson's house that evening, we might see the Prince at supper.' She claps her hands in glee at the memory. 'And he was handsome, too, the officer, as fair as the Prince though with a touch of red. Except he had a lazy eye that gave him a somewhat naughty, lewd look.'

'He was not improper with you, I hope, Miss Byrom?' I say solicitously.

'Oh, no, he was politeness itself, though,' - here she leans in close, putting her hand confidentially upon my forearm – 'he almost made us fuddled with drinking the Prince's health, for we had had no dinner, you see. Then, when the Prince had done supper and was at leisure, we were all introduced and had the honour to kiss his hand, myself and Papa and Dr Deacon - and then we went to Mr Fletcher's where Mama was waiting for us and then we went home,' she finishes with a long sigh, gazing rapturously into the distance.

I take advantage of her reverie to ask, 'And did you learn the name of the gallant officer who acted as your guide?'

'Alas, no, though I saw him again – though only at a distance - with my cousin Emma and her husband.' Suddenly she puts her hand to her mouth in shocked recall. 'The very day poor David died, in fact. The Sunday the Prince's army left.'

'David was your cousin?'

She smiles sadly. 'He was married to Emma, who is

cousin more through friendship than through blood. Aunt Feilden and Mama are very close.'

'And he died? That must have been distressing for you.'

'Indeed it was. Such a shock! To be seized with convulsions, foaming at the mouth, on the very road the Prince had rode along not two days before! Poor David had never ailed a thing in his life!'

At the other side of the garden, the string quartet, whose dissonant sawing has provided the background to our conversation, end their piece with a jangling flourish to a ragged smattering of polite, though I suspect relieved, applause. And Beppy, shaking off her melancholy, suggests we rejoin the others.

'Ah, Mr Lindsay, still alive I see,' says Mr Byrom as we re-enter. 'Beppy has not talked you to death,' he laughs.

'Indeed not, sir,' I reply amicably. 'We have enjoyed a very enjoyable and informative half hour in each other's company.'

The Pretend Rebel

The following morning we attend Mr Joshua Feilden at his shop upon the corner of Market Square and Hanging Ditch.

He issued the invitation as we were leaving Mr Dickenson's house last night. 'Perhaps you might like to see how we do business here, Mr Lindsay. Small fry compared to your own, I dare say...'

'I hope I have not inadvertently misled you, Mr Feilden. It was the Garrick's business. I was associated with it in a very minor way, and for a very short time...'

'That is of no matter, Mr Lindsay. To tell truth, the real reason I am inviting you is for my daughter Emma's sake. She has been so down of late and is in sore need of diversion. You would be doing me a favour if you and your family would honour us with your company.'

Not the most appealing invitation, to be sure, to attempt to cheer up a melancholy woman. But one which I was only too happy to accept, hoping it might shed further light our enquiries.

Feilden himself meets us at the door of his shop and, perhaps feeling himself absolved by my admission last night from any responsibility to discuss the ins and outs of the wine trade in any great detail, invites a very cursory inspection of casks and bottles before conducting us up a staircase to his living quarters which occupy the two floors above the shop.

In a large but homely parlour with a window overlooking the Market Place, we find three ladies and a little girl of about four years old.

The older lady, whom I take to be Mrs Feilden, is doing her best to take an interest in what the child is doing, cutting out coloured paper shapes with the help of her nursemaid and, using flour paste, sticking them into a scrapbook to make patterns.

A younger lady, dressed in black, sits in the window seat, a half-finished sampler on her knee, gazing listlessly at the little girl at play.

Mrs Feilden rises as we enter, smoothing down her skirts.

'Take Lizzie to the playroom, Annie,' she says to the nursemaid, 'and tell cook to bring tea – or would you prefer something else, Mrs Lindsay – chocolate or coffee, we have both?'

She is beaming, over-anxious to please. A marked contrast with the younger women whose strained smile cannot mask the deep sadness in her eyes as she murmurs her greeting.

Once the child and her guardian have departed, Mrs Feilden brushes a few stray shreds of paper from the settee. 'Pray, have a seat, Mrs Lindsay, gentlemen – wherever you please – this chair is most comfortable – though you may prefer to sit by the window for the view...?'

'Here will be most acceptable, Mrs Feilden,' says Agnes, seating herself in an armchair near the fireplace.

Once we are all settled, I say, 'You were not at Mr Dickenson's yesterday evening, Ma'am?'

She gives me a simpering smile. 'No, Mr Lindsay, of late I find myself disinclined to such occasions.' Here she gives a quick glance at her daughter. 'Emma and I spent the evening quietly at home. Was the concert to your taste?'

Her husband gives a cough which, in someone less straight-faced, might be mistaken for a laugh. 'Nicholls and his fiddlers played to their usual standard, my dear. We cannot expect our guests to perjure themselves by complimenting them.'

'I confess I did not pay them much attention,' I reply diplomatically.

'Nor I,' adds Agnes. 'Mrs Dickenson and Mrs Byrom were such diverting company, we hardly noticed the music.'

'And you, Master Charles?' enquires Mrs Feilden.

Charlie gives a broad grin. 'Me? I was otherwise occupied, Mrs Feilden. Mr Byrom introduced me to several young ladies. A gigglesome bunch, and no mistake.'

Agnes gives me a quick look and then says, 'My husband talked to Mr Byrom's daughter. She told him of your sad loss.'

Mrs Feilden looks uncomfortable. 'Elizabeth, yes – she is a chatterbox – lets her tongue run away with her...'

'I hope I have not offended you by mentioning it?' says Agnes gravely. 'Only I have found from experience that it is often a comfort to talk of these things once the initial pain has eased – I myself suffered a sudden and unexpected bereavement before I met William.'

I nod in sympathetic agreement, though in fact what she says is not strictly true. The bereavement she speaks of was of her clandestine lover in a coach crash from which she escaped. The two of them had tricked me and left me to face a charge of murder. But that is another story.

'Emma finds it difficult to speak of,' says Mrs Feilden, looking sadly at her daughter. 'It was so unexpected, you see.'

'In the public street.' It is hardly above a whisper, but instantly all eyes turn to the young woman in the window. 'He died among strangers and I was not there. I can never forgive myself for that.'

Quickly Agnes rises and goes over to sit beside her on the window seat, taking her hands in hers. 'It was not your fault, my dear. There is nothing to forgive. You must not torture yourself so.'

'Mrs Lindsay is right, Emma,' says her mother with surprising gentleness. 'It is time to let go, my love.'

Emma Ross raises her head and looks slowly around at all of us. The sadness in her eyes turns to a look of determination.

'You are right, mother. I cannot grieve for ever. David is gone and I must reconcile myself to his loss. It is not fair to Lizzie. She has lost a father, she should not lose a mother, too. And it is not fair to you and Papa.'

She is trembling with the effort to be strong.

Agnes presses her hand reassuringly.

'It is best to remember him as he was,' she says softly. 'Tell me about him.'

Emma Ross's face relaxes into a sad, half-smile. 'He was the kindest and gentlest of men,' she says. 'Such a good father to Lizzie. And a diligent partner in the business, was he not, Papa?'

Mr Feilden is clearly affected by the change in his daughter. It is as if the austere lines of his face are melting away. 'Yes, my dear, David was always a hard worker. I shall sorely miss him. He had the touch which I lacked, of persuasive conversation. Why, even the morning he d-,' he swallows loudly, 'the morning he left us, he had agreed a contract with Mr Munro...'

'Munro? That sounds like a Scottish name,' I say. 'That is a coincidence, is it not? Miss Byrom said the Highland army was in Manchester about that time?'

'The rebel army,' Feilden corrects me with disdain. 'Yes, this Munro was an officer with them. I was against the idea, but David persuaded me. Sorry, my dear,' he says with an apologetic glance at his daughter. 'Munro was a glib talker. A wine-merchant himself before he decided to throw in his lot with the Pretender. David said the Scots weren't all bad – after all, he was of Scottish descent himself – and that we must look to business once this war was ended.'

'John Munro was the last person David saw,' says Emma with tears starting to her eyes. 'It should have been me. We should have gone to church together, it was Sunday morning. But Munro said the army was leaving that afternoon and requested they seal their agreement with a drink together. They walked a little way with me and then I left them.'

'That must have been when Miss Byrom saw you?'

Emma Ross's face crumples into tears, 'Oh, Beppy, poor Beppy, I've sadly neglected her – and she has tried...'

Agnes seeks to console her, putting her arm around her shoulders, but the young woman shakes her off, turning her face to the wall.

187

Mrs Feilden goes over to them and takes Agnes's place beside her sobbing daughter.

'My apologies, Mrs Feilden,' says Agnes in distress, ' but I thought it was for the best.'

'Pray, do not discomfit yourself, Mrs Lindsay,' says Mrs Feilden with a smile. 'This can only be to the good and it is entirely thanks to yourself. She has not cried since it happened, and now the floodgates have burst she will be on the mend for sure. Her mention of Beppy just now – she would not countenance her company these past five months, but now... Her lighthearted chatter is what she needs – yes, all will be well from now on.'

She leads her daughter from the room, leaving Mr Feilden somewhat embarrassed at this sudden surge of female emotion.

'I – er, Mrs Lindsay – er – gentlemen – I...'

Agnes smooths over the awkwardness. 'I am sure your daughter will be recovered shortly, Mr Feilden. We ladies can be oversensitive at times.' She gives him her most winning smile. 'William is often quite disconcerted by my moods, so he tells me.'

I pretend to ignore her. 'This Munro fellow,' I say assuming a bluff, manly tone to distract from the recent upset. 'You didn't take to him?'

'No, Mr Lindsay, I did not,' he replies. 'A plausible,

silken-tongued fellow that I wouldn't trust as far as I could throw him! A squint-eyed, sneaking fellow as ever I saw. Could charm the ladies, I've no doubt, and managed to fool my late son-in-law, but he didn't fool me. Fortunately I've heard no more of him since the damned Pretender's army left. But I'd soon tell him what he can do with his so-called contract if he ever dares to show his face again!'

'I think you may be assured that will not happen, Mr Feilden. With the rebel army defeated and the Pretender in hiding, I think you may safely assume you have seen the last of Mr Munro.'

Letters

Moments after we return to the *Angel* the innkeeper comes to our room.

He is in a great fluster. 'Ah, Mr Lindsay, pray accept my sincerest apologies, sir,' he gabbles. 'You see, I was called away this morning, or I would most certainly have given you these before you went out. The gentleman who was here – Mr Grey – who departed yesterday, he left them for you with instructions that I give them directly into your hands.'

He hands me a parcel of letters.

'As I say,' he continues, 'I am most truly sorry, I should have given you them this morning...'

'Pray do not discompose yourself, sir,' I interrupt, seeking to stem his torrent of apology. 'They are delivered now, and I'm sure they can contain nothing so urgent that a delay of two hours in their delivery will be of any consequence.'

He retires, still bowing. I close the door and come back into the room to examine the package.

It consists of a large envelope with the superscription *W. Lindsay Esq.* Breaking the seal, I find it contains a loose page of writing and three sealed letters.

The loose sheet is in Nathaniel Grey's precise, neat

handwriting:

Archer,

Find enclosed your detailed instructions from Sir William which, I would remind you, must be destroyed as soon as you have read and thoroughly digested the contents.

Also enclosed are two items of personal correspondence which he has arranged to be passed on to you through official channels. (Take good note that this is a great favour on his part. You should not presume upon his generosity to provide safe passage for any further private communications.)

N.G.

His typical terse style with an equally typical barb at the end! I hand it across for the others to read as I break the seal on Hervey's instructions, which are relayed with appropriate guardedness.

To Wm Lindsay

Nathaniel will by now have told you of the change in plans and provided you with the resources to accomplish the necessary change in status for yourself and your companions.

I fancy you will not be entirely reluctant to abandon the Hodges family, but I suspect you will have some regrets about having to abandon the Ross affair. It is, I'm afraid, a case of needs must. More pressing matters must take precedence.

Once you have reported all you have found out about the Ross business to Nathaniel and become accustomed to your new identities, you should repair with all haste towards Scotland.

I know that, as you are in Manchester, the western route up through Carlisle would seem the most convenient route. But it is also the route most affected by the recent troubles and may prove unduly hazardous. Therefore, I would have you go across country towards Newcastle, where you should enquire after a Mr John Armstrong at the Three Tuns Inn in Pilgrim Street. He may have further information and you may safely entrust any necessary correspondence to him.

Thence, you should proceed to Edinburgh and present yourselves to Mr Duncan Forbes, Lord President of the Court of Session. Feel free to impart to him, at first hand, the fruits of your inquiries concerning the misfortunes of his kinsmen.

More importantly, however, he will appraise you of the latest news concerning the gentleman whose safe passage is of concern to us.

What he has to tell you will determine the direction of your journey from there onwards, but as to the manner in which you pursue it, I leave that up to you and Mrs Lindsay, trusting that you will do your best to ensure a successful outcome.

Yrs,

Wm. Hervey.

'Newcastle,' says Charlie. 'Where's that?'

Although having previously travelled with me to Dublin and to Yorkshire – far further than most Londoners born in similar circumstances to him – the far north of England is an unknown region to him.

And hardly less so to myself and Agnes.

'It is over on the other side of the country, is it not?' asks Agnes.

'I think so,' I reply. 'A good five days' journey, at least. And then another five to Edinburgh. But at least we shall have good horses and, with luck, soft beds to sleep in, rather than a shambling cart and hard ground.'

'Aye,' says Charlie, 'but we've also a rare glut of baggage that we didn't 'ave before. Valises and such, and more clothes than you can shake a stick at. 'Ow we goin' to manage all that on just three horses?'

'Charlie's right,' says Agnes. 'We didn't think of that when we were buying it. And if we are to keep up appearances, we cannot leave it all behind.'

There follows a discussion upon how to resolve our dilemma. It will clearly be impractical to carry all our new wardrobe stuffed into saddlebags. The only solution is to travel in our most sturdy garments – fortunately, as May gives way to June, the weather promises fair for riding – carrying perhaps one change of clothes with us, and entrust the rest of our luggage to a carrier.'

'We must find someone reputable and trustworthy, then,' cautions Agnes, 'else we may find it all goes missing en route.'

'It is a risk we must take,' I reply, disconsolately. 'I cannot see any other way.'

'Unless I go with it,' chirps up Charlie. 'We can tell the carrier I'm your valet. I can wear the plainest coat and britches – I know they're still a mite showy, but that's what valets are like, ain't they? Fancies theirselves above their station. An' I'll be a deal more convincin' playing a manservant than pretendin' to be a gent all the time.'

'We-e-ll,' I hesitate, 'I don't like the idea of us splitting up... What do you think, Agnes?'

She considers for a moment, then says, 'I understand your unease, Will, but I think Charlie is resourceful enough to carry it off. And when we arrive at Newcastle, we can re-consider the situation, if necessary. There may be a stage from Newcastle to Edinburgh that we can all take.'

I relent somewhat. 'It is a possibility, I suppose. We can think on it. Meanwhile,' I continue, taking up the two remaining letters, 'let's see what these contain.'

Both envelopes address me by my real name, and it is with an inner sense of pleasure that I recognise the hands.

The first is from Mr Garrick:

My Dear Will,

What a pleasure to receive your letter! It arrived just two days before I departed Dublin. And what generosity on your part to offer me the use of your newly acquired abode in Soho Square! My only regret is that I am obliged to express my gratitude by letter rather than in person.

Where are your adventures taking you this time, my dear boy? Susan and her young man (who, by the way, are looking after me splendidly!) maintain a tight-lipped silence and express total ignorance of your whereabouts. As does your engagingly efficient agent, Mr Jem Bennett, who is, in all other respects, doing his best to ensure my comfort. (You have found a sound fellow there, Will. Hold fast to him!)

I am half inclined to use him in my latest project. As a result of the Rebellion, Lacy's backers have gone bankrupt.

He cannot, I am positive, hold on to Drury Lane without them. If Jem may help me wriggle into the patent on good terms, I shall be made forever!

In the meantime, the city is returned to normal and is in the mood to celebrate the defeat of the rebels. Rich has approached me to appear at Covent Garden. I am under no illusion that we like each other or can ever be friends, but there is money to be made.

Macklin and Peg are propping up Fleetwood at Drury Lane, but it is a sinking ship, I fear. With Quin and Susanna Cibber here with me at Covent Garden, we shall reign supreme. Quin and I are like chalk and cheese in our approach to the art of acting, but we have agreed to be civil and to alternate the roles of Othello and Richard III in the coming season.

All in all, I am quite sanguine about the next few months, and the security you have afforded me in letting me use your home adds greatly to that confidence. Lord knows I need it after the tribulations of this last year!

One thing would top all, and that would be for you to return from wherever you are gadding so that I may thank you in person. Return soon, my dear boy.

(In the absence of an address, I am entrusting this to Mr Bennett to send. He tells me he may be able to contact you through a third party though, in true lawyerly fashion, he

will not tell me who or what that third party is!)
Yr very true and grateful friend,
David Garrick

It cheers me greatly to hear that my master is returned to London in apparently such good spirits and with such a sense of optimism after his year of illness and misfortune. But at the same time, this reminder of how life in London is proceeding without me rouses such emotion that I have to dash aside a tear from my eye.

'Why, what's the matter, Will,' asks Agnes in concern. 'It is not bad news, I hope?'

'No, not bad,' say I with a quick shake of my head, 'the very opposite, in fact. My master, Mr Garrick, is returned from Ireland in good health and spirits and all is well. Here, you may read for yourselves.'

While they are doing that, I open the remaining letter which is from Jem Bennett.

Dear Will,

If this and the accompanying letter from Mr Garrick reach you, it will be through the kind offices of Mr Nathaniel Grey. (Though perhaps 'kind' is too generous a word - to be candid, he struck me as more officious than generous in nature.)

He came to my office a week or so after you left and fortunately I remembered him as Sir William's associate from the time you and I were involved in the Elias affair, or he would have received short shrift.

Grey informed me that should I ever need to contact you, he would undertake to deliver any correspondence safely, though he was not at liberty to tell me where you were or what you were engaged in. To which end, he left me his card.

He also asked me if anyone had been enquiring after you in your absence.

At the time, I thought this a strange question. But only two days later, by a strange coincidence, someone did enquire about you. A gentleman who said he was an acquaintance of yours but did not give his name. A man of breeding, well-dressed and, like so many fashionable men about town, with a penchant for rosewater perfume, my office smelt of it the whole day!

Of course, I told him nothing, for I had nothing to tell. But he said, if I should happen to hear from you, to remember your mutual friend John Munro to you.

I do not know if this is important, Will, but I pass it on anyway.

More to the point is an incident that occurred a day or two later and was reported to me by Joseph and Susan who are looking after your house. Someone attempted to break in but fortunately Joseph saw him off and nothing was damaged or stolen.

Mr Garrick took up residence the next day, but I thought it best not to worry him with the news, merely instructing Joseph to be extra vigilant and to carry out his evening routine of locking up with extra care.

As a consequence the impudent fellow has demanded more money. I said I could not authorise that without your assent, but appeased him with an extra shilling a week for him and Susan to treat themselves.

Otherwise, all is going well here. I hope it is the same with you and young Charlie.

I look forward to your return and in the meantime assure you that I have your best interests at heart here in London.

Best regards,

Jem.

'What's the matter, Will?' asks Agnes. 'You've gone pale.'

It takes me a moment to realise she has spoken to me. But then she puts her hand on my arm. 'Will? Is it bad news?'

'I thought I was rid of him, ' I murmur.

'Rid of who?'

'My unknown enemy,' I reply.

A frown creases her brow. 'Is this to do with the fellow who tried to kill you at Dettingen? I thought he was dead?'

'*He* is,' I say. 'But he was acting under orders to eliminate me. Even he did not know who my persecutor is. All he said was that I had offended someone powerful and must pay the price. Luckily for me, he was not the one to exact that payment.'

Agnes has taken Jem's letter from me. 'A stranger inquiring after you, and an attempted robbery at your house – do you think they were connected?'

'I don't know. But the thing that worries me is Jem mentioning the man's perfume.'

'Rosewater? That is common enough, surely?' says Agnes.

'Rosewater scent?' interrupts Charlie. 'The cove wot chucked you down the sewer that time, and the one wot was there when you was press-ganged – didn't 'e whiff of that?'

'Exactly! And I thought I smelt him again at the Elias's funeral.'

'Have you no idea who he may be?' asks Agnes, concerned.

'Hervey thinks he may be associated with the Jacobite cause. Or some faction in the Prince of Wales's rival court at Leicester House. Whoever it was tried to drown me whilst

I was investigating things at Kensington Palace. And it was immediately after I'd foiled a Jacobite plot to kill King George that I was kidnapped and press-ganged into the army.'

Agnes glances at the letter again. 'Munro was the name Mr Feilden gave us, the man who was seen with David Ross.'

'The cove who probably poisoned 'im,' adds Charlie.

'Do you think this stranger who inquired your whereabouts from Jem and the Ross murderer could be one and the same?' asks Agnes, worried. 'Hervey suspects your persecutor is a Jacobite – and the man we think killed Robert Ross in Derby and David Ross here in Manchester is also a Jacobite.'

'Is he?' I say. 'Can we be sure of that? All we know is that the killer posed as a rebel soldier. And nobody mentioned that Munro used rosewater perfume. No, I don't think my enemy and our killer are the same man. It's more likely my enemy has somehow found out that I'm looking into the Ross deaths and has made his own inquiries, which is how he's learned Munro's name. He's using it to taunt me and tell me he's still around...'

'He might even be here now!' cries Charlie, more in excitement than alarm. 'D'you think he knows where we are? Or where we're heading? If 'e's been following us, 'e could be lyin' in wait !'

I suddenly recall the feeling I had on our first day in Manchester that we were being followed.

'You may be right, Charlie,' I say, gravely. 'In which case, we'll all need to be on our guard – especially if we're thinking of splitting up. It may be me he's after, but he won't balk at harming those closest to me, knowing how much it would hurt me. Both you and Agnes might be in danger, too.'

Dr Deacon

Despite this disturbing news, we are obliged to postpone any plans to hasten our departure from Manchester because a second visit from our landlord brings an invitation to dine at Mr John Byrom's house in Hanging Ditch.

'Oh Lord!' exclaims Charlie. 'Will that Miss Beppy be there? I don't think I can stand another evening of her chatter!'

Agnes laughs. 'Alas, one of the perils of being in society is having to make polite conversation with people one does not particularly care for. Now you are Mr Charles Lindsay and an eligible bachelor,' she teases him, 'you're required to charm the flighty and endure the foolish.'

Charlie groans and I endeavour to put him out of his misery.

'I can decline the invitation on your behalf,' I suggest. 'I'll say you are not well, that the change of water has not agreed with you In fact, it may be for the best. We do not know who may be there, and if Mr Charles Lindsay, gentleman, is to transform into Charles the valet tomorrow to accompany the carrier, the less you're seen in the meantime the better.'

And so it is arranged. Charlie will keep to his room this

evening and have a light meal sent up. He is not over-keen on the idea at first, but the dismal prospect of thin broth is eventually outweighed by the relief of avoiding the fervour of Miss Beppy's advances.

As it transpires, Beppy is not present at the dinner.

She is at a friend's house, engaged in what her father indulgently calls 'some coven of gossips tittle-tattling over a game of quadrille where they will be sipping watered claret and devouring reputations whole'.

Those present include Croxton, who was at yesterday evening's concert, together with the hosts of that occasion, Mr John Dickenson and his wife, Isobel. The company also includes three new faces: a Mr Cattell and his mouse-like wife, neither of whom speak more than a dozen words during the whole evening; and a hatchet-faced clergyman whom Byrom introduces as 'Dr Deacon, Bishop of Manchester'.

I look at him with interest. This is the man whom Caleb, our late travelling companion, described as the 'stiff-necked old Puritan' who is a staunch Jacobite, preaches against the evils of drink and rejoiced in a most un-Christian way at the death of David Ross. Also the man who has lost all three of his sons to the Jacobite cause.

As the evening progresses, it becomes ever more

obvious that all here are, in some degree, supporters of Charles Stuart. Deacon and Croxton are the most zealous, whilst Byrom and the Dickensons are more equivocal. And the Cattells simply agree with everybody.

A thing that strikes me during the evening's conversation is how loyalty to the exiled Stuarts seems to supersede religious allegiance.

'I thought it brave of the Revd Clayton to make such a public display of his admiration for the Prince,' remarks Croxton at one point. He goes on to explain for our benefit, 'He is the Master of Salford Grammar School, Mr Lindsay, and as the Prince passed by he fell to his knee and cried out, "God bless His Royal Highness Prince Charles!" at which the Prince doffed his bonnet in thanks.'

'Aye,' acknowledges Deacon acerbically, 'the fellow showed sense in that respect at least. Though his high-church Anglicanism and his foolish persistence in educating the young prove beyond doubt that the man is deluded in every other way.'

'You do not believe in education, sir?' asks Agnes, with deceptive innocence.

'I do not, ma'am. What purpose can possibly be served by educating farmers' and shopkeepers' sons above their station in life?'

Out of the corner of my eye, I see the ghost of a weary

smile flit across Byrom's face as if this is an all too familiar tirade.

Deacon continues, as if in a metaphorical pulpit, 'The Lord ordained that some shall be exalted and that others shall ever be hewers of wood and drawers of water. It is at peril of his immortal soul that sinful man defies the Divine Commandment. Has not history shown that calamity ensues when ignorant men presume to abuse the natural order? Does not the traitor Cromwell rot in Hell? And will not the foul conspirators who deny the Divinely appointed succession of our Rightful King also suffer eternal torment?'

His voice is all but shaking the walls when Byrom diplomatically steps in. 'Fie, Dr Deacon, you will alarm the ladies with your visions of Hellfire. And you may upset our guests who perhaps are not used to such views being aired with such vehemence in polite company.'

Deacon's bushy brows contract into a scowl as he mutters gruffly, 'My apologies, Mr and Mrs Lindsay. I forget myself sometimes and speak with too much ardour.'

'It is understandable, Dr Deacon,' says Isobel Dickenson soothingly. 'We have all of us been burdened these last few months – and you more than most.'

If she was sitting next to him, I am sure she would have put a consoling hand upon his arm. She turns and addresses us directly in a hushed voice. 'All three of the Bishop's sons

206

fought for the Prince. Poor Robert died of fever while imprisoned at Carlisle, and the other two are now held prisoner, their fates hanging in the balance.'

'Nay, not in the balance,' interjects Deacon. 'My sons' lives are in God's hands. He knows their cause was just and if He decrees that they must die, then it will be not as criminals but as glorious martyrs.'

'Come now,' cuts in Croxton, attempting to lighten the atmosphere, 'let us not dwell upon such doom-laden matters – we are neglecting our host's splendid fare! This beef is excellent, John. Did it come from Hardcastle's?'

The Dickensons, and even the taciturn Cattells, take the opportunity to move the talk into less contentious pathways, singing the praises of the local butcher.

'And did you know, Mr Lindsay,' says Dickenson, once that topic has been exhausted, 'that John here has a claim to fame that is all his own? He has invented a secret cypher!'

Byrom gives a self-deprecatory laugh. 'Hardly a secret cypher, Dickenson. 'Tis merely a method of shorthand writing, designed for commerce.'

'Aye,' pursues Dickenson with a wink that earns him a severe look from his wife, 'and not just financial commerce, eh John?'

Judging by the amusement on several faces, the nature of his insinuation is clearly common knowledge to everyone but Agnes and myself. Even the Cattells permit themselves a timid smile, whilst Deacon scowls even more.

Byrom shakes his head, laughing. 'Pay him no heed, Mr Lindsay. 'Tis naught but a scurrilous rumour from the time I spent in London.'

Agnes joins in the laughter. 'Pray tell us more, Mr Byrom. You cannot tease us thus.'

'Oh, very well, ma'am,' replies Byrom with a theatrical sigh. 'Folk will have it that my system of writing was designed for clandestine correspondence, and that I was involved in plots and intrigues. There is, I assure you, no truth in it.'

'So you say,' says Croxton. 'But he has not told you the best bit.'

It is clear that the wine has loosened Croxton's tongue, for his habitual dour demeanour has now become quite skittish. 'Here, Mr and Mrs Lindsay,' he announces with a flourish, 'you have the lover of the late Queen Caroline!'

'Enough Croxton!' thunders Deacon. 'Enough of this salacious talk! For shame!'

His outburst subdues the company for several minutes and, like rebuked children, we all eat our meal in chastened silence. But from Mrs Byrom's pursed lips and the surreptitious, apologetic glance that her husband bestows on her, I don't doubt the truth of Croxton's assertion.

Eventually, when the atmosphere is becoming uncomfortable, I venture, 'Have you been out of Manchester yourself, Dr Deacon?'

'Only once,' he growls. 'Several years ago, I was obliged to travel to the Gomorrah which you call London. Such a sink of sin and depravity I have never seen!'

Croxton stifles a snigger, turning it into a cough. But he is clearly still indignant at being rebuked, and is ready to goad Deacon again.

'But I heard you had a visitor from London a while ago, though?' he says slyly. 'A fine gentleman, dressed in the latest fashion, by all accounts.'

A single glance at the Bishop's severe black attire, and a single whiff of its fusty odour is enough to know how such a remark will provoke him.

'You heard aright,' admits Deacon frostily. 'And, yes, he was a mighty fine gentleman and very well-spoken. A vain creature, far too steeped in the vanities of this world for an envoy of the church.'

'He was on church business, though?' persists Croxton, feigning interest.

Deacon frowns and juts out his chin aggressively. 'If you must know,' he says brusquely, 'he came to sound out how the town might be inclined to the Prince's advance and to inquire of those who might be for or against him. He sought me out upon instructions from Bishop Gordon who is of the Prince's party.'

The mention of Bishop Gordon sends a shot of ice through me, pitching me back to when I helped foil the plot to kill King George at Kensington Palace some three or four years ago. In the mayhem, I clearly remember seeing Bishop Gordon pointing a pistol at His Majesty.

Afterwards, Hervey told me that Gordon had been diplomatically exiled to Aberdeen. And he also told me that it was very likely my enemy and Bishop Gordon would be known to each other. *Could he have been Deacon's fine, well-spoken visitor?*

I come back to the present to hear Mr Dickenson saying with gentle mockery, 'Sure, my dear Doctor, you would not damn a man for aspiring to look presentable?'

'The righteous have no need of fine raiment,' replies Deacon, once more in sonorous, oratorical mode. 'Does not the Gospel enjoin us to consider the lilies of the field and see how even Solomon in all his glory is not arrayed like one of them? There is no merit in silks and satins where good fustian will serve, and honest sweat is sweeter far than stinking perfume.'

The ladies in the party seem about to demur, but I break in quickly, 'You are friends with Bishop Gordon, sir? Whilst in London last, I heard he had been obliged to leave the capital in some disgrace. Can that be true?'

'There is no disgrace, Mr Lindsay, in holding true to one's beliefs,' he bridles. 'He was driven out because he expressed loyalty to God's ordained king and refused to grovel before the Hanoverian usurper.'

One might argue, think I to myself, *that there's a difference between refusing to grovel and attempting to shoot King George dead.*

'But he must still exert some influence in the capital?' I humour him. 'The envoy came from London, you say?'

'Aye, he had the affectation that that foul city breeds,' says he with distaste. 'I hearkened to his request, told him that the Prince might find many well-disposed towards him in Manchester, and sent him on his way.'

'He didn't go, though, did he?' needles Croxton. 'Or at least, if he did, he came back again. I'll swear I saw him in town a few weeks later. He was with that fellow that Feilden says nearly swindled him – what was his name again, Byrom?'

'I'm not sure I recall,' says Mr Byrom, wrinkling his brow with the effort to remember. 'Moreton, was it? Or Morley? No, I have it – Munro!'

'Aye, that was it. 'Twas after the Prince's army had come and gone again.' The drink is starting to make Croxton slur his words, 'Yes, the two of them, hard by the Exchange – I think it was him – but then again, I can't be certain, they were some distance away...'

'Perhaps they were old acquaintances,' interjects Agnes brightly as Croxton tails off into a drunken mumble. 'They may even have been related. What was your envoy called, Dr Deacon?'

'Nay, I don't recall, ma'am,' he replies haughtily. ' 'Twas at least five months ago and the fellow was only with me for a day. If he gave a name, 'tis slipped completely from my memory.'

Agnes and I leave Mr Byrom's house in Hanging Ditch feeling yet more uneasy. An uneasiness that turns to real apprehension when we return to the Angel and hear what Charlie has to tell us.

Contrary to our arrangement, he slipped secretly out of the Angel whilst we were at Byrom's house.

'I couldn't abide bein' shut up no longer,' he protests, 'and what with all this talk o' someone follerin' us, and knowin' we's a-leavin' tomorrer, I just 'ad to see Rosie one last time. See she was alright.'

'That was a stupid thing to do, Charlie,' I say angrily. 'You were supposed to stay out of sight. And I told you Grey said the horse and wagon would be taken care of.'

'Aye,' he retorts hotly, his voice breaking with tears,

'they've been taken care off, sure enough. When I got to Parsonage Croft, the cart was a blackened shell. It 'ad been burnt out – and Rosie lay dead beside it! So much for that damned black beetle's promises!'

'This is Grey's doing,' I say, perturbed. 'He may not like me, but he would not flout Sir William Hervey's orders in such a way. No, this is my enemy's work. It means he's closer than we think. Before Caleb left, I thought someone was following us. I said nothing because I couldn't be sure. But now it seems I was right. We must leave tomorrow without fail.'

'Let's not be too hasty,' interrupts Agnes. 'All must be done with due care. There is no reason to suspect your enemy – *our* enemy - knows about our changed disguise. It was the Hodges that he followed, and against them that his revenge - by destroying the cart - was aimed, not the Lindsays. Certainly we must leave tomorrow, but we must do it in a calm and controlled manner, not be panicked into rash action.'

'You're right,' I say, heartened by her good sense. 'All the same, I shall see the landlord tonight, before we go to bed, and ask him to have horses at our disposal as early as possible. And to have a gunsmith call first thing so that we may travel suitably armed.'

Across the Pennines

The landlord of the Angel informs us next morning after breakfast that horses are ready for us in the stable yard behind the inn, together with an ostler who awaits our instructions.

And that Mr Dent, the gunsmith, is in the parlour

Only Agnes and myself have come down for breakfast. We are still keeping Charlie out of sight under the pretence of being unwell. Our host offers to send up some more beef broth, but we decline, smuggling up a goodly hunk of bread and ham once we've finished our meal.

Leaving him to devour it in our room, we go down to the parlour where Mr Dent, a small, astute man, shows us several firearms which he assures us will meet our needs. I purchase two brace of pistols; a pair for Charlie, which can be secreted about his person and a pair for myself which may either fit in the skirts of my riding coat or in a holster attached to a belt, which I also purchase. Agnes chooses a small, silver weapon more suitable for a lady.

Then, while Agnes carries our purchases up to our room, I go out to the stable yard where I find two fine stallions and a roan mare tethered, contentedly munching oats from nosebags.

Their ostler is a grizzled, nut-brown fellow barely two-thirds my height and with legs so bowed he would hardly stop a pig in an alley.

He greets the news that I shall only be requiring two of the mounts with a resignation that suggests he's well used to the whims of gentlemen. Any disappointment, however, is dispelled by a half sovereign for the inconvenience.

When I ask if he knows of an honest and trustworthy carrier who'd be willing to transport our luggage to Newcastle for us, I'm rewarded by a gap-toothed grin and a frantic nodding of his head as his grubby hand closes over the coin.

'Aye, cock, mi own son, 'Arry. 'E's a sound feller, up fer owt. Ah'll vouch fer 'is honesty, don' you fret. Shall ah send 'im round? We lives under a mile away.'

'No need to bring his cart here,' I say. 'If you can get a barrow for our bags, my manservant, Charles, will go with you when you take your horse back. I want him to accompany your son and be answerable to me for the safe conveyance of our luggage on the journey, if that's alright?'

'Whatsoever yer 'onour says. Ah'll be about it straight.'

Within five minutes, he is back with a wooden barrow onto which Charlie and he load our baggage. I give Charlie half the money to hand over when he and Harry are ready to depart.

'I shall personally pay Harry the remainder when we meet up again in Newcastle,' I tell his father. 'And there'll be an extra two guineas if he and Charles arrive before my wife and myself.'

The ostler tugs his forelock and offers another gap-toothed grin of thanks.

'Take care,' I say, clasping Charlie's hand. 'Stay alert for highwaymen.'

'Never fear, Wi – er, sir, I have the best argument against robbery right here,' says he, slapping his breast where the pistols lie concealed.

'Make the best time you can,' I tell him. 'I'm reposing all my trust in you. Don't let me down. I'll see you in Newcastle in five days or so.'

If the ostler were not at our elbow, and if we were not keeping up the pretence of master and servant, I would hug him to me. As it is, I can only firmly shake his hand.

'Don't worry, sir, you can trust me, I won't let you down. Have a safe journey, you and the mistress,' he replies with a brave nod and resolute set of his lips. But I detect the faint tremor in his voice and do not fail to see the slight dampness in his eye when he winks.

Then, while the ostler hefts the handles of the barrow, Charlie reaches up and takes the horse's rein, slaps its flank and with a click of his tongue urges it into a gentle trot beside him.

I watch them till they're out of sight, then turn with a heavy heart and go back up into the inn.

'Do not fret, Will,' says Agnes gently as I return disconsolately to our room. 'I am sure Charlie will come to no harm. He is quick-witted and capable. You'll see, all will be well.'

'I hope so,' I say, putting on a brave smile.

But I feel like a fond parent who has just parted from their only child for the first time.

Gradually, as we gather together everything necessary for our journey, activity abates the ache of unease.

Then, once we have finally checked each item - topcoats, saddle-bags, money wallet, the pistols for me and for Agnes – she takes me in her arms and softly kisses my lips.

'Now, Will,' she murmurs, 'we are ready to start upon our great adventure. But before we embark on the unknown, let us make the most of a few last precious moments together...'

Slowly, she starts unlacing my shirt and I feel desire stirring as her eyes lovingly search my own, her breath warm upon my cheek. Swiftly stripping off my shirt, I fumble with the ties of her dress and within a few moments we are naked on the bed together.

Then, as the sounds of the town drift through the open window from the street below, and as the late morning sunlight traces flickering patterns on the whitewashed wall, Agnes and I lose ourselves in the secret pathways of each other's bodies.

We make love with the same breathless joy of discovery which marked that first occasion so many months ago – but it is a joy underscored by melancholy, for we are both only too aware that this could be our last opportunity for some time to come. Once our ardour has reached its peak, we lie for some while quietly in each other's arms, passing the time with soft murmurs and tender caresses.

A little too long, perhaps, for it is past noon before we ride out of town.

The day is hot and for the first stage of our journey we discard our heavy riding topcoats, rolling them up and buckling them to the saddlebags. I tuck one pistol into my belt whilst Agnes secretes her daintier weapon amidst her skirts.

For the next few days, our daily travel takes on a regular pattern. Setting out in the rising morning mist from whatever inn we have lodged at overnight, we maintain a steady pace along winding, uneven pack-roads through wide open vistas of moor and heath, or negotiating the closer confines of densely wooded countryside. Occasionally it is hard-going, for as we travel further north and eastwards, the land becomes mountainous and we are sometimes obliged to dismount and lead our horses along steep, rutted tracks.

This is a wild and sparsely populated country, where forests clothe the craggy hillsides and rivers run, sparkling, through deep valleys. It has a rugged beauty all its own but, nevertheless, it is with a sense of relief that we at last descend into the gentler hills of Yorkshire. Not into the vast level plain of the Vale of York where I was born and where my mother still lives with the family of the childhood friend who now manages my estates for me – but towards the more northerly rolling hills of Dales country.

It is a sore temptation to divert our journey and ride south for the few miles which would allow me to visit my family. But I know I cannot. Time and the urgency of our quest press too hard upon us. It has already taken us three days, and though we are now arrived at Harrogate, it will likely be the best part of another two before we reach our destination. Therefore, much as I would like to see my family and friends again, it cannot be.

At least in Harrogate we are assured of a softer bed and a better night's sleep than in some of lodgings on the way. The Queen's Head is a prosperous and well-provided establishment, the equal of any in Manchester or Derby and the landlord could not be more accommodating.

Here is none of the suspicion that has met us during other parts of our journey. The Pretender's rebellion has seemingly had little or no impact in this part of the country. Although Marshal Wade's forces passed near here when he marched up to Newcastle last autumn, when it was feared the rebels might choose to invade England via the eastern route from Edinburgh, and although a goodly number of rebel prisoners now languish in York prison only a few miles away, life in Harrogate has proceeded as if nothing untoward has happened.

The well-to-do still come here to take the supposedly health-giving waters from the chalybeate springs, and as we ride into the town, Agnes comments on the number of invalids being pushed around in wheeled chairs.

'It is almost like the aftermath of a battle, except that they all look too old to have set foot on a battlefield these last fifty years!'

As we ride past a small group of these conveyances gathered about a fountain or well, I hear a cry of 'Strong sulphur water, a penny a cup!' and see a matronly woman dispensing pewter cups of the spring-water to the assembled crowd.

Its reputed health-giving benefits aren't immediately

obvious, judging from the remarkable range of grimaces and expressions of disgust on the recipients' faces.

I therefore decline the lady's invitation to sample it, even though she extols its merits in glowing terms. 'A most sovereign remedy for all complaints of the liver and of the bowels, sir! I take it every day and I am in my seventieth year, though my skin is as smooth and blemish-free as any wench of thirty!'

'You look very well on it, ma'am,' says Agnes. But she, too, resists the offer to partake.

That evening at dinner I beg a copy of the local newspaper from the landlord.

A jolly fellow with a rubicund visage and well-proportioned belly, he hands it over with an apologetic warning. 'There be not much to divert a body, sir. 'Tis all gloom and doom about executions down in London. I know this late rebellion was a terrible thing, sir, and I know the rebels have to be punished. But all these executions – to be sure it makes me wonder if we really are as civilised as we pretend to be. The Duke of Cumberland is a noble and worthy gentleman, I'm sure, but to harry whole families from their homes, to slaughter the menfolk and leave their wives with their babbies and bairns destitute, 'tis a crying shame in my opinion.'

He retires, tutting in dismay.

The news sheet proves to be as disheartening as he says. Its front page is taken up with a full account of a mass execution of rebel leaders at Kennington Common in London.

Amongst the list of the condemned I see the name of Thomas Deacon who, with seven others had been sentenced to be hanged, drawn and quartered.

The crowd assembled round the gallows began to jeer as the wretched procession drew nigh. While the prisoners were removed from the sledges and assisted on to the cart from which they would be hanged, the faggots were lit ready for the burning of the entrails...

It is not pleasant reading to accompany a fine dinner, and I relay only selected parts of the account to Agnes.

'There is at least some humanity, even among executioners,' I say. 'They hanged Colonel Towneley for three minutes but when they cut him down he was still showing signs of life, so the executioner dispatched him by cutting his throat before embarking on his bloody work.'

I do not let her read the grisly details that follow.

The corpse being laid on the block, first the genitalia were removed and cast into the fire. Then, the torso being sliced asunder, bowels and heart were consigned to the flames. Finally, the executioner used a cleaver to sever the head from the body.

Each traitor's corpse was so served, at the conclusion of which, the executioner, steeped in gore from his labours, held up his dripping arms and cried "God save King George!" to which the crowd responded in like fashion.

The heads of Towneley and Fletcher will be displayed on Temple Bar. Those of the other rebels are to be preserved in spirit until they may carried to Manchester and Carlisle to be similarly displayed.

So this is the fate suffered by Thomas Deacon, the second of Dr Deacon's ill-starred sons – to have his head displayed upon the walls of the city where he was born.

'Poor man,' says Agnes in distress. 'No matter how stiff-necked a zealot the old man may be, one cannot help but feel pity for him. But tell me, Will, does it give no further news of the Pretender's whereabouts?'

I run my eye over the columns of tightly packet print, but find no mention other than that the rebel Charles Stuart is still believed to be in hiding somewhere in the north of Scotland.

'None,' I reply. 'But the Duke of Cumberland has returned to London, leaving the task of pacifying the Highlands to Lord Albermarle.

'His arrival was marked by the ringing of bells, gun salutes, illuminations, bonfires and all other demonstrations

of the greatest of joy from people of all ranks,' I read out to her, scanning on ahead as I do so. 'Apparently his first act on returning was to attend the Prince of Wales at St James's Palace. The pair of them appeared at a window and embraced each other to the cheers of the crowd below.'

'Prince Frederick basking in his younger brother's glory. He'll like that,' remarks Agnes cuttingly.

I laugh as another short piece catches my eye. 'Yes, considering that *his* only contribution to the war effort seems to have been to order a model of Carlisle Castle in sugar which guests were encouraged to bombard with sugar-plums in imitation of the siege!'

'At least London finds cause to celebrate,' says Agnes scornfully. 'It's a pity they can't see the destruction it's caused up here. And we haven't even seen the worst of it yet.'

I am still skimming over the other items of news.

'And the Highlands are likely to suffer even more, it seems. Parliament is drafting laws to outlaw the Clans and Highland tartan dress. All Scots are to be forbidden to carry arms...'

'But not all Scots are Jacobites,' protests Agnes. 'It is as Sir William says - such measures are more like to incite than to quell resentment and possible insurrection.'

'But you'll be pleased to know,' say I with a smile,

folding the paper and laying it aside, 'that Mr Handel has composed a new oratorio in celebration of the victory over the rebels. Something to do with some obscure Jewish hero called Maccabeus. People are already singing the main tune, *See the Conquering Hero Comes*, in the streets.'

'Well,' says Agnes, 'let the Duke of Cumberland enjoy it while he may, but I do not think any Scotsman whose home he has razed, or any highland widows and orphans with husbands and fathers exiled or executed will be joining in the singing. I expect they see him more as a butcher than a conquering hero!'

Her sigh of pity turns into a delicately stifled yawn. 'But the hour gets late, Will, and it is high time we were abed.' Then, with a mischievous twinkle, 'Time for my own particular conquering hero to come, don't you think?'

The Three Tuns

We arrive in Newcastle late in the afternoon two and a half days after our departure from Harrogate.

The day is the hottest so far, the air heavy and thick. It is so hot and oppressive that we are obliged to rest for a while in the middle of the day and take refreshment at a very pleasant inn within sight of the great cathedral in Durham before completing our journey.

By the time we come near to Newcastle, the heat is somewhat abated, but there is a sultriness in the air that presages an oncoming storm.

The town lies in the bottom of a valley and from a high hill about two miles distant it is possible to see it laid out before us like a map. It is situated on the banks of the River Tyne which winds like a pewter coloured ribbon through the middle and on for a distance of five miles or so to the sea which lies leaden calm under a sky almost purple with the reflection of the declining sun behind us.

For the last few miles, the air has been thick with the reek of sulphur from countless coal pits which dot the countryside and on the road is an abundance of small horse-drawn carts, laden with coal, conveying it from the pits to barges moored on the river.

Agnes has also remarked upon the numerous squat, brick-built structures along our way, some of which billow smoke like chimneys bereft of the house that should support them.

'I think they're lime-kilns,' I tell her, 'for making quicklime. They're often built near coal mines. They layer coal and chunks of limestone and set it alight for days, then the lime is raked out and used for fertiliser or in mortar for building. It's also useful for disposing of bodies more quickly. There'll have been more call than usual for it after recent events,' I say grimly.

As we ride into the town, we find the streets broad and handsome with many tall and impressive buildings and water conduits running into large stone cisterns for public use. We enter through the West Gate, passing a large brick building which, from the numerous figures in lawyers gowns milling about, I take to be the hall for assizes.

In the middle of the town is the Exchange, with rows of stone pillars and a court-room and council-chamber in the upper storey, and a balcony which looks out over the river and the quay.

The quay itself is broad and runs to a great length, with flights of steps running down to the water for the convenience of loading or landing goods. Even at this hour of the day it is busy with merchants, porters and boatmen bustling about the cellars and warehouses which line the dockside.

Having enquired our way to Pilgrim Street and the Three Tuns Inn, we find it to be a well-appointed establishment and we book a room for the night.

Not a moment too soon, for hardly have we handed over our horses to a groom for stabling than a blazing fork of lightning splits the lowering sky. A tremendous crack of thunder echoes round the surrounding buildings. And the heavens open.

A familiar voice greets us as we hurry indoors, escaping the deluge which would have soaked us to the skin within a minute.

'You two certainly took your time. What kept you?'

I hug a grinning Charlie to my bosom before I recall that we are supposed to be master and valet and quickly release him. Fortunately everyone else is so occupied with escaping, or deciding whether to brave, the rain that no-one seems to notice.

'You have made very good time,' says Agnes. 'How long have you been here?'

'An hour at most,' admits Charlie. 'Harry's unloaded your luggage and is stowing the wagon round the back as we speak. He was so keen to earn his extra two guineas that we made the most of every hour of daylight – and borrowed an hour or two of night as well! He's a good fellow is Harry, and 'e can certainly 'andle himself in a sticky situation.'

'You had trouble on the way?' I ask.

We have repaired to a cosy parlour away from the bustle of the entrance hall, but all the same Charlie lowers his voice.

'Second day out, it was. These two rough-looking coves overtook us and blocked our way.'

'Highwaymen?' asks Agnes.

'That's what we thought at first, but when they didn't produce no shooters and didn't make no demands to rob us, it was clear they was after somethin' else entirely. Told us the way up ahead was blocked and led us along a different road. Harry weren't 'appy, but we went along wi' 'em. Then this other fellow turns up, a gentleman to all intents and purposes. An' 'e knew who we were. Leastways, 'e thought 'e did. Thought we was the Hodges 'oo'd got another wagon an' wanted to know where the lady was.'

'He'd followed you from Manchester?' I say with alarm.

'Looks that way,' replies Charlie. 'Well o' course I feigned ignorance, and Harry didn't ave to pretend, 'cos he knew nothin' about it anyways. But this fellow wasn't 'avin it. Produced a pistol and ordered us down from the cart, then ordered his bully-boys to search it while he held us at gunpoint.'

'How did you get away?' asks Agnes.

'When they said there was nothin' there, 'e ordered 'em to search us. An' that was 'is mistake, see? Cos, once they was close to us, Harry showed 'em 'ow good 'e was with 'is fists. I've never seen anyone as fast. 'E saw off the first one with an elbow to the belly followed by an almighty crack on his jaw as he doubled up. Then as the second came at us, Harry grabbed his arm and twisted it at an angle like I've never seen and – crack! - the ruffian was down on the ground, yelling like a stuck pig.'

'What did the gentleman with the pistol do?'

'Well, 'e tried aiming it, but with all the to-do, 'e could've hit anyone. So, while he hesitated, I outs wi' my own gun and shoots 'im in the thigh, causin' 'im to topple from his 'orse. His gun went off as he fell and his horse took fright, settin' the other two bolting likewise. Our cart-horse would 'ave follered, 'cept Harry got there sharpish and took 'old of 'er. Then we got on the cart and made ourselves scarce.'

'And that was the only trouble you had? They didn't follow you?'

'One shot in the leg, one with a broken arm and t'other out cold – hardly!'

'And they only asked about the Hodges? They didn't know about the Lindsays, or mention our real names?'

Charlie pulls his face into an exaggerated grimace. 'Well, funnily enough, Will, we didn't get chance to have a conversation about all that – sorry if that disappoints you.'

Agnes laughs at his mockery. 'You did very well, Charlie. And Harry, too.'

'Glad someone appreciates me,' says Charlie with a grin. 'Now, have you by any chance ordered dinner yet? I'm starvin' and I'm sure Harry wouldn't say no if we was to invite 'im to sup wi' us.'

We order dinner to be brought up to our room and a little while later, Charlie turns up with a damp-looking Harry who is a sturdier version of his father, though with less bandy legs. He has a square jaw, darting, inquisitive eyes and solid muscles. Yet he carries himself with a light, almost feline ease which gives credence to Charlie's account of his skill at fisticuffs.

The rain is still pounding on the roof and pouring in streams down the windows, but we manage to be a fairly convivial little band over a hearty meal of beef stew and game pie followed by a lemon posset of which Mrs Wiggins, our erstwhile cook back in London, would be proud.

Once I have paid Harry the remainder of his fee, not forgetting the two guinea bonus for arriving before Agnes and myself, he departs to spend the night sleeping in his wagon before returning to Manchester in the morning.

Then, while Agnes and Charlie chatter, I compose replies to the letters that Grey delivered to me in Manchester.

To Mr Garrick I write that I am well but do not envisage returning to London for some time, by when I trust that his efforts to take over the management of Drury Lane will have been crowned with success.

To Jem I express my thanks for his management of my affairs so far, and apologise that I must continue to impose upon him for some time to come. Whilst not wishing to alarm him about the break-in at Soho Square and the stranger who was inquiring after me, I nevertheless commend him for mentioning them and trust that he will continue to inform me of any other unusual occurrences.

My letter to Sir William Hervey is longer. I report that the supposed Jacobite officer with the lazy eye goes under the name of Munro and, having been seen by various witnesses in company with both Robert and David Ross immediately before their deaths, is most likely their murderer.

I also tell him that my enemy with a penchant for rosewater scent has been making enquiries about my whereabouts from Jem in London. Also that he is – or has been acting the part – of an emissary of the Jacobite cause at the behest of Bishop Gordon. And that I suspect he has made an unsuccessful attempt to apprehend us, but was luckily foiled by Charlie, who wounded him in the leg.

I show Agnes what I have written, to check that I have omitted nothing of import, then seal the letters ready to hand over to John Armstrong, the gentleman whom Nathaniel Grey said would meet us here.

I then seek out our landlord to enquire after the said gentleman and am informed that it is his habit to come most mornings about eleven to take a drink and smoke a pipe of tobacco.

After which, with the remnants of the storm still rumbling in the distance, we all retire for the night – Charlie to his own room, and myself and Agnes to the warmth of a feather bed where we fall asleep in each other's arms.

John Armstrong is a long-limbed fellow, all angles and craggy features, who would seem more at home striding the hills than puffing a pipe and perusing the daily news sheet in a hotel parlour.

He rises as I say his name, coat hanging loosely about his lanky frame, bony wrist projecting a good three inches from his cuff as he extends his hand to greet me, mouth cracking open in a wide smile like a fissure opening in a rock face.

I account myself tall, but he towers several inches above me.

'Pleased to meet ye, Mr Lindsay, and this must be yer bonny wife and yer brother, hey?'

His local accent is broad, his huge hand engulfing my own and making Agnes's appear no more than a doll's in its hearty clasp.

The landlord bustles in with a dish of tea and a platter of flat, fruited griddle scones.

'Ah took the liberty o' orderin' some singin' hinnies,' says Armstrong. His voice is deep and friendly with a hint of humour. 'Ah doan't doot they'll be to the lady's taste, if not to yer own.'

Plates, cups and a bowl of creamy butter are laid before us and, having exhorted us to enjoy the cakes whilst they're still warm, the landlord leaves us to our business.

Charlie sets to without delay. He takes a bite, expresses satisfaction, then liberally be-daubs the sugary surface with butter. 'Mmm,' he sighs, mouth full, 'rum scones these. Didn't realise I was so peckish. Here, try one, they're bene.'

'Ah'm told you may have some letters that need delivering safely?' says Armstrong once we are settled. 'Ah've a reliable fellow standin' by who'll set off with all dispatch this afternoon.'

'Aye, and we were told you might have further information about the matter on which we are embarked,' I reply.

'Why, I doan know about information,' says he, 'but what ah do 'ave, is three tickets for the fast stage to Edinburgh, wi' orders to get yer on it by two-thirty this afternoon. Yers all have an appointment wi' Lord President Forbes day after tomorrow. An' ah've bin told to tell yer to travel light as 'is Lordship will provide you with all necessaries for the continuation of yer journey once you get there. So, if you've 'ad yer fill o' cake ma bonny lad, we'd best get cracking.'

He reaches into his pocket and gives me the three tickets and I hand him my three letters in return. 'I thank you, Mr Armstrong. I regret that our acquaintance has been so short. We would, I'm sure, have welcomed the opportunity to get to know each other better. You seem an open, honest fellow that I could get to like.'

Again his craggy face cracks open into a grin. 'Aye, well, appearances can be deceptive, can't they, Mr – er – *Lindsay?'* he replies with a knowing wink. 'For all you know, I might be the subtlest and most deceitful of rogues. But, in our line o'work, that's just one o' the hazards we face, eh? Now, if the three o' yer are ready...?

Lord President Duncan Forbes

Two days later, after overnight stops in Alnwick and Berwick upon Tweed, we arrive in Edinburgh.

We have taken John Armstrong's advice and travelled light with but two bags between us. One for Agnes and the other with a spare coat and a change of linen for Charlie and me. The rest of our luggage we have left at the *Three Tuns* back in Newcastle to be collected on our return journey. Or, if we do not return within a six-month, to be disposed of by the landlord as he thinks fit.

In Edinburgh we are met off the coach by a dapper little man. Dressed all in black and politely brusque, he guides us through the bustle of alighting passengers to a secluded alleyway off the main thoroughfare where a pony trap stands waiting.

His Lordship, he informs us, awaits us at his mansion in Musselburgh, an hour's ride out of town.

As it is a fine day, the journey in the open carriage passes pleasantly enough, though our guide, now turned driver, is reticence incarnate, so we are left to admire the passing scenery and, by the time he turns into a long, gravelled driveway leading up to a fine mansion overlooking the sea, we are no wiser about its owner than we were at the start of our journey.

We are ushered into a wood-panelled room by a maidservant. 'The maister's on the links the'noo,' she tells us in a lilting Scottish accent, 'but ye may tarry here awhile. He'll be here anon.'

It is not a room in which one can be at ease. The upright wooden chairs are not built for comfort, and there are no cushions to alleviate their hardness.

Agnes strolls over to the window to look out at the view, whilst I examine the pictures upon the panelled walls. A series of portraits of austere-looking be-wigged men who must, I guess, be Lord Forbes's ancestors. All display a family likeness in their high foreheads and long, equine noses.

'Links?' says Charlie after a few moments puzzling over the departed maid's words. 'What the hell are *links?'*

Agnes beckons him over to the window which looks out over the garden and a stretch of open, gently undulating greensward beyond, with the sea in the distance.

A small group of men with sticks are walking between the hillocks. But rather than using the sticks in the manner of walking canes, they pause occasionally and take it in turns to congregate around one or other of their companions whilst he wields his stick, which I see has a bulbous end, holding it high and bringing it down in a curving arc to strike a small ball that lies upon the ground. Then all watch the missile's flight to see where it lands before walking on towards the spot and repeating the process all over again.

'What on earth are they doing?' asks Charlie, in bewilderment.

'Playing some sort of game, it would seem,' suggests Agnes.

And, even as we watch, it appears that the contest reaches its conclusion. One of the distant figures stoops to gather up the balls, which he puts into bag at his waist. It is clear that he is a servant for the other three then hand him their sticks, which he gathers together in a kind of vertical bag that he hitches over his shoulder by its strap. He then plods in the direction of the house, leaving the others to stroll in a more leisurely manner after him.

Arriving at the perimeter of the grounds, they stop a while in conversation. Shortly a carriage appears from somewhere behind the house. Two of the gentlemen get in and the vehicle moves off.

The remaining gentleman, after raising his hand in farewell, turns and marches briskly towards the house where, a few moments later, he presents himself at the doorway of our chamber.

'Mr William Archer?' he says, striding towards me and holding out his hand. His handshake is as strong as his tone is authoritative. 'And Miss Agnes Mayer?' He gives a polite bow to which Agnes returns a low curtsey. 'I have been expecting you. And this young gentleman is...?'

'Charlie Stubbs, at your service, sir.'

'Splendid! And you all know who I am, I take it?'

'Indeed, sir,' I reply. 'You are Mr Duncan Forbes of Culloden, Lord President of the Court of Session and valued friend of the British Government and British State. We are honoured to make your acquaintance, sir.'

'Aye, aye,' he replies, waving a dismissive hand, 'a simple Mr Forbes will suffice. I stand on no ceremony here in my own home.'

He looks around the room as if seeing it for the first time. 'God bless me! What was Maisie thinking of, showing you all in here. Come, let us retire to somewhere more comfortable.'

He bids us follow, apologising on the way for not being here to meet us. 'The round of golf took longer than I planned. My companions were in a mood for conversation and that made us tardy.' He sees our puzzled faces. '*Golf!* Do you not know the game?'

'I have not seen it played in England, sir. It is peculiar to Scotland perhaps?'

He is all amazement. 'Well, Master Archer, you English do not know what you're missing! Now,' says he decisively once we are arrived in a more congenial sunlit parlour, 'pray make yourselves comfortable and tell me, do you know why you are here?'

'Partly, Mr Forbes,' I say. 'We have information to impart regarding the unfortunate demise of various of your relatives. And I believe you may also have information to give us relating to the task assigned to us by Sir William Hervey.'

'Admirably succinct, Master Archer. Straight to the point. I like that in a man,' he says. 'Would some of the lawyers who appear before me in the Court of Sessions cultivate similar brevity! Now, did MacPherson tell you anything of arrangements?'

'MacPherson, sir?'

'The dapper little fellow who brought you here. Did he say nothing about what was to happen?'

'Nothing, Mr Forbes. He barely spoke above a dozen words the whole journey.'

'Aye, well done MacPherson!' says he with a hearty laugh. 'Like all the men in my employ, his job is to listen, not to speak. And you, I am sure, are the same for I expect Sir William is of a similar mind. It does not do to be careless with words in our business.' He pauses, regarding us keenly. 'None of you has remarked upon the fact that I have addressed you by your real names?'

'We assume you are in Sir William's confidence, sir.'

'You assume correctly, Master Archer. He and I are on the same side - the side of the rightful head of the United Kingdom of Great Britain, his Majesty King George II. And both of us are most desirous that this Kingdom shall remain united. Which is why,' he adds with furrowed brow, 'we are sending you to ensure that the gentleman whose late abortive rebellion attempted to disrupt that unity successfully eludes his English pursuers and escapes safely to France.' He pauses, raising a quizzical eyebrow. 'You understand the paradox, I take it?'

'I would guess that you and Sir William are prepared to countenance his escape in the hope that a failed adventurer is unlikely to command as great a following as a martyred hero?'

Forbes gives an admiring beam. 'Again, most succinctly put, Master Archer. I see why Sir William sets such store by you. If only a young man of sense such as yourself had His Majesty's ear rather than that impetuous young puppy, the Duke of Cumberland...' He broods a moment, then becomes serious. 'Our hope is also that, with young Charles Edward Stuart safely back in Rome, Sir William and I may do our best to curb the Duke's misguided revengeful excesses here at home.'

'I thought the Duke was back in London, Mr Forbes?'

'Aye, he is, where he has ensured that the captured rebel leaders suffered the utmost humiliation through public execution.'

'We read the account of the executions at Kennington on our journey hither,' says Agnes with a shudder. 'It was horrible.'

'Scarcely more horrible than all that has happened here since the rebels were routed at Culloden,' replies Forbes sadly. 'It will be a matter of eternal regret to me that my family home will be forever tarnished with the memory of that bloody encounter. Culloden House has been our family seat for generations. It was from there that I tried to assess the severity of the the threat just after the Pretender landed, and tried in vain to convince the powers in London that 'twould be no mere fire of straw. And it was from thence that I was obliged to take flight just before the rebel Prince seized possession of it and put a price upon my head.'

'The Pretender took your family home?' exclaims Agnes in surprise.

'Aye, ma'am, he and his generals. 'Twas there they stayed the days before the battle. Yet I allow him this – he and his followers did no damage. For all they had possession of the home of their enemy, they acted honourably and with respect.'

'You sound almost as if you admire him?' I say.

Forbes gives a weary smile. 'I abhor what he has done – set father against son, brother against brother and brought such disaster upon this country of mine that I fear will not be expunged in my lifetime – but, like many who followed him, he is not, I believe a bad man. He may be deluded, but he acted as a gentleman, according to his own beliefs and principles, and displayed a respect for those he considered his enemies. Behaviour that some of our own leaders might do well to emulate.'

'You refer to the Duke of Cumberland, sir?'

'Aye, Master Archer, and to Lord Albermarle and others, whom he has left to carry on his work here in Scotland, and who are pursuing the Duke's policy of crushing my poor countrymen with equal, if not greater, rigour,' he says sorrowfully.

'But,' he exclaims, clapping his hands together, 'I am neglecting my duties as host. What MacPherson might have told you, had he been so inclined, was that you are all three to be my guests tonight. We shall dine shortly and you shall tell me all you have discovered about the deaths of my Ross kinsmen. Then I shall brief you upon where your journey will take you over the next few weeks. So, ma'am and gentlemen, if you would care to follow me, I shall see you safely accommodated for this night at least.'

* * *

He and the three of us comprise all the company at dinner, which we take in a splendid dining room around a table large enough for a dozen or more. The high windows afford a view across the Firth of Forth where the setting sun throws a gilded path across the calm, sparkling water.

'Mrs Forbes is not joining us?' asks Agnes.

A shadow passes across his face. 'My wife has been dead this five and thirty years, Miss Mayer, though I still miss her as if it had been but yesterday. You will think me foolish, ma'am. We were childhood sweethearts and she was taken from us not long after our only son was born. I was a widower ere I was twenty three years old.'

'That is indeed tragic, sir,' says Agnes sympathetically. 'And you never thought to re-marry?'

Forbes smiles sadly. 'Never, ma'am. No other could replace my Mary Rose. And, as a constant reminder of her, I have my son, John. A finer son no man could wish for. But come, Master Archer, tell me what you have found out about the deaths you have been investigating.'

For the next half hour, with Agnes's and Charlie's assistance, I recount all we have discovered about the deaths of Robert Ross in Derby, David Ross in Manchester and Alexander Ross in London.

From time to time, Mr Forbes puts in a question or two, mainly relating to the supposed Jacobite officer.

'He went by the name of Munro in Manchester you say?'

'Yes, according to Mr Feilden, David's business partner.'

'And various people commented upon his appearance, saying that though he might be considered well-looking, one eye drooped slightly or had a slight squint?'

'That is so. I asked Sir William to inquire if such a man had been observed around the time of Mr Alexander Ross's murder in London, but he has so far not replied.'

'Hmmn,' Mr Forbes strokes his chin thoughtfully. Then, with no apparent rhyme or reason, he asks, 'What do you know about Scottish Clans, Master Archer?'

'Next to nothing, Mr Forbes.'

'Then I will keep it as simple as I can. Clans are gatherings of people who claim kinship. Like ancient tribes, they claim and defend their own territory. The head of the clan, or Chief, is usually a powerful Lord and everyone who lives in his territory is regarded as a member of his clan, often taking on his name. The history of Scotland is a history of rivalry, wars or allegiances forged between clans. So powerful is this bond of kinship that the Young Pretender was obliged to organise his army into clan-based regiments, for they would not accept orders from any but their own clan chiefs.'

'That sounds like a recipe for chaos and indiscipline,' I say. 'No wonder many in London called it the Highland rabble!'

'Rabble they are not, Mister Archer. They are fierce and formidable fighters, as the English found to their cost,' replies Mr Forbes with a touch of asperity. 'And the Clan system, far from being a recipe for chaos and indiscipline is, in fact, the very opposite. It represents a tenacity and loyalty which will make a Scotsman fight to the death. Which is why Parliament is even now, rashly in my view, enacting laws to eradicate it.'

He muses for a moment. 'But I am diverging from my subject, which is the villain who seems to be ruthlessly murdering my relations – all, as you probably realise, members of Clan Ross. The clan to which I, despite my surname being Forbes, also belong.'

'You think the murderer may be a member of a rival clan?' I ask.

Mr Forbes grimaces, 'Nearer to home, I'm afraid. I believe he may be a treacherous member of Clan Ross itself.'

'How can that be?' asks Agnes in surprise.

'You must understand, Miss Mayer, that most of Clan Ross sided with King George. My nephew, Alexander Ross of Pitcalnie is the present Chief. Together we raised a force to defend Inverness castle against the rebels. But loyalties can be divided within clans as well as elsewhere – as I know to my regret. My great nephew, Malcolm Forbes of Pitcalnie, deserted the English army and went over to the rebels at Prestonpans. I wrote to try and dissuade him, telling him that such misguided rashness would earn him not glory but a halter, But driven by the hot-headed certainty of youth he went his own way. So after Culloden, when the Duke of Cumberland gave orders to root out all deserters from the Government forces who had gone over to the Jacobites and to deal out summary justice, poor Malcolm was one of thirty-six who were hanged in Inverness in those first few vicious days after the battle.'

'I'm so sorry, Mr Forbes,' says Agnes sympathetically.

'Nay, ma'am, we all make our own choices in life and, in times like these, we must be prepared to face the consequences. I, too, have made choices which I fear my son may live to reprehend me for. I am near penniless from furnishing money for government business this past year, and as my entreaties to deal mercifully with the rebels find little favour at this present time I doubt I shall leave John anything but debts. But though I shall go to my grave with regrets, I shall go with a clear conscience, knowing I have served my King and my fellow men with justice and compassion. But,' says he, casting off his melancholy tone, 'once more I digress. We were talking of who might have murdered my three relatives.'

'Indeed, sir, you were saying that you thought he could be, like his victims, a member of Clan Ross himself?'

'Yes. As I said, my nephew, Malcolm, was hanged at Inverness. Which means there is no longer a direct heir.' He pauses a moment before continuing, 'But young Malcolm had a cousin, about the same age. John Ross. Not so much a hot-head as an ambitious schemer, skilled from an early age at turning a situation to his advantage. He was born out of wedlock, but I suspect bastardy sharpened rather than inhibited his ambition. And in light of what you've told me, I fear that his ambition is now to be named chief of Clan Ross and master of all the Balnagowan Estates. He fits the physical description: well-looking but for that lazy eye.'

'You think this John Ross has been disposing of prospective rivals, sir?' asks Agnes, shocked.

'Knowing his character as I do, it is the inescapable conclusion,' replies Forbes, sombrely.

'But the murders were committed before his cousin Malcolm was hanged,' I say. 'Surely he could not have known that would happen?'

'John is as unscrupulous as he is devious, Master Archer. He was obviously preparing the ground, removing possible obstacles in his path. Then, with his route to the title unimpeded, if Fate had not removed Malcolm, I have no doubt that John would have gone on to engineer his death himself. I have it on good authority that both men fought at Culloden but, whilst Malcolm was captured, John escaped. Where he is now, I do not know.'

'Could he have fled with the Pretender?' I ask.

'If he did not, I should think he is even now seeking Charles Stuart out in order to petition for rights and titles of Clan Ross,' says Forbes.

Special Envoys

Retiring to the parlour after dinner, Mr Forbes urges upon us large glasses of malt liquor which I sip but find too fiery for my taste and, after lingering out the first glass, I politely decline his offer of a refill, feeling already light-headed.

He, however, more attuned to its bold flavour, partakes of several more glasses without any noticeable effect upon his faculties.

Then, in the comfortable warmth of his parlour and with all of us replete from a fine meal, he outlines the future course of our journey.

'I have recently received a letter from Lady Margaret MacDonald in which she entreats me to intercede on behalf of her kinsman Alexander MacDonald of Kingsburgh.'

He goes to a writing desk and takes a sheet of paper from one of the drawers.

'She writes as follows: "Your Lordship can't yet be a stranger to the trouble which has lately been brought upon this island by the indiscretion of a foolish girl with whom the unhappy disturber of this Kingdom landed at this place." By this, of course she means Charles Stuart, the rebel Prince.'

'And the 'foolish girl'?' asks Agnes.

'One Flora MacDonald, step-daughter of Hugh MacDonald who commands the Skye Militia, which is, in name at least, loyal to the Government.'

'And in what respect has this Flora MacDonald been indiscreet, Mr Forbes?'

'She aided the Pretender to evade his pursuers shortly after Culloden by transporting him to the Isle of Skye in the guise of a female servant. Lady Margaret's letter seeks to absolve her from blame, maintaining that, as the young man was in disguise, no one knew anything about it until he had left.' He pauses and regards us with cynically raised brows. 'A claim that is at best disingenuous, and at worst downright false. Her aim, of course is to escape reprisals.'

'You think they were all complicit in aiding his escape?'

'I have no doubt of it,' replies Mr Forbes. 'I have it on good authority that Captain John Fergusson, who has been in close pursuit of the Pretender these last two months has, in his own words, been on several occasions within an hour of capturing him. Fergusson is a brute and a boor and it shames me to own him as a fellow Scotsman. The manner in which he has persecuted those suspected of harbouring the fugitive prince – burning their houses and cruelly mistreating their womenfolk – is execrable. But I have no reason to doubt the truth of his claims. Unfortunately, since Lady Margaret wrote to me, he has arrested Kingsburgh, the

251

kinsman whose cause she would have me plead. Which is why I intend to send you as my special envoys to convey my reply, assuring her that I shall do my utmost on his behalf.'

'You would do that, even though you know he is guilty?' says Agnes.

'There are many degrees of guilt, Miss Mayer,' replies Mr Forbes philosophically, 'just as there are many forms of justice. The MacDonalds in Skye did not throw in their lot with the Jacobite cause, they remained loyal to King George. But, like myself, they saw the ferocity with which, following the battle at Culloden, our government forces have pursued our fellow countrymen; such vengeful carnage cannot but appall. There is no doubt in my mind that the memory of it will afflict Scotland for countless generations to come. Flora MacDonald and her family acted not from any partisan allegiance, but from a deeper allegiance to humanity itself. And can we, in all conscience, condemn them when we ourselves are about to embark upon just such a plan – to aid the rebel Prince in making his escape to France?'

'So you intend to send us to Skye, Mr Forbes?' I say. 'I have heard the name, but I have no idea where it is. Is it far from here?'

'It is an island to the north west of Scotland a week's ride at least. But I think you will not have to go so far. My latest intelligence is that our man is returned to the mainland and is somewhere in the vicinity of Loch Arkaig and Ben Alder forest, though exactly where I do not know. I shall give you letters of authorisation which will ensure safe passage as far as Fort William, which is close to the area where we believe the Pretender to be. From there I and Sir William put our trust in you to decide how to pursue your quest further. '

'Will there be anyone at Fort William who may be able to supply us with information about the Prince's whereabouts?' I ask.

'There will be many, I should think, for all there will be employed in the search for him,' replies Forbes grimly. 'Captain Caroline Frederick Scott, the Government commander of the garrison, is an ardent enemy of the Stuarts and viciously zealous in his desire to apprehend him, but I would most earnestly counsel you not to ask *him* for information. For calling Charles Stuart 'the Prince' as you have just inadvertently done, he would have you stripped and flogged naked in the street. Captain Caroline Scott is as bad, if not worse than Captain Fergusson.'

'His name is *Caroline?'* says Charlie with a snigger.

'Aye, in honour of Queen Caroline, his godmother,' replies Forbes with a blackly humorous smile, 'and one might argue, perhaps, that his pitiless nature may in some measure be a counteraction to the humiliation that his name, so unusual for a man, must have caused throughout his life.'

'And we are to tell him the purpose of our journey is to deliver the letter to Lady Margaret MacDonald? What if he questions that?'

'Show him the letter I shall give you, requiring your safe passage. He may not like it, but he will not dare refuse it. But you must give him no cause to suspect that Skye is not your real destination.'

'How are we to deliver the letter to Lady Margaret MacDonald, then?' asks Agnes.

'If needs be, you may appoint a courier. How you contrive that is up to you. But this,' says he, once more going to the writing desk and returning with a folded document sealed with an official seal, 'is a letter which you *must* deliver in person. And this must be kept close until that moment arrives. If it is discovered before then, I cannot answer either for your safety or your lives.'

He holds it out. The superscription reads *Charles Edward Stuart, Esquire.*

For the next four and a half days we ride through country the likes of which I have never seen before. Our route takes us north and west through a land of towering mountains and plunging valleys, where dense forests clothe the lower reaches of precipitous slopes which rear up in rocky peaks and ridges, or plummet down to deep rushing rivers or long vistas of clear, calm lakes.

It is fortunate that Lord President Forbes has provided us with an escort of two cavalrymen as far as Fort William, for otherwise we would surely lose our way in this wild, inhospitable land where any direct route seems to be blocked either by fearsome crags or impassable waters.

As it is, our guides appear to know the circuitous paths and roundabout ways that wind about the feet of the mountains or around great lakes, and are familiar with fords and bridges across innumerable rivers.

Having them as our escort is not an entirely unmixed blessing, however. Though we encounter but few people on our journey, the sight of our companions' red-coats seems to inspire a deep antipathy. At best, they favour us with a few surly words, at worst they spit on the ground as we ride past. On one or two occasions, we see ragged bands of armed men high on a ridge observing us, and once a puff of smoke and distant report shows they have fired at us, though no shot from such a distance could possible come close.

It is not difficult to understand why the red uniform should be so reviled. Every so often we come across a ravaged huddle of deserted houses, their walls blackened, roofs caved in and a sorry litter of discarded possessions strewn across the surrounding ground.

This is the legacy of our Government's 'pacification' policy. Everyone tarred with the same brush, all classed as rebels by reason of being Scottish, and all to be driven out, made homeless and forced to fly or seek refuge where they can.

The further we travel through this depopulated countryside, the more we begin to dislike our guides, not for themselves - they are decent enough fellows - but for what they represent: agents of a wholesale persecution not only of fellow human beings, but those who are, in effect, our own countrymen.

And, seeing this, the greater grows the realisation of how difficult our task will be. With every mile we ride, it becomes clearer that we are entering a country where everyone will be our enemy. Where simmering resentment may at any moment flare into deadly peril.

Fortunately, Mr Forbes has anticipated this state of affairs. The riding dress he has provided for us all contains several cleverly concealed and padded secret pockets wherein are hidden both pistols and daggers, and in the coats for Charlie and myself, even a place where a rapier is secreted.

Also concealed in one of the secret pockets is the letter to the Pretender, which bears not just one but two official seals. One bearing the crest of Mr Forbes, the other that of Sir William Hervey.

So skilfully are the garments tailored that they appear no different from normal riding coats, and even if we should be so unfortunate as to be subjected to a search of our persons, it is doubtful that either the vital missive or our secret arsenals would be discovered.

Just before noon of the fifth day since we left Lord Justice Forbes' house near Edinburgh, we come within sight of Fort William.

For near two hours we have been riding with a wide expanse of water on our left, whilst in the near distance to our right blue hills line up behind each other, with one particularly grand one seeming to rise up almost menacingly to overlook the walled town that nestles at its foot.

'That,' one of our escort informs us, 'is called Ben Nevis. Some say 'tis the highest peak in this godforsaken land.'

Ben we have learned is a Gaelic term for *Mount,* just as the expanses of water we call *lakes* the Scots give the name of *lochs.*

'And what loch is this beside which we have been riding this past hour?' I ask him.

'This is called Loch Linnhe,' he replies, 'though in truth 'tis more of a strait than a loch, for it gives the only access to the open sea hereabouts, which is why Fort William is so well located. With Ben Nevis to its back and able to command the sea from its front, it is well-nigh impregnable – as those damned Jacobite rebels found to their cost a couple of months back when they tried to besiege it. But Captain Scott saw them off, no trouble.'

'Captain Scott is a skilful fighter?' I ask.

'Don't know about skill, but he's a damn plaguey thorn in the side of them blasted rebel scum. Put here by the Duke of Cumberland himself to scour out all those confounded renegades. He's a hard man, but he gets things done.'

A similar assessment to that which Mr Forbes gave, but here spoken with admiration rather than distaste. It does not make me any more sanguine about our forthcoming meeting.

It is a meeting that cannot be avoided, however. The arrival of three strangers with an official military escort cannot pass unnoticed, and within half an hour of our entry into the town we are shown into Captain Scott's presence.

He is a coarse-looking man, his chin rough with two days' growth, his eyes suspicious, who wears the trappings of civilisation, his close-cut wig and military uniform, with little grace.

His manner is less gracious still.

'Forbes sent you?' he says brusquely. 'Show me his letter of authorisation.' He holds out his hand impatiently.

I produce the Lord Justice's letter which he takes without ceremony and, breaking its seal strides away a pace or two, turning his back on us as he digests its contents.

'You're bound for Skye to that nest o' vipers, the MacDonalds, you say?'

'To deliver His Lordship's greetings to Lady Margaret, yes.'

'You know they're traitors?' he snarls, giving us a scowl from under his dark brows.

I shape my reply as diplomatically as I can. 'My information is that they have always expressed loyalty to His Hanoverian Majesty,' I say with a slightly puzzled air.

'Words mean nothing to these Highland scum,' he scoffs. 'They'll stab you in the back while swearing allegiance. I wouldn't trust a one o' them!'

He stares at each of us in turn before addressing me again. 'You're English to judge from your accent. Though such an ale and porter tongue as I cannot hazard whether north or south.'

I swallow my anger at the gibe and reply civilly, 'Yorkshire born but London raised, sir,'

'Yes, that would account for your mongrel speech. And your two companions? Are they common tykes as well?

Speak, ma'am, so that I may judge.'

'What would you have me say, sir?'

'That will suffice,' he sneers. 'You're clearly no damned Scot, nor North-Englander. Not English at all, I'd say?'

'My family is of Dutch extraction, sir.'

'Aye, I thought I detected a tang of Orange,' says he offensively. 'And you, sir, are you a dyke-jumper, too?' he asks Charlie.

'No, sir, a Londoner born and bred.'

'And low-born and low-bred, too, judging by your Cockney whine.'

I see Charlie bridle, but he has the good sense to hold his tongue.

'Well,' the abusive Captain continues contemptuously, flinging Mr Forbes's letter back at me, 'I don't know where His Lordship dug up such a motley crew to run his errands for him, but I certainly can't spare any of my men to nursemaid you all on your way to that damned bitch in Skye. Not when there's Highland vermin to hunt down.'

'You'll not object to us staying overnight here in Fort William, sir?' asks Agnes acidly.

'You may do as you please, ma'am. There's an Inn in town that I believe is not totally lice-infested. But see that you're gone by mid-day tomorrow, or I shall want to know the reason why,' says he, stalking from the room.

An Old Acquaintance

For the next hour, left to our own devices, we have opportunity enough to discover that, as our guide hither told us, Fort William is near impregnable from land or water.

And that it is almost as inhospitable to guests as to invaders.

The one or two soldiers we approach to inquire about the whereabouts of the inn express ignorance of any such place. To them the fort, its barracks and its parade ground mark the boundaries of their life and knowledge. Anything beyond its walls is unworthy of note.

Some apologise half-heartedly for their inability to assist us, others grunt their lack of knowledge with only the barest civility. The one good consequence of such unhelpfulness is that we are let to roam almost at will.

Thus, by dint of walking about and climbing the ramparts unhindered, we see that the fort itself is situated upon a sort of natural bulwark of land formed at a point where a river runs into the loch. Its walls, which look to have been recently strengthened are thick and high, with several bastions giving a clear view over all the waters to the front and side, and over what looks like bare and scrubby marshland behind.

It is by far the best kept building of the little settlement to which it gives its name. Beyond its walls on the landward side is a scattering of houses which comprise the town, though village might be a more apt description for there are signs of neither pride nor wealth in the mean and neglected-looking dwellings.

'If there is anything that calls itself an inn down there, it will be a poor place indeed,' complains Agnes. 'Might we not be better continuing our journey at once, there is a good five or six hours of daylight left and we may chance upon somewhere more accommodating?'

'And in what direction would you propose we travel?' I answer, somewhat more snappishly than I intend. The interview with Captain Scott has put me out of sorts and made me irritable. 'We know not where our quarry is and in the meantime we have no choice but to stay and learn what we can.'

'And how do you propose we do that?' retorts Agnes, equally irritably. 'The Commander of the Garrison is a boorish bully who wants us gone and every soldier we have met is barely civil enough to give us the time of day! Where do you propose we find such information?'

'Hey, you two!' says Charlie reprovingly. 'This is no time to be a'fratching! You're both right, though – we don't know where we're headed, and it don't look like anyone's likely to tell us. So what're we goin' to do?'

His rebuke brings us to our senses. We descend from our position on the ramparts overlooking the town and start across the open expanse of the central parade ground, threading our way through the innumerable red-coated soldiers to whom we are all but invisible for all the notice they take of us.

Whilst there may be little prospect of decent accommodation outside the walls of the fort, we may at least hope to gain a little more information, for it seems impossible to get any here.

We are within a dozen yards of the main gate when I hear a voice calling me.

But not by my own name, nor either of the aliases I've assumed over the last few months.

'Stap me! Jack Weaver? Is it really you?'

The next moment I am engulfed by a brawny bear of a man who near squeezes the breath from my body, his eyes shining, his mop of fair hair doing its best to escape from under his tricorne hat.

Jack Weaver. The name my enemy gave to the recruiting sergeant when his hired ruffians dragged me, half unconscious, to be pressed into the army. The name under which I served in the British army as we toiled across the breadth of Europe , and under which I fought in the Battle of

Dettingen. A name which, though imposed upon me, I found convenient not to change until I was freed from my unsought-for military servitude.

And the big, blond bear who is only now releasing me from his enthusiastic embrace is none other than Tom Hooper, who befriended me during that campaign and saved me from imminent death at the hands of another whom we both thought was a friend.

And who is now holding me at arms' length, surveying me as if he cannot believe his eyes.

'By God, it is you! What the devil are you doing here?'

'A good question, Tom,' I say, heaving a deep sigh, 'but one which cannot be easily answered. Know you of anywhere private, away from prying ears and eyes? Then I can introduce you to my two companions, and satisfy your curiosity in full measure.'

'I have the very place,' says he. He looks at Agnes and Charlie with curiosity, then with a broad wink at me, he adds, 'and I'd hazard that victuals and a dram or two of strong liquor would aid the telling of the tale?'

He bids us follow him, which we do, attracting as usual hardly any attention from the milling soldiers all intent on their own business.

The Fort is like a town in miniature. Around the central open space which is roughly triangular in shape, with the main gate at its apex, are ranged numerous tall buildings. Mostly three storeys high and similar to the mill at Derby in the regularity of their windows and the length of their frontages, they are the barracks for the hundreds of troops stationed here. The place where they go about most of their daily tasks, consort during their leisure time and sleep each night.

Of the few other buildings all have a specific purpose. Close by the main gate is a walled enclosure which Tom informs us is the powder store and shot yard, and next to it a building, not much bigger than a small house, with several of its windows barred that I guess is the guard house.

We come to a building to our left where lines of soldiers wait in relaxed but orderly fashion. 'That's the mess-hall,' says Tom, 'and if you'll excuse me...'

He strides over to the entrance and we see him parleying with those at the front of the queue. Heads briefly turn, disinterestedly, in our direction as they allow him through.

A few minutes later, he emerges carrying baskets covered with muslin cloths and hurries back to us.

'Beef stew,' he says. 'I hope you like gristle! But there's fruit duff for afters. And,' he continues, showing the necks of a couple of flasks protruding from the cover, 'a little something to warm the cockles!'

So saying, he takes us in tow again towards the far side

of the open space, heading for a somewhat dilapidated building in the corner.

'An old barrack block,' he explains. 'Disused since the new block was built over there, and fallen into decay. But serviceable for our purpose.'

Which, indeed, it proves, for there are tables and chairs still, albeit a little dusty and rickety, but adequate for our needs.

Our host has brought wooden spoons and a couple of bowls, into which he ladles stew before handing them to Agnes and myself. 'I'm afraid they only had the two bowls spare,' says he to Charlie, so you and me will have to dip in together, if thats's all right by you?'

'I'd eat it straight from the cow,' laughs Charlie. 'My stomach's beginning to think my throat's cut!'

And without further ado, we all set to. The sauce is savoury and nourishing, though the chunks of meat take a deal of chewing.

'So, Jack Weaver,' mumbles Tom with his mouth full, 'how come you here, and with such a fine lady and this strapping lad?'

I wipe a trickle of gravy from my mouth with the back of my hand. 'It's a long story, Tom, but first 'tis only right I clear up a misunderstanding. My real name is not Jack Weaver, but Will Archer. I meant to tell you when we were in Flanders together, but somehow the chance never arose.'

Tom nods enthusiastically. 'Can't say as I didn't have a notion you weren't all you seemed,' says he with a grin. All that secret followin' of folks and that villain Woodrow a-tryin' to kill you. A dark horse you were – but a good friend all the same. So Weaver or Archer, 'tis all the same to me, so you still be the same worthy fellow,' says he giving me a slap upon the back that near makes me choke upon a piece of gristle. 'And these, your fellow travellers?'

I introduce Agnes and Charlie.

Tom regards Agnes closely, his brow furrowed. 'Ain't I seen you somewhere before, ma'am? Your face looks mighty familiar.'

'I, too, was in Flanders at the same time as Will and yourself. Mayhap you chanced to see us together.'

'Aye, that's likely it,' he replies, 'you sly dog, Jack – sorry, Will. Damn me, I'll not get used to this!' he laughs.

'Then I'm afraid I shall have to maze you even more, Tom,' I say. 'Whilst 'tis true what I told you about being pressed into the army against my will, there is more that I was unable to tell you, and you can have no notion how guilty that makes me feel. We became good friends, you and I, and it grieves me that I was obliged to deceive you so. But now, as a measure of my trust in you, I can tell you that I was on government business. Tasked with uncovering a plot against King George himself.'

Tom lets forth a whistle of amazement, emitting a fine spray of gravy in the process.

Before he can further express his surprise in words, I continue, 'Now I am engaged in such a business again. All three of us are, Agnes, Charlie and myself. Which is why this chance encounter with you is so fortunate. I couldn't imagine Fate would be so kind! How comes it that you are here so opportunely?'

'Nay, that is soon told,' says he, taking our empty bowls and wiping them with one of the muslin cloths before dividing the pudding into pieces. 'After you disappeared without a word, - and shame on you for that, 'twas unfriendly done, I thought you were dead.'

I mutter renewed apologies.

'Aye, well 'tis no matter, 'tis all in the past now. As I was saying, because of casualties and wounded, the regiments that fought at Dettingen had to re-group. I was enlisted in the Duke of Cumberland's men and spent a few more months chasing the French round Europe. But when he was called back to quell the Highland Rebels, I came with him. Now he's returned to London, and we're left here to harry the remaining Highland stragglers.'

'Your commander, Captain Scott, is rigorous in their pursuit, I've heard?' says Agnes.

Tom's face clouds. He leans closer and lowers his voice, though there is no one to overhear us in this deserted building. 'The man is a very devil, without a shred of mercy,' he says scathingly, 'without even the least respect for civilised behaviour.'

'That is strong language, Tom.'

'He is a monster, I tell you. I have seen it with my own eyes.' He does not wait for us to query it but presses on with feeling. 'We heard that the rebel, Stewart of Ardsheal, was in hiding near his family home. So what does that demon, Scott do? He raids his house. There's only the wife and frightened children there, but after terrorising them, Scott orders us to round up all the cattle, and to confiscate her meagre supply of cheese and butter. Then we were made to strip the house bare – everything: doors taken off their hinges, panelling stripped from the walls, slates from the roof. And 'twas all done very slowly and carefully so that everything, even straightened out nails, could be sold at market. He even took the children's school books. When nought but a shell remained, he asked the poor woman for her keys which she had no choice but to hand over, surrounded as she was with her terrified children, and big with another. Then, aping the gentleman, he takes her by the hand, leads her to where the front door once stood, her children clinging to her skirts. "You have no business here any more, Madam," says he. "Ardsheal House is no longer your home." Then he casts them out with nothing more than the clothes upon their backs. There was not one of us could look the poor woman in the eye and such was the feeling amongst us that, had that bastard not been our commanding officer, and had we courage enough, he'd not have lived to see another day!'

'Truly a most despicable act,' I say in sympathy. 'And your confirmation of his viciousness only serves to make our business the more urgent.'

'Your business is to do with Captain Scott?' asks Tom, wide-eyed.

'Only in that we - and my master who works for the interests of the British Government – seek to thwart him in his main desire.'

'Ah,' says Tom, his face lighting up with realisation, 'you mean his determination to hunt down the Pretender? You aim to capture him first?'

'We-e-ell, in a manner of speaking,' say I evasively. 'And this is where you may help us, if you are willing, Tom?'

'If serving his Majesty helps to take that monster down a peg or two, then I'm your man! What do you want me to do?'

I explain to him that, while our ostensible task is to

270

deliver Lord Justice Forbes's missive to Lady Margaret MacDonald on Skye, we think our real aim lies in the opposite direction.

'Our true purpose being to find the fugitive Prince before Scott does.'

'You must make haste then,' says Tom. 'There's a detachment of troops setting out at noon tomorrow,with the express purpose of apprehending him. The latest rumour is that he's hiding out in Ben Alder forest with the renegade Cluny MacPherson. The forest is fifteen or so miles north east of here and Scott is leading the party himself. But it's desolate and deserted country, part thick forest, part open moorland, with rebels round every bush ready to take a shot at you.'

'Are you in the party, Tom?'

'Not this time.'

'Good,' I say decisively. 'As you say, time is of the essence. So here's what I propose we do.'

They draw close as I outline my plan to them.

The Hunt Begins

First thing next morning, banking on the fact that he won't want to risk offending Lord Justice Forbes's envoy, I request to see Captain Caroline Scott again.

He is not best pleased, but the very fact that he agrees to see me only confirms my assumption that, like most bullies, he is also a coward.

'Not gone yet, Archer,' he says with a sneer. 'I told you I wanted to see the back of you before noon.'

'And you shall, sir,' I say boldly, holding my ground, 'but you must provide me with an escort...'

'*Must,* sirrah!' he explodes, red-faced. 'There is no *must* about it! Who do you think you are, marching in here and giving your orders?'

His fury only strengthens my resolve to stay calm. I hold his gaze and speak with quiet determination. 'I know very well who I am, Captain Scott. I am Lord Justice Forbes's special envoy. And *he* in turn is second only to the Duke of Albermarle, Commander in Chief in Scotland, appointed by His Majesty himself. Neither gentleman, I think, would look kindly upon your refusing to supply an escort for a messenger upon Government business through dangerous country in such perilous times.'

His brow contracts thunderously, 'You dare to threaten me, sirrah?' He bunches a fist as if he would like to strike me.

'No threat, Captain. Merely a statement of the situation,' I reply coolly. Then I change my tone, affecting an appeal to reason. 'All I need is one soldier, Captain. Surely that is not a lot to ask? Why risk the disapprobation of your superiors over such a trivial matter? And you may be sure that, if you accede to my request, I shall commend your co-operation to His Lordship upon my return.'

He glowers at me, but I compose my features into a look of understanding expectation.

'Very well, ' he growls at last, 'you may take the first man you see and be damned to you.'

'With respect, Captain Scott, I can hardly expect one of your men to obey me...'

'The Devil take you, sir!' he storms, flinging himself towards the door and wrenching it open. 'You, soldier!' he yells to the nearest body. 'You're to escort this fellow and his companions as far as the ferry to the Isle of Skye. Do you understand? There, you confounded nuisance,' he spits at me, 'there's your man. Now get out of my sight.'

With that, he manhandles me from the room and slams the door behind me.

Tom Hooper who, in accordance with my plan, has

273

made sure he is the first person the impulsive Captain sets eyes upon, salutes me smartly for the benefit of those around, giving me a huge wink as he does so.

We set off within the hour, Tom bringing us provisions from the mess-hall to start our journey. A night spent in the disused barrack block under mildewed blankets on dusty floors has left Charlie, Agnes and myself grubby and dishevelled, but that is all to the good for our forthcoming journey. The less we draw attention to ourselves the better, and from what Tom tells us of the countryside we'll be travelling through, it is likely we'll get more unkempt and bedraggled yet.

It is not yet ten o'clock and Tom is keen to put as much distance as possible between us and Fort William before Captain Scott's search party sets out at noon.

To start with we travel west as if heading towards Skye, but once out of sight of the fort, we double back east, fording rivers and streams until we reach an area of thick woods on rising ground. Scott's soldiers, Tom tells us will keep to the main track at the foot of the hills for the first part of their march.

As we are on horseback we could easily outpace them on that main track. But it is not desirable we should follow the same route as they will take, for fear some stray patrol might see us and report our presence.

So, although it is not as easy going, Tom leads us on a parallel route, along heavily wooded ridges a mile or two to the south where there is less chance of our being spotted. Our going may be slow, but we can only hope that theirs on foot will be slower.

It is as wild and desolate a land as any we have encountered on our journey so far. We ride when possible, but for most of the time we are forced to dismount and lead our horses through the tangled undergrowth. We travel for hours without sight or sign of habitation or another human being. And, more often than not, when we do suddenly come upon some rude hut in a clearing, we find it deserted or burnt out, its occupants fled or ousted by Scott's raiding parties.

Yet there are people in the woods. We catch glimpses from the corner of our eyes, flickers of movement between the trunks of trees, no sooner seen than gone.

Our hope is that they are dispossessed villagers forced to eke what meagre existence they can in the forest, but wary enough at the sight of Tom's red-coat to avoid us.

Our fear – which increases the further we get from Fort William and the nearer to the wild country where fugitives are known to be hiding – is that there could also be bands of armed rebels to whom a solitary red-coat would be a target to attack. My hand several times steals towards the secret pocket in my greatcoat, the presence of the weapons that lie concealed there providing slight but welcome reassurance.

We make, by Tom's reckoning, not above nine miles by the time dusk begins to encroach, which it does even sooner here under the forest canopy. We make our camp for the night in a dense thicket of trees and eat some of the provisions that Tom has brought. Dried strips of meat and hard biscuit.

Charlie's face is a picture. 'Bloody hell, even that gristle stew was better'n this!' Pity we ain't horses, they've got the best of it,' he says, looking across to where the animals are contentedly munching thick clumps of grass in the gloaming.

'Be grateful for what you've got,' I say with a laugh. 'Leaves aren't as tasty as you think, as Tom and I can tell you from our time in Dettingen.'

'Aye,' agrees Tom. 'Time many we were grateful for the odd worm or beetle we found among 'em!'

'Urrgh!' says Charlie disgustedly and returns to his gnawing.

That night we get what sleep we can, making beds from bracken, with our coats to cover us, while we all, Agnes included, take it in turns to keep watch.

I am assigned the last watch from three o'clock in the

morning until daybreak begins to penetrate the ceiling of branches above us.

The first faint traces of dawn reveal a world which is still in shades of grey. My companions are three darker mounds on the forest floor. Nearby, the horses stir and snort in the growing light.

I heave myself to my feet from where I have been sitting against a knotty tree trunk. My limbs which have become stiff during my vigil. I yawn and stretch.

By my reckoning August is not yet ended, yet the leaves are already in places tinged with the onset of autumn, And this dawn is colder than any I have known in London at this time of year. It is as if here, in this wild northern wilderness, time runs away faster than down south.

I walk a few paces to the edge of the copse in which we have camped overnight in hope of spying out where our journey will take us today.

Suddenly, from somewhere down below in the still morning air, there comes the whinny of a horse and I flatten myself against the nearest tree trunk.

Carefully I peer round it. Further down the slope at a distance of half a mile or so, I see shapes moving in the morning mist which swirls like a cloud fallen to earth. Gradually as the day lightens and the mist begins to disperse, I make out blurs of red.

This must be Captain Scott's search party. They must have arrived some time after us last night and encamped on the flatter ground below us.

I hear a rustle of bracken behind me and turn to see Tom, his shirt rumpled and untucked, rising from his woodland bed. He rubs his eyes, stretches his arms as I did not five minutes ago, then walks over to the nearest tree and, unfastening his britches lets forth a copious, steaming stream against its trunk.

I wait for him to re-lace before drawing his attention with a loud whisper. 'Hist! Tom, over here!'

He weaves his way through the trees towards me and follows the direction of my pointing finger.

The mist has cleared somewhat and the detachment of grenadiers can now clearly be seen making their morning preparations. Half a dozen of them are dismantling a tent that Scott and his junior officer have slept in overnight. Others are shovelling earth over the embers of fires and filling in a shallow trench dug for a latrine.

'Just the two mounted men,' mutters Tom beside me, 'Scott and his adjutant. And about thirty foot-soldiers I reckon. He must be expecting trouble. There's usually only a dozen or so. Just as well we didn't light us a fire last night.'

'And just as well you haven't put your coat on yet. Red is a very conspicuous colour.'

'Aye, 'tis all very well for hiding the blood on a battlefield, but damn little use up here in the woods. Come on, Jack - er, Will – damn me, it sits ungainly on the tongue after I've got so used to the other! - we'd best make a move. Let's rouse the others.'

I shake Agnes awake, putting a finger on her lips to prevent her speaking, whilst Tom does the same to Charlie.

Once we are all ready, Tom signs that we should aim for the top of the ridge and proceed on the other side where we will be out of sight of the troops below.

We walk slowly, leading the horses over turf or soft bracken as much as possible, to avoid their hooves making a noise. Not until we are safely over the crest of the hill do we consider mounting them or speaking in anything above a whisper.

In a hollow upon the other side, Tom gathers us all together.

'You see that mountain yonder? That's Ben Alder, and 'tis rumoured that Cluny MacPherson has a secret bolt-hole thereabouts, which is where our information says the Pretender is likely to be hiding.'

'How far away is it?' asks Agnes, shading her eyes against the rising sun. 'It's so difficult to tell.'

'Seven, eight miles,' hazards Tom, 'ten at most. I'll come with you for the first couple, but then, I regret I must leave you.'

'Why, Tom?' says she in dismay.

'I'm supposed to be conducting you to the Skye ferry. If I'm not back by nightfall, there'll be questions asked. Also,' he adds, 'the country between here and Ben Alder is crawling with rebels. My uniform makes us all a target. If I stay with you, it grieves me to say I'll more likely prove your death-warrant than your protector.'

'Can't you cast aside your uniform?' asks Charlie. 'We could lend you one of our coats...'

Tom looks at him and laughs. 'A generous thought, lad. But look at me – I'm as big as you and Will put together. No,' he continues sadly, 'if we'd thought this out properly, I could have brought something that might have served, but as it is...,' he spreads his arms in disappointment.

'No, Tom,' I say, slapping him upon the back. 'We have no right to put you in danger. You have done more than enough to help us, but this quest is ours alone. God grant we may be successful and that we shall meet again.'

'Aye, amen to that,' grins Tom. 'But we need not part just yet. I'll set you well on your way before I wish you godspeed.'

Ben Alder Forest

We travel on for another two hours, picking our way carefully through the woods and covering perhaps two miles and a half before the trees begin to thin and we come to the edge of a vast expanse of open moorland.

The hills and hollows are purple with heather, but apart from the occasional copse of trees, there is no cover at all. Any traveller can be seen from miles around.

From here on Tom's red coat would stand out like a beacon.

'This is where I must leave you,' he says. 'I'd wish you a safe journey, but we all know that isn't likely. The most I can do is advise you to take care.'

'Never fear, Tom, we shall trust to our wits. We have our story prepared if any challenge us. We shall say we are bound for Inverness to fetch home a kinsman wounded in the great battle.'

'There is a grain of possibility in that,' he concedes doubtfully, 'but it is a flimsy tale in my opinion and not one to dissuade these wild Highlanders from taking you hostage.'

'That is the risk we must run. But with luck they will see from our clothes and our horses that we are no mere peasants and carry us to someone higher in authority. And that may play to our advantage in getting us closer to the fugitive Prince.'

'Well, if anyone can do it, you can,' he concedes. 'As Jack Weaver you had a silver tongue to get you out of trouble, as well as the luck of the devil! Let's hope neither has deserted you.'

He shakes us all heartily by the hand and reluctantly takes his leave. Having watched until his red-coat has disappeared entirely in the gloom of the forest, we mount our horses and trot out into the open countryside.

I cannot speak for my two companions, but from the look upon their faces, I am sure they are experiencing the same apprehension as myself. That same emptiness in the pit of the stomach, the fluttering in the chest and a vague nagging sense of impending disaster.

It is not long in coming.

Our horses are feeling their way gingerly down a fell-side, placing their hooves carefully amidst the springy heather to avoid hidden rocks. I am leading, Agnes a couple of yards behind me and Charlie bringing up the rear when of a sudden the heather around us erupts into life.

Before we know it, our mounts' reins are seized, we are hauled off and thrown to the ground and within seconds we are lying on our backs, each with a dirk at our throat.

I look up into the face of my assailant. It is black with weeks of dirt and exposure to the sun, its very blackness emphasising the piercing light blue eyes that are glaring at me.

I look back at him with as much composure as I can muster.

He utters something incomprehensible in an unfamiliar, outlandish sounding tongue and when I don't reply, he grabs my collar, shaking me and digging the point of his knife so hard against my throat that I feel it draw blood.

'We – are – English,' I manage to gasp. 'I don't understand...'

He thrusts me roughly down on the ground and twists about, calling to one of his fellows.

They speak amongst themselves for a few moments in their wild language, until one seems to take the lead.

This one signals to the others to drag Agnes, Charlie and myself to our feet, three of them holding us, arms pinioned behind, so that we are facing him. He, like all the others is dressed in ragged, filthy clothes and his face is unwashed and weather-beaten.

He seems to be struggling to find words. Meanwhile, the three who have us captive and another who holds our horses' reins bunched in his fist, lean forward expectantly, urging him on.

'Whae are ye? An' wheer gang ye?' he eventually blurts, the words awkward as pebbles in his mouth.

'We are going to Inverness,' I say slowly and clearly.

There is another burst of conversation between them.

'Whae foor?' he asks.

'We seek a kinsman hurt in the great battle,' I reply. 'We mean you no harm. Let us go on our way.'

Again they consult each other in a growling contentious manner, clearly arguing what is best to be done with us.

Having come to a conclusion, they roughly bundle us together, sitting us back to back in the heather, directing the one with a smattering of English to guard us. The remaining four then set off, taking our horses with them.

Thus we sit for more than an hour, time enough for the sun to reach its zenith and start its decline into the afternoon. All this while, our guard sits at a distance of a few feet, pistol in one hand, drawn sword in the other, watching from under fierce brows but avoiding looking directly at us.

After a few minutes, Agnes turns her head to me. 'Where do you think they've...?' but gets no further.

Our captor springs to his feet and looms over her, brandishing his blade. 'Whisht! Dinnae talk tae each ither.'

We all remain obediently silent for another ten minutes or so and he returns to his post, scowling in our direction but never making direct eye contact.

'Gone to get the boss, 'ave they?' Charlie blurts out without warning.

'Haud yer gab!' retorts the Highlander. Then, as if this enforced silence is making him as uneasy as it is us, he says more calmly, 'Ye'll see soon enow. They'll no' be lang the noo.'

Charlie waits another five minutes or so. Then, 'Got a name, 'as 'e, this boss o' yours?'

'Aye, that he has, an' a noble one at that,' replies our guard a little more equably, 'but I cannae tell ye, 'tis no' ma place.'

Taking heart at his easier mood, I only wait a couple of minutes before I venture, 'Would it be Cluny MacPherson, by any chance?'

For the first time the man looks at me directly, startled. 'Ye know the Laird?'

'We've heard of him – who hasn't? This is MacPherson land is it not?'

'It is, but dinnae ask me tae say more because I willnae.'

And, true to his word he relapses into silence for the rest of the time until a crackling and rustling of the heather heralds the return of two of his comrades.

After a brief exchange of words, we are ordered to our feet and searched. Fortunately, the secret pockets are well enough concealed and padded so skilfully that our hidden weapons are not discovered.

Then we are led onwards. Deeming us no threat, they make no move to bind us or even to hold our arms, merely marching along beside us in silence.

About half an hour later, we surmount the brow of a hill and see a secluded valley before us. All but invisible from the land over which we have been travelling, it slopes sharply downwards and is enclosed on the other side by a near perpendicular cliff.

Descending the slope is not easy, so steep is it, and we are obliged to clutch on to clumps of heather as we search to find footholds in the rocky soil. By the time we reach the bottom, where a little winding stream trickles over pebbles, our hands are scratched and cut and our clothes scuffed and snagged.

As we ford the stream, I surreptitiously check that the damage has not gone anywhere near the secret pockets in my coat and am relieved to find them intact.

It is not until we are several yards beyond the stream that we notice what looks like a cliff-fall composed of heaped up stones and boulders. Coming nearer, it is apparent that this is a man-made structure built in front of a natural under-hang of the cliff.

Although impossible to see from the top of the valley,

the space behind forms a large chamber capable, I would say, of housing up to thirty men in comparative comfort. And, indeed, as we are guided inside, I judge there must be near that number in here now.

It appears that this hideout has been in existence for some time. Flaming torches light the deeper parts of the interior and there are tables and chairs which must, in the past, have been transported from a grand house, for they are no rough-hewn country stuff, but elegantly carved pieces. I guess that, before the recent troubles made it a refuge for rebels, it may once have served as a curious sylvan retreat for some local nobleman to amuse his guests.

That thought is quickly followed by a realisation that perhaps not all that much may have changed, for the young man who rises from behind a table as our captors push us forward is no rough Highlander. His clothes, though stained with rough living, are those of a gentleman, and he speaks to us not in incomprehensible Gaelic but in English.

Is he a nobleman turned fugitive?

'Your name, if you please, sir, and your business here?'

'First, I would know by what right you demand it, sir,' I reply with an affronted air, 'and why we have been brought here, captured and misused by your ruffians.'

'An Englishman?' says he, raising his eyebrow. 'You are either very brave or very foolish to be venturing in these parts.' He beckons to one of our captors to fetch a seat for Agnes and invites her to sit. 'Let it not be said that John MacDonald of Borrodale cannot remember his manners, even in such circumstances.'

'That is your name, sir?' I say.

'Aye, and this is my cousin, Alexander,' says he, indicating the fine-looking fellow beside him. 'MacDonalds both and proud to own it. Now, will you do me the honour of reciprocating?'

We each give our names as he glances at us in turn.

'A strange trio,' he muses, 'yet travelling together upon the same business it seems. The ghillie said something about a kinsman in Inverness?'

'That is what I told him, yes,' I say.

He picks up the implication of my words giving me a penetrating look. 'By that I take you to mean that that is not the real reason why you are here?'

I give a small shake of my head.

'You realise the danger you put yourself in by such prevarication?' he says menacingly. 'I could have you all killed, and no-one the wiser. Three more deaths amongst so many - in these troubled times, it would scarcely merit a second thought.'

'We are aware of that,' I reply. 'But I do not think you will do it when you hear what I have to say.'

'Well, say on,' he says, leaning back in his chair, and opening his arms wide to include all around, 'we are all ears.'

'It would be safer, sir,' says Agnes softly, 'if it were told in private, for your ears only. You are MacDonalds, you say, and will have heard of the suspicion that has fallen upon your kinsfolk in Skye?'

Alexander MacDonald stiffens, taking a step forward, his hand upon the hilt of his sword. 'If you have come to spy and lay information against our clansmen, you may fall to your prayers now, for you will not leave here alive.'

His cousin stays him with an outstretched hand. 'Peace, Xander. Let us hear what they have to say.'

'Be not alarmed, gentlemen,' I say, 'we are no enemies to the Clan MacDonald. Nor,' I add with great significance, 'to the noble gentleman who was recently your kinsmen's guest.'

John MacDonald rises, exchanging a glance with Alexander and laying his hand upon his cousin's arm. 'Come, Mr Archer. Bring your companions. We will retire somewhere more private.'

He leads us to a far corner of the cave, curtained off from the main chamber with piece of faded but richly patterned brocade that may once have graced a casement in some stately home.

There are three chairs and a small table within this enclosed space. Taking one, John MacDonald invites Agnes and I to take the other two. Alexander MacDonald and Charlie remain standing.

'Now Mr Archer, no more mystery, if you please. Speak. And make your words convincing – for you are talking for your life, and those of your two companions.

To emphasise his words, he lays a pistol on the desk between us and from behind me I hear his cousin draw his sword from its scabbard.

Checkmate

Although our acquaintance has been brief, my instinct tells me that John MacDonald is a man to be trusted. Much more so than his impulsive cousin.

I therefore decide to tell him all – or nearly all – of our purpose.

'May I speak candidly, sir?'

'Not only *may*, but *must* Mr Archer, if you value your life. You alluded to the noble gentleman who was our guest. Many better men than you have given their lives for his cause. Candour is the least I shall expect.'

'Very well, Mr MacDonald. Then the truth you shall have.' I pause momentarily, glancing at Agnes and Charlie, silently enlisting their support. Agnes gives a serious nod. Charlie shrugs and grimaces as much as to say, 'Your choice, 's all the same by me'.

I embark upon my explanation. I tell MacDonald that the story about going to Inverness in search of an injured relative is false, at which he nods in satisfaction but makes no comment.

'We were given a letter by Lord Justice Forbes in Edinburgh to deliver to Lady Margaret MacDonald in Skye. She had written to His Lordship shortly after certain events of which you may be aware? Events involving an escape by boat...?'

MacDonald nods again, his lips tight, ' Go on.'

'Lady Margaret implored Mr Forbes to intercede upon behalf of her kinsman, Alexander MacDonald of Kingsburgh and his daughter, Flora, who had been implicated in the flight of one 'Betty Burke' who was passed off as her lady's maid,' I say guardedly. 'In the letter entrusted to us, the Lord President promises to do whatever is in his power to petition the relevant authorities.'

Again, John MacDonald nods. 'Forbes is not of our persuasion, but I believe he is a good man at heart.'

'Good-hearted or not, his pleas are too little and too late,' bursts out Alexander. 'Kingsburgh and his daughter are already arrested and sent to London by that devil Fergusson. The man is a vile wretch who brings disgrace upon his country!'

John MacDonald ignores his cousin's outburst. 'You have that letter on you?' He holds out his hand.

'I do, sir, together with another affording us safe passage.' I take them from my pocket, putting the safe conduct one open before him, but do not immediately hand the other one over.

Having scanned the former, John MacDonald tuts in irritation and waggles his fingers for the latter. 'Do not fear,

Archer, I shall not open it. All I require is to see His Lordship's seal and the superscription. The contents are no longer of relevance. As Xander has said, Kingsburgh and Flora are already in custody.'

He examines the letter, then hands them both back.

'So far, your story has the ring of truth,' he says. 'But I find it strange how, if Skye is your destination, you come to be so far out of your way – and I fail to see why, when a single Scotsman with His Lordship's guarantee of safe conduct could have performed the task perfectly well, he chose three foreigners to deliver a single letter? What is it that you are not telling me?' He gives me a hard stare, his eyes suspicious.

Again I look to Agnes and Charlie before I divulge the true purpose of our journey. But Agnes saves me the trouble.

'You are most astute, Mr MacDonald. More perceptive than the majority of King George's representatives that we have met on the way. You are the first to question why there are three of us. And you are correct in suspecting that there is more to tell.'

He is not taken in by her flattery, but cannot resist the charm of her smile.

'In that case, ma'am, pray tell it.'

'Our commission comes not only from Lord Justice

Forbes in Edinburgh. We also work for Sir William Hervey, head of King George's secret service.'

'Dammit, John!' explodes Alexander. 'I told you they were spies!'

He seizes Charlie next to him, pinioning him with an arm about his throat and thrusting his sword point in our direction. 'The whole truth now, or this snivelling wretch dies!'

Charlie splutters and chokes under Alexander MacDonald's steely grip and clutches at the arm that is throttling him, but the sword never wavers.

In front of us, John MacDonald has taken up his pistol. 'Well, Archer?'

I know I must make my next words count if we are to survive.

I hold up my hands in submission. 'All we have told you so far is true. And yes, you might call us spies. But hear us out. It is not what you think.'

'Convince us, then,' says he grimly, the pistol still firmly pointed at us.

Agnes takes up the story. Despite Charlie gasping for breath behind her and the muzzle of a pistol facing her, she speaks boldly.

'We are here to help you, Mr MacDonald. And not only you but Prince Charles as well.'

I hear Alexander's grunt of disbelief. John Macdonald's face expresses amazement. And uncertainty. Agnes's use of the word 'Prince' has caught them off-guard.

She follows up her advantage quickly. 'Yes, sir, there are those in England who would, like you, have your Prince safely out of the country. Not everyone supports the Duke of Cumberland's drive to humiliate the Scottish nation. The vindictiveness and cruelty of such as Captain Fergusson and Captain Scott revolt not only Lord Justice Forbes, but also Sir William Hervey.'

MacDonald's pistol droops still further as Agnes's clarity and passion take effect.

I back up her account. 'That is why Sir William has sent us, Mr MacDonald, to give what assistance we can in getting the Prince safely out of the country. He and Mr Forbes are humane men, sir. They deplore the blood that has already been spilt and would see no more of it. Once Prince Charles is out of the country, they believe the persecution of your people will lose its force and more moderate counsels may prevail.'

'These are fine words, Mr Archer,' replies John MacDonald, 'but what proof can you offer that they are true?'

'With regard to the hoped-for consequences, only time will tell,' says Agnes pacifically. 'But there can be no doubting Mr Forbes's and Sir William's sincerity. In acting counter to government policy, both are putting themselves in the greatest danger. They would not do it if they did not ardently believe in the benefits that would ensue.'

'Aye,' sneers Alexander MacDonald. 'The chief benefit being that the damned Hanoverian usurper would be secure upon his stolen throne.'

'But another would be that your Prince would be alive – and perhaps, with France's promised help, able to fight again another day?' I remind him.

That gives them pause for thought and Agnes intervenes, 'Time is short, gentlemen. Even now, Captain Caroline Scott is in the area with a force of thirty or more redcoats, intent on capturing the Prince. If you know where he is, you must warn him immediately.'

'Or better still, take us to him, that we may lay good reasons before him why he should trust our masters,' I add. 'And to aid you in conveying him to safety with all speed.'

'It is a trick, cousin,' Alexander interrupts. He shifts his hold on Charlie, moving the tip of his sword to prick the side of his neck. 'Let them lay these *'good reason'* before us if they value this boy's life.'

I feel for Charlie's distress, but I know I must be resolute if we are to have any hope of meeting Charles Stuart face to face.

'I am under strict orders that these matters must be delivered to the Prince and to him alone, sir,' I say to John MacDonald, relying upon him to be the more reasonable of the two. 'Miss Mayer and I have told you the truth. Trust us, and you may lessen the persecution of your fellow Scots. But if you kill us, that persecution may redouble in its fury.'

I can see John MacDonald wavering. He signals to Alexander to release his hold on Charlie, which he does, thrusting him away so that he staggers and all but loses his balance, nursing his bruised neck with a malevolent glare.

But some doubts still linger in MacDonald's mind. 'What possible assistance could you give that we, his friends, cannot?' says he scathingly.

'We have Lord Justice Forbes's letter of safe conduct, and if the Prince were to travel in disguise, he might pass as one of our party. Government soldiers will be less likely to suspect an English 'family'.'

'His disguise must be more convincing than that of Betty Burke, then,' scoffs Alexander. 'I actually saw him, traipsing about like a great maypole in a flowered dress. Wouldn't convince a fly!'

John MacDonald strokes his chin, pondering. 'You expect us to take you to him?' he says with a doubtful frown.

'We expect nothing, sir,' I reply neutrally. 'But I firmly

believe it would be to your, and his, advantage.'

MacDonald shakes his head dubiously. 'It is a great thing you ask, and I am still not certain I can trust you. What say you, Xander?'

'I am with you, cousin. It is your decision. But to make matters sure, how say we hold this young fellow here as a guarantee.' He gives me a bold, challenging stare. 'Is that agreeable to you, Archer? His life and safety as earnest of your good faith?'

John MacDonald sees the look that passes between Charlie and me. 'Well,' says he with a grim smile, 'What say you to that proposal, Archer. Trust, it seems, may be made to work both ways.'

It is Charlie who overcomes the checkmate. 'Yeah,' he croaks, his throat still hoarse, 'that's fine by me.' He turns to John MacDonald. 'You see, sir, I trust Will with my life. I know he'll stick by what 'e says. You can trust 'im, sir. Question is, can I trust your cousin 'ere?'

Alexander bridles at the insult and raises his hand, but his cousin orders him to desist.

'Enough, Xander!' Then he turns to us. 'Very well, you have your bargain, Mr Archer, thanks to this young man. I will take you to the Prince. But be sure that, at the least sign of treachery, I shall not hesitate in killing both you and Miss Mayer. My cousin, for his part,' says he sternly to

Alexander, 'shall treat Master Stubbs with all due respect and kindness until our mission is accomplished. Then he will be returned to you unharmed.'

He rises and comes round the table, 'Now, I suggest you both get what rest you may. We must journey by night and it is already within a few hours of sunset.'

Night Journey

We set out as soon as night falls. The dusk to the west is red-rimmed with the last faint traces of day and owls are starting their nocturnal hunt, their eerie screeches echoing over the wild moor.

The night is not entirely black. A moon, no more than a few days on the wane, shines bright in a sky clear and chill with the onset of autumn. It is both a blessing and a danger. We can see more easily, but we can also be more easily seen.

We are joined by one of MacDonald's ghillies. 'Hamish knows this land,' John MacDonald tells us. 'Follow his lead, do as he does and obey what he says. For tonight he, not I, will be our guide.'

Once we have climbed out of the valley that hides the MacDonalds' cave, we find ourselves upon a wilderness of heathland. What by day would be red and purple with heather is, under the cool moonlight, a dun palate of browns and greys.

We set off into a rolling, undulating plain covered with a carpet of springy, spiky brush punctuated by occasional waist-high bushes, its far edges swallowed by the night. Unseen rills and pools lurk beneath, laying ambush for our unwary feet, ready to soak them. Hidden snags lie dormant in the rock-pitted earth under the brush, waiting to trip and turn our ankles or rip our hems and coat tails.

It would not be so bad if we could walk at a moderate pace and upright. But telling MacDonald about the thirty-strong detachment of Scott's men that are in the area prompts Hamish to be even more vigilant for unseen watchers, making him insist that we continually seek out the hollows and gullies, necessitating us zig-zagging erratically across the moor.

When no rift or gap presents itself, we are obliged to bend double or sink on to all fours, scuttling from bush to bush, or even to crawl on our bellies through the scratchy broom.

It is exhausting work, made worse by the fact that whole patches of the heathland, burnt black from summer fires, are covered in dust and ash, fine as powder, that rises to clog our throats and nostrils and blacken our faces.

So parched are we from the dust and so sweaty from exertion that we need to stop from time to time to seek out one of the innumerable streams that trickle below the heather and scoop the ice-cold water up in our palms to slake our thirst and lave our grimy faces.

After several hours of this punishing progress, Agnes and I are near exhausted, our clothes torn and our faces scratched and filthy.

When we come to a shallow depression in the land, with a clump of stunted trees along its edge, we beg a few moments respite.

Hamish grudgingly agrees. He, infuriatingly, seems as fresh and untired as when we set out. Watching him dart and scurry over the moor, I have wondered at times if this was his natural gait, so easily he does it.

MacDonald, though less unflagging than Hamish, is still not as bone-weary as Agnes and myself. The months on the run since Culloden have obviously instilled a certain hardiness in him.

While we rest and draw our breath, Hamish crawls up to the top of the ridge to spy out the land before us.

A few moments later he scurries back and an urgent, whispered conversation in Gaelic with MacDonald alerts us to the fact that something is amiss.

MacDonald shuffles across to us.

'There is a group of people half a mile distant. Probably soldiers, but hard to tell from here,' he tells us, keeping his voice low. 'Our way lies past them, there is no other route.'

Cautiously, we all clamber to the crest of the gully and peer into the distance.

Out on the moor, a flickering glow marks a camp-fire. Though difficult to see from this distance, it looks as if there are a couple of seated figures silhouetted against it.

'We have no way of knowing how many more may be sleeping,' whispers MacDonald. 'If, as we suspect, they are soldiers, it is likely that they will have set a sentry, or even two, so we must proceed in absolute silence.'

He points ahead to a dark mass that rears black against a sky now mottled with scudding clouds.

'The mountain yonder is Ben Alder. That is our destination.'

For the first time, I look around the horizon of the land we have been traversing. With my concentration perpetually fixed upon the two or three feet of ground before me for the last seven hours, I have not noticed that there are now hills on all sides. And, looking across the open countryside before us, I notice how it is becoming more wooded. No large patches of woodland, but odd clumps of trees here and there.

Hamish raises an arm, beckoning us onward and we crawl quietly over the ridge and out into the open moorland.

Now we must move even more carefully, placing hands and feet lightly at first before trusting our weight to them and inching forward. It is slow laborious work which strains every sinew of mind and body.

It is near twenty minutes of this painful exertion before we approach near enough to judge the extent of the threat before us.

Lying prone in the heather, I cautiously raise my head to look.

Around a low campfire of glowing embers with blue and orange flames flickering over its surface are five men. The light from the fire reveals their red coats, so they are definitely government troops.

All are lying down which gives us hope that they are asleep. The two seated figures we saw earlier must either have lain down with them, or have moved out on to the moor.

Hamish scans the gloom for sight of any movement and after a moment points silently to a darker shadow in the blackness of the night.

A sentry.

He is sitting side on to us in the heather about twenty yards away, his musket laid across his knees. And he is directly in our path.

Hamish gestures that we must veer off to the side in order to make a detour behind his back.

And so our cautious, silent crawling begins again.

We have nearly put him behind us when, whether from carelessness brought on by fatigue, or premature confidence that the danger is past, my carefully placed hand slips on a hidden stone, painfully jarring my wrist.

It collapses under me and I subside with the full weight of my body upon a clump of heather. The slight rustling might escape unnoticed – just the scuffle of some nocturnal moorland creature – but not my hastily stifled gasp of pain.

All four of us freeze, hoping beyond hope that the sentry has not heard. But no such luck!

To be sure he is not as alert as he should be - probably dozing upon duty – but he clambers to his feet and issues a befuddled challenge, 'Who goes there?' His voice is querulous and uncertain. Loud enough in the silence of the night. But low enough, we hope, not to wake his companions.

We remain, rigid as the rocks beneath the heather, hoping that his uncertainty will convince him he's mistaken.

For what seems an eternity, he stands, turning his head slowly about, Then, musket held out in front of him, he begins, step by wary step, to move towards where we lay hidden.

I feel Agnes's fingers twine themselves with mine in the darkness. I squeeze them with a reassurance I myself don't feel.

Another five yards and the soldier cannot fail to see us, darker mounds huddled in the heather.

But fate, it seems, is on our side.

As he approaches, one of the gathering clouds sails

opportunely across the face of the moon, blanketing everything in true darkness.

We hear him stop, waiting for the cloud to pass.

And it is then than Hamish acts. Snatching up a stone, he hurls it off to the sentry's right.

The soldier spins round, yelling out his challenge more forcibly - 'Stop! Who goes there?' - and aims his musket towards the noise.

Hamish leaps to his feet and, taking little care to disguise his flight, he hares off the opposite way, straight back in the direction we have come from.

With a shout, the sentry takes up the pursuit, sending a shot towards the crackling sound of fleeing feet.

John MacDonald stretches out an arm, warning us to remain still.

Then, as his cries and gunshots recede into the distance, the sentry is joined after a few minutes by his roused but still drowsy companions, who follow in blundering pursuit.

It is not until this moment that MacDonald urges us onwards with a whispered command to proceed as quickly and quietly as possible.

Only when we are out of earshot does he let us rest in a small brake of bushes.

'Such loyalty and bravery,' says Agnes sorrowfully. 'A noble fellow to sacrifice himself for our safety.'

'Sacrifice?' laughs John MacDonald softly. 'No such thing! Hamish knows these heathlands better than the hares their nests! He'll lead those redcoats round about till they be thoroughly mazed. Do not worry your heads about Hamish.'

An hour or so later, as the dawn is just starting to lighten in the east, we come within sight of our destination.

For some time the land has been rising, heather giving way to greener foliage and small copses of trees.

Eventually we come to the foot of a steep wood which scrambles up a craggy hillside where rocky outcrops tower among the branches, joining eventually into a sheer, naked precipice which rears beyond the topmost trees.

'It is here,' says MacDonald, pointing upwards to the rock-face.

Peer as I can, I can discern no habitation in this vertiginous crag.

But MacDonald is already ascending through the wood. So steep is the slope that the trees cling upon it more horizontal than vertical. We use their trunks almost like rungs upon a giant's ladder, grasping at convenient boughs to haul ourselves up.

Agnes's skirts, already much ripped and bedraggled by our flight across the moor, suffer further depredations from projecting twigs and branches and I have, on several occasions, to reach out an arm for her to grasp, or bend a shoulder for her to clamber on.

Finally, as the trees begin to thin, unable to find any further purchase in the unfruitful soil, we come to the place where the bare precipice rises sheer above us.

And here, as MacDonald promised, we find the strangest dwelling.

In front of us stands a fence or barricade constructed from felled tree trunks, laid horizontally one atop another and supported with stout stakes driven vertically into the ground.

Above and behind it is suspended what I can only describe as a huge wasps' nest. From a tree growing out of the cliff-face and thus forming a living centre beam for the roof, depends an egg-shaped structure. Constructed with panels of wattle covered with moss, it half hangs, half stands upon the ground behind the barricade.

While Agnes and I gaze in amazement at this curious house, MacDonald goes cautiously towards the barricade to announce our presence.

His wary advance proves unnecessary. It seems we are expected. A ladder is already being lowered upon this side of the barricade, allowing us to climb up and over into the compound beyond.

Behind the wall, the ground has been levelled up with

earth to make a floor a good six foot above the level of the ground outside the fence so we are able to step down easily with no need of a ladder.

MacDonald ushers us inside the strange habitation, which is bigger than it first appeared. There is room, I judge for five or six persons to live quite comfortably. In a corner – or rather a curve within the egg-shape – abutting the cliff, a fireplace has been cleverly constructed from a projection in the cliff-face, where the smoke can ascend unseen, being virtually the same colour as the natural rock.

It is sparsely furnished. A table, a few chairs, piles of plaids as makeshift beds. A metal pot stands on the fire, tended by a wild looking fellow with long, unkempt red hair and a beard to match. Beside him stands a tall, lean man, grey and craggy as the cliff itself.

The quaint habitation, Macdonald informs us, is known as Cluny's Cage and the man before us is its owner, Cluny MacPherson.

'Come awa' in, Mr MacDonald,' says this man. 'And you, ma'am and sir. Welcome to my house, which is a queer, rude place for sartain, but fit for royalty nonetheless.'

Beside us, John MacDonald has fallen on to one knee.

'Your Highness,' he says.

I look about, bewildered, to seek the presence of another person in the room. But there is none.

'Pray, John, stand not on ceremony.'

My jaw drops in amazement. It is the red-haired man by the fire who has spoken, but his voice is not that of a wild highlander. It is clear and refined, with the slightest hint of a foreign accent.

It appears that we are in the presence of Charles Edward Stuart himself!

In Cluny's Cage

I am caught off guard. 'Your Highness,' I stutter, giving a low bow. I persuade myself that in my position and in these circumstances, even Sir William Hervey would do likewise.

Certainly Agnes does, curtseying low, though she says nothing.

As the red-haired man rises, I see he is dressed in the common Highland garb. A black kilt, grubby shirt and a length of faded plaid over his shoulder.

'No ceremony,' he repeats. 'It is hardly warranted in my present condition. For the moment, Cluny is master here and I am but a guest like yourselves.'

He turns to John MacDonald. 'What news, John? Why have you brought these people here?'

MacDonald gives him a brief account of our capture, who we are and what we have stated our purpose to be.

'I considered there to be enough truth in their story to risk bringing them here,' he concludes 'But Your Grace will judge for yourself.'

Charles Stuart has seated himself next to the table, his duty as pot-watcher taken over by the servant who has returned from stowing the ladder. But our host, Cluny MacPherson, defers the forthcoming inquisition a few moments longer.

'Come awa' gentlemen – and fair lady! - mak yersels comfortable. We s'll hae some parridge when my man maks a shift tae serve us, an' a wee dram tae warm us 'll no' come amiss, I reckon.'

He draws out a chair for Agnes and myself. MacDonald seats himself upon the pile of plaids and Cluny returns to his post near the fire.

'So, Mister Archer,' says the Prince, 'state your business.'

'Mr MacDonald has given you the main import, sir. We told him that we would lay reasons before you to merit your trust.' I take from my secret pocket the letter from Sir William Hervey.

John MacDonald springs up, drawing his sword.

'Another letter! You said nothing of this, Archer. You said all was in your head and that was why you must see His Majesty in person. You are a liar after all! Forgive me, sire, I have brought you into danger. But I shall remedy my fault...'

I have barely chance to rise before his sword point is at my breast. I hear Agnes's chair topple as she backs away in alarm.

The Prince holds up his hand. 'Put up, John MacDonald. Would you commit murder before your Prince! Sheathe your sword, man. Let no man say Charles Stuart did not give him fair hearing. Well, Archer?'

'I am no liar, Your Grace. I withheld knowledge of this letter so that I might ensure a meeting. I mean no harm to any here – as witness of which...'

Taking care not to provoke a further assault from MacDonald, I slowly withdraw the weapons which have lain concealed in my coat and lay them on the table in front of the Prince. I nod to Agnes to do the same with her hidden pistol.

'Had we intended mischief, we could have used these at any time. Now we lay them before you to show that they are at your service.'

MacDonald's face is a picture of furious amazement. 'But...but... my men – they searched you...?'

'And did so very thoroughly,' says Agnes. 'But they were no match for cunning tailors.'

There is a great laugh from near the fireplace. Cluny MacPherson steps forward and claps MacDonald on the shoulder. 'Well awa', John –   ye hae been bested by a seamstress! Step up to the table now and get some honest Scots parridge in you whilst oor Prince reads what the Sassenach has to say.'

As the Prince breaks the seal and starts to read Hervey's letter, Cluny's serving man doles out the boiled oatmeal into wooden bowls. It is plain fare, but more than welcome after our perilous night on the moor and we set to with an appetite.

Cluny follows it up by pouring a fiery spirit into glasses and handing them round. 'A wee dram o' usquabae, gentlemen – and lady! To your health!'

He and MacDonald toss the honey-coloured liquor back in one mouthful. But having experienced its potency back at Mr Forbes's house in Musselbrough, Agnes and I approach it more cautiously.

By the time bowls and glasses are cleared away and the manservant has taken them out to rinse them with water from a nearby spring, the Prince has read and re-read Sir William's letter.

He regards me narrowly. 'Duncan Forbes, the co-signatory of this missive is well-known to me. But I have not heard of this fellow, Hervey, before. What is he, Archer?'

'I suppose you might call him a Spymaster-in-Chief, Your Highness. And I am sure he would take your ignorance of him as a great tribute to his success in that role,' I reply with a smile.

'He is a lackey of the Hanoverian usurper, then?' says the Prince suspiciously.

I shake my head. 'Sir William Hervey is no man's lackey. His only master is the British State, and his chief care is to ensure its security – which he does regardless of whichever party may be in power or,' I say with careful emphasis, 'whichever King sits on the throne. Like yourself, sir, few know of his existence, and that is usually because they have nothing to hide. But anyone who plots harm against our country's security, or seeks to subvert it for personal gain – be sure they will learn of his existence, and rue the day that they did.'

'Surely Sir William must count me among such people?' says he warily. 'In that case, why would he seek to help me?'

'Do *you* count yourself among their number, sir? Do *you* regard yourself as an enemy of the British State and the British people?'

Perplexity gives way to anger. 'Am I not the rightful King? It is my country, the people are my people – how could I wish them harm?'

'Then there is the answer to your question, sir.'

His brow furrows with confusion. 'You are saying he would aid me in my quest for the throne?'

'I do not presume to fathom his mind. Your Grace must look to what he writes in his letter to answer that question. All I know is that he most heartily desires that neither you nor your followers should suffer further oppression at the hands of some who profess to act for the present occupant of it.'

315

His mouth twists in a grim smile. 'An ambiguous answer, Mister Archer. But I suppose you could give no other.' He glances down at the letter. 'This Hervey - would he, in your opinion, work as diligently on behalf of the state if I were King as he does for the Hanoverian usurper?'

'I have not a shadow of doubt, sir.'

He nods, satisfied. 'You think very highly of him, Mister Archer. And in this letter,' he says holding it up, 'he speaks very highly of *you* and presents many compelling reasons why I should place my trust in you.'

I feel the colour rise to my face and lower my eyes modestly, but say nothing.

He returns to the letter. 'He also adds this postscript: *The agent who delivers this letter is also in pursuit of one whom we suspect has espoused your cause solely for his own personal gain – and has committed murder several times in order to ensure it. I am most desirous, as I trust you will be, to see this person brought to justice.* What can you tell me of this person?'

I start to give him a rapid summary of our pursuit and of the Ross murders.

Whilst I am in the telling of it, however, my tale is interrupted by a low whistle from somewhere outside and, before I can conclude my account, Cluny's ghillie comes in and exchanges a few whispered words with his master.

'My apologies, Mister Archer,' says Cluny, interrupting me. He turns to the Prince. 'My man says Lochiel and his brother are approaching with news o' the French ships, Your Highness.'

Any further discussion of the Ross killings is forgotten as we prepare for the new arrivals.

Whilst the manservant puts the ladder in place at one end of the barricade, Cluny and MacDonald busy themselves at the other. At first I am at a loss what they are about, but soon I learn that Donald Cameron of Lochiel received hurt in both ankles from an exploding shell at the Battle of Culloden. Three months on the run and in hiding have done little to aid his healing, making him unable to scale the ladder. Cluny and MacDonald enlist my help to lift him over the barricade in a kind of rough and ready hammock of tied-together plaids.

He is accompanied by his brother, Dr Archibald Cameron, who ascends by the normal means. As soon as being deposited safely inside Cluny's hideout, Lochiel attempts to kneel in front of his Prince.

Charles seizes him by the arms and raises him up. 'By no means, old friend. You have already suffered enough on my behalf.'

Cluny ushers us all back inside where Dr Archibald Cameron casts a curious look in our direction.

The Prince tells him our presence will be explained anon. 'But first, gentlemen, tell me your news. The French ships are on their way?'

'The *Prince de Conti* and *L'Heureux,* with Colonel Richard Warren and young Sheridan aboard are within a day's sail of Lochnanuagh. They come with the express intention of rescuing Your Highness. We must make our way to Borrodale with all despatch, for you may be sure that if that wretch Fergusson hears of their arrival, he will hasten to intercept them.'

'The man's a blackguard,' exclaims MacDonald angrily, 'a disgrace to Scotland and a traitor to his countrymen!'

The Prince has turned to Cluny. 'You must attend us. You know this country better than all, for it is MacPherson land. How long to Borrodale?'

'Two days if we could go direct,' replies Cluny. 'But as oor guests here hae said, the land is crawling wi' redcoats, so we maun flit by night. I ken a hoose or twae where we can lie up by day. An' proceedin' so, I guess 'twill tak the best part o' five or six days.'

'Then we must leave at once,' says the Prince.

'Aye, at set o' sun,' agrees MacPherson.

That gives us six or seven hours to plan how we will proceed.

It is agreed that Cluny MacPherson shall guide us for

the first part of the journey until we reach the Cameron lands around Borrodale and Lochnanuagh beyond.

I also suggest that the Prince adopt the guise of a Highland guide hired by Agnes and myself. To which end, he submits himself to have his hair and beard trimmed by Agnes. And Cluny sends one of his ghillies to collect some clean shirts from his sisters who still live nearby in a family property that has not yet been raided or confiscated.

Agnes and myself spend much of the day wrapped in plaids. After washing our clothes at the nearby spring and drying them, draped over the barricade in the sunlight, we both set to with brush and needle to repair the depredations of the journey through the heather. By the time the sun is sinking towards the horizon, we have managed to make them look vaguely presentable, scuffed by travel rather than ravaged by flight.

Thus we hope to avoid too close a scrutiny by any government troops we may encounter on the way. The Prince is no longer recognisable as the handsome, well-complexioned, fair-haired, god-like hero that Widow Ward entertained in Derby and so entranced the heart of Beppy Byrom in Manchester. Humbly dressed, in the guise of servant to a 'married' English couple, I am confident he should not attract too much attention. As long as he maintains a humble demeanour and keeps his mouth shut!

I cannot say that any of the Prince's confederates yet trust Agnes and me entirely, but they see the wisdom of the stratagem, and it is the Prince himself who, having studied himself in a clouded glass produced by Cluny, expresses himself delighted by his new imposture and hands us back our weapons to conceal once more in our secret pockets.

The Journey to Lochnanuagh

As soon as the sun dips behind the horizon, we set out once again. In the failing evening light, the descent from Cluny's Cage is even more hazardous than the ascent twelve hours before. Then, at least, we had the brightening dawn to help us – and we were not slowed down by an invalid.

Though Donald Cameron exerts himself to the utmost of his ability, his injuries make for slow progress. For much of the descent, he is carried in the makeshift hammock by four of Cluny's men who appear as if by magic from the woods shortly after we leave the Cage.

These scouts must, I suppose, have been there last night, observing us and MacDonald approaching, relaying the news to their master, just as one of their number brought the news this morning of the Camerons' arrival.

As soon as we come to more level ground at the foot of the incline, they vanish once again, melting away into the forest.

Lochiel limps valiantly along, supported in turn by his brother Archie and John MacDonald, and though he protests his continued vigour, we deem it necessary to stop at regular intervals to let him rest. Cluny, out of respect, declares these pauses to be necessary for reconnoitring the way ahead, and he duly creeps off for a few minutes each time, but we all know the real reason.

Fortunately the sky is overcast and the waning moon not so bright as last night so we are able to walk upright, though still making use of what cover the heathland provides.

By the time the eastern horizon begins to lighten with the coming day, I estimate that we have traversed a little over half a dozen miles.

Six miles, that is, closer to our destination. In reality we have covered at least twice that number wandering by circuitous routes to avoid any bands of redcoats. One of which diversions we are currently embarked upon in search of a house where Cluny hopes we may lie up for the day.

He leads us up a gentle slope of moorland in which I can see no habitation for miles around and I begin to worry that with dawn rapidly coming on, we shall soon be sitting ducks for any redcoat patrols.

Suddenly it is as if the ground swallows him. He disappears from view and, as we follow, I see that he has descended a narrow gulley which leads into an unseen hollow. Nestling at the bottom of the hollow is a stone built house. Bigger than a crofter's cottage, but not as grand as a landowner's farmhouse.

Cluny bids us wait under the lee of the overhanging bank and sets off at a loping run down the narrow track. I see him knock at the door – three sharp knocks, then a gentle knock and, after a pause of three seconds, two more sharp knocks.

After a few moments the door is opened a crack and a conversation, inaudible from this distance, takes place. Then Cluny turns, beckons us to come down and disappears inside the house.

Within a few minutes the householder, a wiry, agitated fellow, is hurrying us inside, looking fearfully to all sides of the valley before slamming and bolting the door behind us.

'Ye cannae bide lang,' he whines. 'The country's rife wi' redcoats, an' they reck nought o' bargin' in wi' no let or hindrance tae search a place. Ah've ma wife an' bairns tae think of.'

The lady in question is cowering in a corner with two mewling little ones clinging to her skirts, her face a picture of dread.

'Wheesht, Neil,' chides Cluny. 'A day's respite is all we ask. Have ye no hidey-hole where we may bide?'

The man expresses incredulity. 'For seven of ye? 'Tis impossible!' But then, seeing the look upon his laird's face, he relents slightly. 'There's three or four might lie concealed in the attic, but nae more.'

Cluny falls into urgent discussion with the Camerons and John MacDonald. The Prince, whose true identity has

323

clearly not been divulged to our reluctant host, stands with Agnes and me, relegated to a mere observer.

'Very well,' says Cluny as they arrive at a decision. He takes us and the Prince aside and speaks low. 'We are obliged, it seems, to move on. John and Archie shall stay here wi' Donald, for he is fair done in by the night's work. We four must borrow a half hour o' daylight to reach the next safe place. You, sir, must rehearse your role as servant to William and his 'wife' in case we are challenged.' He turns to me, 'You have the letter of safe passage?'

When I nod confirmation, he returns to our reluctant host. 'I charge you on your life, Neil Mackie, to keep these gentlemen safe. If you fail, be sure I shall hold you to account.'

'Have nae fear, Mr MacPherson,' replies the terrified householder, nodding frantically.

'And directly after sundown tonight, you shall bring them to Wullie MacLintock's, you understand?'

'Aye, sir, aye. I s'all do't.'

Then, after a brief farewell to MacDonald and the Camerons, we set out once more.

The sun is now peeping above the horizon and the dawn mist lying low upon the heather.

Cluny advises us that we must walk not too speedily but with confidence, as travellers with every right to be here.

And we must keep to the worn pathways.

'You, Mister Archer, must take the lead should we encounter anyone. Are you up to that?'

I assure him that my time spent as an actor with Mr Garrick will stand me in good stead.

'And you, Your Highness,' says Cluny with a wry smile, 'you must stay silent and defer to Mister Archer.'

'Ever the humble servant,' replies the Prince ironically. 'And what of you, Cluny? How will Mr Archer explain your presence in our little band?'

'With luck, there may be no need.'

And with this enigmatic pronouncement, we continue on our way.

Ten minutes later, while skirting round a copse of trees, we catch a glimpse of red-clad soldiers approaching.

'Make sure you merit the trust we've placed in you, Archer,' hisses Cluny, falling in behind me. 'Our Prince's life is in your hands. I have a pistol in mine. One wrong move and be sure I shall use it!'

As we draw nearer, Agnes links her arm through mine, for all the world like a comfortable married couple out for a morning walk. The Prince walks alongside, head down.

We meet just where the trees end.

There are four of them. The first holds up a hand,

commanding us to halt.

'Explain your business, fellow,' says he.

'I am not your fellow, sir. I am a chandler on my way to Fort William to arrange the supply of candles to the regiment stationed there.' I extract Mr Forbes letter of safe conduct. 'I have papers here...'

He glances at the official seal and seems satisfied. He waves them aside. Obviously he cannot read.

'And this?' he says, indicating Agnes with a leer. 'Your doxy?'

'I am his wife, sir,' says Agnes with dignified affront. 'And you, sir, are impertinent. Be sure I shall mention you to the commanding officer when we arrive at Fort William.'

He has the grace to look abashed. 'My apologies, ma'am.' Then a doubtful look steals over his face. 'But neither of you looks - well, like what I'd say was...'

'Well-to-do merchants? You think us too shabby?' I finish for him. 'As I said, I'm a chandler. 'Tis not a moneyed profession, which is why we travel on foot rather than a fine carriage. And why our clothes are travel stained.'

'As you have no doubt observed,' adds Agnes, 'we are English, like yourself. And, in a time of war, do we not all seek to earn a living as best we may?'

The appeal to shared hardship seems to work.

'And who's he?' asks the soldier, turning his attention to

the Prince who stands, shoulders bowed, face downturned, for all the world like a surly Scotsman faced with the hated English soldiery.

'A man we hired at the last town, to guide us over the moor,' says Agnes.

The soldier affords him a cursory glance, then peers over my shoulder. 'I thought I saw a fourth person with you?'

I turn round in surprise to find no trace of Cluny.

Agnes covers my confusion. 'Our factor, sir. These last two days, he has been troubled with the flux. He is answering the call of nature in the trees yonder if you wish to examine him, too,' she says tartly.

'No need,' mutters the man. 'Fort William's a day or two away. You'd best hope he's better by then – they'll not thank you for bringing him otherwise. Come, men!'

Rallying his three companions, they continue their march onwards, leaving us to continue ours.

As soon as the soldiers are out of sight, Cluny reappears, rejoining us as silently and as mysteriously as he vanished, and within another half hour we arrive at another safe house, the abode of Wullie MacLintock, another adherent of the Clan MacPherson.

Although, by royal decree after the Battle of Culloden the Clan system is to be outlawed, the old allegiances still hold firm. 'Nae scribble on a scrap o' parchment can wipe oot centuries o' oor history!' asserts Cluny. 'Isn't that the truth, Wullie?'

MacLintock provides us with refuge for that day and in the evening, true to his word, a very agitated Neil Mackie delivers John MacDonald, Lochiel and Dr Cameron in time for us all to continue on our way to the coast. Then, having fulfilled his reluctant duty, he departs with almost indecent haste.

Our journey continues in this fashion, travelling by night and resting by day, for another three days. On four more occasions we are challenged by government patrols. Each time, our party splits as soon as they are sighted, the Prince, Agnes and myself facing the soldiers out whilst the others remain hidden – and each time Lord Justice Forbes's letter sees us through.

But Progress, which is already slow because of Lochiel's injuries, is further hampered by the fact that the weather turns against us.

On the third night, soaked to the skin and chilled to the bone, we reach Achnacarry House, seat of the Chiefs of Clan Cameron and Lochiel's home.

Alas, it is a home no longer. All that remains of the house is a blackened ruin. Cumberland's forces burnt it to the ground back in May. As for the estate, what hasn't been destroyed has been ransacked, cattle sold off and crops flattened.

But the old loyalties are not so easily erased. The erstwhile steward of Lochiel's household still occupies a cottage rescued from the depredations and, after hesitantly opening the door a mere crack in answer to our knock, immediately throws it open upon sight of his lord.

'Maister Donald, can it be you?' he cries with tears in his eyes. 'And Maister Archie, why God be praised! Come awa' in oot o' this dreich weather.'

Alasdair – for that is the old man's name – is not the only one of Lochiel's former servants who has managed to rebuild his life and eke a living since the laird's lands were confiscated. Agnes and I are assigned to a homely woman who was once a cook in the great house. She is of a friendly disposition but as a Gaelic speaker she has very little English. What she lacks in words, however, she makes up for in constant smiles and welcoming gestures.

The Prince and Lochiel stay with Alasdair, whilst John MacDonald, Cluny and Dr Archie lodge for the day in a cottage on the edge of the estate with a grizzled, weather-beaten fellow who I gather was once the gamekeeper.

All our hostess can offer us is a straw-filled mattress by way of bedding, but after a meal of fresh baked bread, new-churned butter and honey from the old estate hives, Agnes and I sleep soundly enough.

We are awakened late in the afternoon by Dr Archibald Cameron, his hair stranded wet across his forehead, his thick woollen cloak beaded with water. The rain has shown no let up all day.

'Cluny and I are going on ahead to Camgharaidh to find a place to stay and arrange provisions for the voyage. You are to attend his majesty in an hour's time at the steward's cottage.'

Then he leaves without another word.

Face to Face

We arrive at the steward's cottage to find two strangers in deep conversation with the Prince and Lochiel.

One is a kinsman of Cluny, Donald MacPherson of Breakachie. The other, a little peacock of a fellow, constantly preening himself, is introduced to us as Colonel John Roy Stewart. Both, it seems, are long-standing, loyal supporters of the Prince.

They bring news that Captain Fergusson's ships have been sighted down the coast, apparently heading towards Lochnanuagh.

'It is imperative that we complete our journey in the utmost haste,' says the Prince. 'What say you, Lochiel?'

'I agree, your Majesty,' he replies. 'And I would therefore suggest that from now on we must travel by day as well as night. There may be redcoats on our trail, but I think we may avoid them, for there are things that may now play to our advantage. '

'What are they?' I ask.

'First, we are now in Cameron country. All here, like Alasdair and the good folk who have sheltered us this day, are loyal to me and to the cause. The English troops will get no help from them. In fact, they will be actively hindered.'

'And second?' asks MacDonald.

'The land between here and the coast is wild and rugged, but no one knows it better than my men. They will ensure our safe passage whilst leading our foes astray. And, as a mark of my confidence, I have arranged that there shall be horses for my Prince and myself, so that he shall travel as a Prince should - and my damned feet shall no longer be an impediment to our progress!'

According to the erstwhile gamekeeper, the rain that has dogged us continuously for the last few days will ease this evening. Deferring to his skill in weather lore, we agree to delay our departure until then.

Sure enough, the sun sets red, promising fine weather tomorrow and as we set out on the final leg of our journey, the rain has stopped, though underfoot the earth is still sodden and boggy, making it still wearisome and heavy going.

Often the Prince insists that, in the most treacherous pathways, Agnes should ride in his stead, an offer which she gladly accepts for, despite her protestations to the contrary, it is clear that the journey is taking a great toll on her.

It is a gesture which speaks volumes for the Prince's generosity.

Now we are safe within Cameron country, the slight security offered by our letter of safe conduct and the cover of our English accents is no longer necessary. No need, either, for the pretence of being our hired guide. He rides at the head of our little band as their acknowledged Prince once more.

Worryingly, I begin to sense a growing coolness from Lochiel and Dr Archie, and barely concealed hostility from the two newcomers, Breakachie and John Roy Stuart, towards the continued presence of Agnes and myself. I am sure their antipathy is caused by the view that we are only accompanying them under enemy orders to bear witness to their beloved leader's departure from British shores. I begin to suspect they would be rid of us if they could.

But the Prince is either too noble – or too politic – to allow it, and I wonder if his continued courtesy to Agnes is his way of gently rebuking those around him.

However uncomfortable they make me feel, though, I refuse to be cowed by them.

For there is another reason I am determined to see the business through to its end. And to me it is the most important one. Charlie's safety depends upon the successful completion of our mission. Only when the Prince arrives safely at the place where the ships await him will John MacDonald see that we have kept our word and restore Charlie to us.

* * *

Lochiel warned us that the land ahead would be wild and rugged, and he was not wrong. We are now in a country of towering peaks and plunging, precipitous valleys. Of steep, narrow pathways amongst what might in fine weather be purling streams and pretty waterfalls but which now, swollen with days of rain, have become tumultuous rushing torrents and crashing, foaming cataracts.

For much of the time the Cameron guides who, like Cluny's sentries a week ago, seem to appear from nowhere and melt back into their surroundings with almost magical ease, manage to circumvent the worst hazards.

Nevertheless, by the following afternoon, I have several times missed my footing on some cramped, winding ledge and am soaked up to waist from fighting against the churning waters of numerous mountain floods.

On several occasions, we catch a glimpse of red military coats at the bottom of a valley or flickering between distant trees causing us to halt and take cover whilst our guides consider the best strategy. Sometimes this is to send a few of their number to create a diversion and lead the soldiers away from us. At others, it is to seek out paths which they know will keep us concealed from watching eyes.

Yet despite the perilous terrain and the secrecy of our journey, followers of the Prince still manage to find us. A web of whispered report and rumour is obviously tracking our progress. A labyrinth of secret communication unseen and unheard by the English invaders.

Humble cottagers emerge from the woods to bow and tug their forelocks, shouting, 'God save Your Majesty!'

And during the course of the day, our number is swelled by several renegade noblemen, fugitives from Culloden who, to judge by the heartfelt greetings, are clearly known to my companions and to the Prince. They fall in with our party and seem intent on accompanying us to see the Prince safely embarked.

By nightfall, our original group of seven has become nearly twenty. A small army of rebels, straggling through the Scottish mountains with their defeated but still defiant Prince at their head.

As more people join us, our presence thankfully attracts less notice. Agnes and I do not deliberately keep ourselves to ourselves. Rather it is that we are ignored by the newcomers who are intent on mixing with their erstwhile comrades and paying their attentions to the Prince.

The only person who regularly keeps company with us is John MacDonald, more to keep his eye upon us than out of comradeship, but even he is occasionally drawn away as he exchanges greetings with old friends.

It gives Agnes and myself the chance not only to merge into the background, but also to observe and to listen.

Much of the conversation laments the ill fortune of the Prince's quest but for every despairing voice there are two that speak of hope and optimism that his star will rise again, and more gloriously than before. The King of France will send a long-promised army. Clans who did not support him before will, now they see English tyranny for what it really is, rise up and support him now. The Hanoverian usurper will be vanquished. The rightful Stuart dynasty will be restored.

Agnes and I listen with a sense of sadness to the repeated litany of vain hopes and unrealisable dreams.

Just after dark, as we make camp for the night, in a small wood upon a steep hillside, the arrival of two men attracts our attention.

Our guides have insisted that, for security, we spread out between the trees and keep any fires or lanterns shielded and dim. The Prince and his immediate party of Lochiel, Breakachie and Colonel Stewart are at the centre of a rough circle of small groups dispersed at a distance of a dozen or so yards around them. Agnes and I have found a place in the shadow of a large oak tree at the very edge of the camp. The only people beyond us are Cameron's sentries.

Gradually the low murmur of voices ceases, allowing the quiet of the night to drift back. Agnes and I are settling down to sleep when the crack of a twig alerts us to further arrivals. Somewhere in the dark a sentry issues a whispered challenge.

'Stay! State your names and business.'

Unseen in the darkness, a low voice replies, 'John Ross and my man, Neil Muir, to pay our compliments to His Majesty.'

The softly spoken reply brings us to full wakefulness.

Our quarry come to state his claim to the chieftainship of Clan Ross!

Beside me, Agnes whispers in my ear, 'It's him! We must get to the Prince before he does.'

But the sentry saves us the trouble.

'His Majesty is abed. Your business must wait till morning.'

Ross makes no protest and a moment later he and his companion pass close by us, two stealthy shadows in the silence of the night.

At first light, I seek out John MacDonald.

'The man who arrived last night,' I tell him, 'he is the one I told you of. He seeks to ingratiate himself with the Prince and obtain royal assent to be officially declared the head of Clan Ross. But he has achieved his ends by deception and murder. The Prince must not grant his request. Ross should be arrested. '

MacDonald stares at me coldly. He does not take kindly to an Englishman accusing one of his fellow countrymen, still less of dictating what his Prince should do.

'His Highness is at breakfast, Archer. I shall take you to him and you may state your case.'

Agnes and I follow him through the trees, only to find Ross and his henchman already in conversation with the Prince.

'That is certainly him,' Agnes whispers in my ear. 'See the drooping eye and the fawning smile.'

MacDonald has stepped forward to crave a word with the Prince in confidence. In response to a regal wave, Ross retires to a short distance while MacDonald and his master converse in an undertone.

Then MacDonald gestures Agnes and myself to come forward.

'What is this you allege?' asks the Prince with a frown.

'This is the man mentioned in the postscript to the letter I gave you from Sir William Hervey, sir,' I remind him. 'The man we suspect espoused your cause solely for his own personal gain – and has murdered several of his kinsmen to achieve it. If you remember, we were interrupted by the arrival of Lochiel and his brother, Dr Archie and we had no further chance to discuss it.'

'It is a serious charge, Archer. Have you proof?'

338

'If you will allow me to question him, you may judge for yourself, sir.'

'I would gladly allow it in normal circumstances,' replies the Prince. 'If it is as you say, then I agree that justice must be done. But time is our enemy. Our ships are waiting. We must embark this afternoon, but we have several miles still to go.'

'You cannot let him go, sir,' I protest.

I see his flash of anger at my presumptuousness. Then his jaw sets and he beckons Ross forward.

'John Ross,' he says imperiously, 'I hear your petition to be recognised as the head of Clan Ross. However, I am not minded at this present time to grant it...'

'Your Highness,' Ross interrupts indignantly, 'it is mine by right. You cannot refuse me.'

I expect the Prince to react with anger to this further example of insubordination. But he remains calm, almost apologetic. 'That may very well be the case, Ross, but we have not at this time the leisure to debate it. Our ships await our arrival. When we return in triumph to finally overthrow the Hanoverian Usurper, we shall address your claim again.' Then his brow darkens in displeasure and he fixes Ross with a severe look. 'And also the accusation that your claim is founded on deceit and foul practice...'

Ross interrupts him furiously. '*Deceit? Foul practice?*

Who thus accuses me?' he cries in passion. He looks desperately around him and his gaze alights on me and Agnes, his drooping eye glaring malevolently. 'Is it these two? What lies have they told Your Highness?'

'No lies, John Ross,' I reply. 'Only truth about your doings at Derby, at Manchester and in London. You cannot deny it.'

His face is pale with fury. 'Your Majesty cannot take the word of this English cur against that of a true Scot loyal to your cause!'

'Enough, sirrah!' commands the Prince. 'The matter is closed. Come, gentlemen, it is time we were away.'

I make one last plea as he and his followers turn to go. 'Will Your Highness not arrest him?'

Charles Stuart mounts his horse. 'My men will not arrest a fellow Scot, Archer. You arrest him if you will, but we have more pressing matters in hand.'

'Arrest me!' yells Ross, drawing his sword. 'Let any man try, he shall feel cold steel in his belly! I will have my right!'

Those around him instinctively retreat a step or two, ranging themselves between him and the Prince, fearing violence against their sovereign. There is a clamour of swords being drawn.

A brief skirmish ensues in which the Prince and Lochiel ride out of harm's way before reining in their steeds and watching to see the outcome.

Ross and his companion stand little chance against so many. But, with their Prince removed from danger, there is no real appetite for a fight. The majority sheathe their weapons, seeing no need to protect two English strangers. They march after their Prince, leaving Agnes and me exposed.

Only a handful of the Prince's men remain, Cluny and MacDonald at their centre, hesitating whether to fight or not.

Taking advantage of their hesitation, Ross and his henchman rush at Agnes and myself.

I fumble in the secret pocket for my hidden weapon. But before I have it out, John MacDonald strides forward, sword drawn, which spurs the rest into action.

The ensuing encounter is short and decisive.

Ross's companion falls, wounded by a chance blow that proves fatal.

Ross, seeing himself outnumbered, turns tail and flees.

A couple of the Prince's men follow halfheartedly until MacDonald calls them back. Then he turns to us.

'Not the outcome you were hoping for, Archer. Still, no matter, he is gone and matters of greater enterprise concern us now.'

Beside me, Agnes gives a small cry and falls upon my arm. The last few days have severely sapped her strength.

'See to Miss Mayer,' continues MacDonald, 'she is your responsibility. I would advise the two of you to keep close for the next few hours. I have sent word to my cousin Xander to bring your boy. By the end of this day, the Prince will be safely aboard and our bargain will be done.'

The Waterfall

It is getting on for noon and we are making our way slowly along a winding ridge overlooking a deep valley. The party is spread out in groups of two or three over a distance of half a mile or so.

To the left of the narrow track, the ground plunges almost sheer to a surging, foaming torrent almost fifty feet below. To our right rises a steep slope covered in trees.

Underfoot, the turf, dotted with small clumps of gorse, is springy, oozing moisture with every footfall and frequently crossed by rills flowing from springs higher up the mountain.

Occasionally these merge into wider, tumbling streams which plunge over the rocky edge into the torrent below.

Though Agnes and I, obeying MacDonald's injunction to keep close to others, started out in the middle of the assemblage, we have gradually fallen back as weariness began to take hold.

Spurred by the prospect of the waiting ship, the Prince has ridden on at a pace that has left many of his followers straggling behind him. He and Lochiel are only just visible far ahead. MacDonald, though initially making the effort to slow his pace to ours, is now some fifty yards in front.

He has already crossed the latest stream, the widest and

deepest channel that we have yet encountered.

It is about a dozen feet wide and at least two feet deep, the water swirling and splashing around outcrops of rock before it plummets in a great, roaring cascade over the edge.

I take Agnes's arm to help her across but she looks at it with dismay.

'I can't go on, Will,' she whimpers, pulling back. 'I must rest awhile.'

Gently I lower her to the ground, looking anxiously ahead to the receding backs of the party. 'Bide a while here while I test which is the safest route across,' I say, trying to raise her spirits. 'Those rocks may act as stepping stones. Once over the other side, we shall quickly catch them up.'

Gingerly I set foot on the nearest stone and peer deep into the eddying water to gauge my next step. Two or three paces on, I turn with a reassuring smile, ready to return and help her across.

And almost lose my footing with horror.

John Ross must have been following us under cover of the trees, awaiting his chance.

He has dragged Agnes to her feet and now holds her tight against his chest, arm clamped about her waist. With his other arm, he forces her head back against his shoulder thrusting a dirk against her delicate neck.

He is saying something I cannot hear, his words lost in

the tumult of the waterfall.

I lurch, splashing to the bank, shouting at him to let her go.

I hope that my shout may have alerted the others. As I near the shore, I cast a swift glance over my shoulder to see if any are coming to our aid. But none have turned, my voice, too, has been lost in the noise of the waters.

Within a foot of the bank, I miss my footing on a slippery rock and my ankle buckles under me. I stagger and fall headlong, reaching out my arms to break my fall.

Ross sees me fall. He laughs harshly and pushes Agnes forward.

This gives her a chance. She is more resourceful than he thinks. Taking advantage of his slightly looser grip on her, she twists away from his knife, hooks her leg backwards round his, and unbalances him.

But her exhaustion makes her weak and it is not enough to bring him down. By the time I have staggered to my feet, the two of them are tussling with each other, she trying desperately to wrest the knife from his grasp.

I know she has not the strength to resist him for long.

And with every second their struggle is bringing them closer and closer to the sheer drop.

I leap forward.

But not quickly enough.

Tripping on a clump of gorse, Ross topples, loosing his grip on Agnes.

She, so suddenly released, stumbles, totters and then pitches helplessly into the rushing stream.

Before my horrified eyes I see her grasp desperately for a hold upon the slippery stones as the torrent buffets her.

With a cry I rush to her aid, but too late!

Even as I reach out, the waters tear her numbed fingers loose and, unable to resist the powerful current, she is whirled with a despairing scream over the edge of the precipice.

I fling myself full length upon the rocky ledge beside the churning torrent, only to see her body tumbling, helpless as a rag doll down the cataract, to be swallowed by the frothing, foaming pool at its base.

'Agnes!' I scream in anguish. 'Agnes!'

Despair grips my heart, but I know she is gone.

Far below, I see a dark shape bob to the surface, only to be swiftly carried away, limp and lifeless, by the surging river.

I scramble forward, peering desperately over the edge, vainly seeking a path down which I might clamber to rescue her. But there is none.

Beyond a slight slope where straggly gorse bushes cling to fissures, the rock face descends sheer to the gorge below, smooth and featureless as marble.

The ice cold realisation of loss turns to a raging fire of anger. I turn my rage upon her killer. Rolling over, I find Ross standing over me.

I lunge forward and grapple his legs, clawing my way up his body, my hatred fuelling my strength. I reach for his throat but he brings his head forward, crashing it into my face.

My nose explodes in blood, temporarily blinding me.

Through a red haze, I grab his hair with one hand and with the other rake his face, searching for his eyes, ready to gouge them out. But my own blood which covers his face causes my fingers to slip and I feel his teeth close upon them.

I bring my knee sharply up into his groin and have the satisfaction of hearing him grunt with pain. His teeth release their hold as he doubles over.

But, in doubling over, he grabs me round the waist, swinging me round dangerously near the edge of the cliff.

Feeling myself thrown off balance, I thrust upwards with my fist, hearing it crack upon his jaw, snapping his head back. But his grip about my waist doesn't loosen.

From somewhere beyond the pounding in my head and the curtain of red that covers my eyes, I think I hear a gunshot and a shout.

Ross hears it too. And sees the puff of earth thrown up next to his foot. He staggers backwards only for his foot to snag in one of the treacherous clumps of gorse.

He topples, pulling me with him. He reaches back with his other foot for firmer ground and finds only empty space. Locked together, we tip over the edge in a flurry of torn earth and pebbles.

His grip loosens momentarily, giving me chance to grab at the rocky lip. My fingers find precarious hold.

But he finds no such purchase. He slides over me, clutching at my clothes as we both slither down the short slope leading to the sheer drop. His weight is dragging me down with him.

Suddenly I am brought up painfully short by one of the meagre crevice-hugging stems of gorse which slams into my crotch, arresting my slide.

The breath is knocked from my body as hot rods of agony shoot up from my groin, rendering me almost insensible.

The sudden jerk of my arrest unfastens his grip on me.

By some miracle I manage to reach up and grasp hold of another of the sparse branches to prevent me sliding further.

But he falls backwards over the precipice.

My face pressed to the earth, my eyes blinded with tears of pain, I do not see him fall. But I hear his yell of terror. I hear it cut short as his body bounces and rebounds down the rock face. In my mind I picture his limbs breaking, his blood fountaining.

I hear the distant thud as his broken body lands.

I lie prostrate, gasping for breath as the pain slowly subsides.

And the full gravity of my position slowly creeps in on me.

Above me stretches three foot of rocky slope. Below me are eighteen inches at most before the cliff drops sheer away. My whole weight is supported by two scraggy bushes rooted insecurely in cracks in the rock. Bushes which, at the slightest attempt at movement, tear a little bit more free of their tenuous hold.

I have a choice: die by inches, or release my hold and plunge down to join the broken body at the foot of the cliff.

It is at this moment, when I am about to give up all hope, when fear at last gives way to a calm acceptance of my imminent death, and my fingers are slowly surrendering their grip, that I am visited by an angel.

And a foul-mouthed one at that!

'Fucking 'ell, Will, wot you got yourself into now?'

I cannot believe my ears. 'Charlie? Is that you?'

'Oo d'yer think it is? The Queen o' Sheba?'

I still can't be certain I'm not dreaming. 'How do you

come to be he- ere?'

The last word is jerked out of me as the bush between my legs loses a bit more of its purchase in the rock fissure, pitching me down a few more inches.

'Wiv all due respect, Will, this ain't the time for catching up. Here, grab a hold o' my hand, will yer?'

So saying, he slides his upper body a foot or so over the edge and reaches out his arms.

'No good, Charlie, I'll only pull you over with me.'

'Don't talk daft! I got Xander 'oldin' on to mi ankles, and 'e's 'olding on to 'is belt wot's tied round a rock. So *haud yoor whisht* as they say round these parts and grab mi fucking hand before them bloody little twiglets give way altogether!'

I let go of the gorse with my right hand, whilst still keeping hold with my left. Averting my eyes from the skitter of dusty grit as yet another strand of root gives way, I slowly edge my free arm up towards Charlie's outstretched fingers.

He clasps my wrist with a firm grip, working his way down my arm until we both have a firm grip above each other's elbows.

Only then do I let go with my other hand and reach for his. At the same moment, the gorse bush between my legs, unable to take the momentary extra weight gives up its struggle for survival. My body jerks downwards, causing

Charlie to grunt in pain as his chest slams against the rock. But he grabs for my other arm, takes firm hold and within seconds I feel myself being hauled upwards.

Then, though I remember being laid on the ground and water from the stream being splashed on my face, it is as if my senses begin to blur, the mental and physical strain of the last few minutes leaving my body drained and wrung out like a wet cloth.

Cluny's face hovers above me. I think it is he who is now wiping it with a damp cloth, washing away the dirt and dried blood. It seems other faces, including that of the Prince crowd behind him in curiosity.

I am vaguely aware of thinking the shot I heard before I went over the edge must have succeeded in attracting their attention.

Cluny's voice echoes, as if from a distance, 'Ye may count yersel fortunate that John's cousin and yoor young man came up when they did, Archer, or ye'd be droonded sure.'

I seem to have drifted upwards out of my actual body, for it is almost as if I am observing all this from a height.

Droonded? Am I drowned? Am I dead?

No – but Agnes is! I see myself push aside Cluny's hand. I see how I try to prop myself on my elbow, raving about Agnes, pleading with them to help me find her.

I see them shake their heads in sympathy. I see them

turn away, one by one, until only I am left, flailing my arms and shouting myself hoarse as Charlie struggles to hold me.

At length, I cry myself into exhaustion. A dismal sense of emptiness overwhelms me.

No longer totally in my own body, I am vaguely aware of Charlie heaving me on to the back of a horse. In a sharp, but fleeting moment of clarity I recognise it - one of those that Agnes and I left at the MacDonald hideout what seems like a lifetime ago. Charlie and Alexander MacDonald must have have brought them back...

There are voices around me, talking about me, talking *to* me? There is the steady, jogging movement of the horse beneath me.

Then all is lost in a dream-like trance of fleeting shadows and hollow, booming echoes.

Return

I cannot vouch with any certainty for the events of the next two days. I have only Charlie's word for them.

He tells me that I have been in a world of my own, spouting nonsense, raving or bursting into tears for no apparent reason.

'You missed all the excitement,' he tells me, 'and all them as kept you company these last weeks 'ave scuttled off back to their hidey holes.'

It is evening, the last of the sun's rays gleaming golden through the window of an unfamiliar room. In answer to my question, Charlie informs me that I'm in the barracks infirmary at Fort William.

'If it weren't for the fact you'd taken leave of your senses, we'd both be as like danglin' from a rope's end. Captain Scott's convinced we 'ad a hand in the Pretender's escape.'

'The Prince is gone?' I ask, sitting up in the truckle bed I'm lying on. The effort is too great. I don't realise how weak I still am.

Charlie casts a worried look over his shoulder. 'Peace, you want-wit!' he hisses, bending over me. 'For god's sake don't let anyone hear you call him that, or we'll be strung up for sure.' He looks anxiously around again and, seeing for the first time my surroundings, I discover that there are other beds and other occupants. Fortunately too ill to pay attention to our conversation.

I lower my voice. 'Scott suspects us?'

'Aye,' replies Charlie, equally softly, 'but like before, 'e daren't do anything for fear o' Lord Justice Forbes. Tomorrow, if you're well enough, 'e's packing us off back to Edinburgh, but with an escort this time.'

'I don't understand,' I say with a frown. 'He wouldn't give us an escort before...'

Charlie clicks his tongue in exasperation. 'Cor, you really 'ave lost your wits, ain't yer! We ain't bein' escorted as official messengers – we're prisoners, you loon, sent back to Mr Forbes, accused of aiding and abetting the Pretender's escape.'

The bewildered question that rises to my lips is prevented by the arrival of an orderly who takes Charlie roughly by the elbow.

'You've 'ad yer time,' he rasps. 'It's back to yer cell for you, mi lad. And *you*,' he sneers over his shoulder with a cruel smile as he marches Charlie away, 'you'd best get what sleep you can. You need's yer strength if you're goin' to Edinburgh to be hanged.'

* * *

As it transpires, it is another two days before, at first light, I am abruptly woken and hauled before Captain Caroline Scott.

'This,' he sneers, holding up a packet, 'is an account of how the pair of you were found at the very spot where the traitor Charles Stuart's ship had just set sail. It will, I hope,' says he with a nasty smile, 'also prove your death warrant. You will die as traitors to your rightful King and to your country.'

He allows us no reply. He merely signals to his men to take us away.

It is as we are preparing to leave - Charlie helping me to mount for, though much recovered from my fevered confusion, I am still weak - that I become aware of a discussion between the four soldiers who are to form our guard.

Another trooper has approached one of our party. Whatever he has asked is now the subject of debate amongst all four, allowing for some show of reluctance and much persuasion. Eventually the one who seemed most opposed walks off with a shrug of his shoulders and prepares his horse for departure.

The soldier originally approached shakes hands with the newcomer, giving him the reins and letting him mount the horse in his place. He then walks away, whistling.

Our small posse take up their positions, two before, two behind with Charlie and me in the middle, and the order is given to ride on.

As we pass under the gateway, our new fourth member, who is in the pair ahead, turns and looks over his shoulder.

It is Tom Hooper. He gives me a broad wink before facing forward again as our mounts settle into a swift trot.

Gradually, during the day's journey, I start to regain some of my faculties, though the dull, aching emptiness of Agnes's loss lies like a lead weight deep inside me.

Charlie attempts to cheer me up, but his prattle is irksome and find myself drifting off into the dream-like state that has possessed me for the last few days.

Fragments of memory waft like leaves on the breeze before my inner eye.

Faces - kindly Hugh Bateman - the laughing features of Beppy Byrom - John Ross's, death-white, his hooded eye glaring accusations at me.

Places - the vast bulk of the pounding silk mill, the streets of Manchester, acre upon acre of rolling hills - and always the frothing, foaming cascade that tore Agnes from me.

Her last cry rings in my ears, her frail body tossed on the flood is perpetually before my eyes. Her loss is the hopeless, helpless emptiness at the heart of me.

But by the time we set up camp on the second night, grief and anger have begun to burn themselves out, to be replaced by the realisation that I shall see her no more. That, if I survive the charge of treason Captain Scott has laid against me, my life must be lived without her playful smiles, her fond caresses – without the love we both shared.

As darkness closes in, I lie down on the hard ground, resigned to accept whatever happens.

Which is why, when Tom Hooper crawls silently over to me once the other men are asleep and whispers plans of escape, I gently refuse.

'I have done running, Tom. I shall take my chance with Justice Forbes for I believe he is kindly inclined to me. And if not, then 'twill be no more nor less than Sir William warned me of at the start of this enterprise. When you and I were soldiers together in Flanders, we knew we had but a tenuous hold upon our lives. And we also knew that we would rather die honourably than live as cowards and runaways. It is no different now.'

He does not try to dissuade me, for he knows my mind is set.

Charlie and I are delivered to Lord Justice Forbes in Edinburgh at noon the next day.

We are kept waiting, under guard, in an ante-room while he reads the report from Captain Scott.

When we are eventually marched into his presence, I am startled to see Sir William Hervey there. His face is blank, his expression unreadable, and for a moment I fear the worst.

I have witnessed in the past how Hervey can cast aside those who have served him, and I wonder if it is now my turn.

Certainly Scott's account is a damning indictment.

He recounts how, being apprised of Charles Stuart's imminent departure from British shores, he and his men hastened to prevent the traitor's escape. They arrived at Lochnanuagh, where two ships rode at anchor a little distance from shore, waiting on the tide. Straightway, they were confronted by a band of foul rebels who put up fierce resistance to prevent His Majesty's troops boarding the vessels to apprehend the Pretender.

Casualties were sustained on both sides, but such was the fanaticism of the savage highlanders that they were prepared to sacrifice their own lives for the preservation of their masters. As a result, three known rebels Cluny MacPherson, John and Alexander MacDonald managed to escape arrest.

By the time Scott and his men had overcome the resistance and taken prisoners, including me and Charlie, the tide had turned and the two ships sent from France to carry off Charles Stuart had set sail.

They were accosted in the Sound by *HMS Furnace* under the command of Captain Fergusson, but at too great a distance to effectuate a capture. Shots were exchanged but no damage done to any vessel.

The encounter, visible from the shore, was witnessed by the rebel prisoners who set up a great huzzah before being subdued by their captors.

'And did you huzzah along with the rest of them?' asks Lord Justice Forbes severely.

'In truth, my lord, I cannot say,' I reply. 'I have no recollection at all of these events.'

'May I speak, your Lordship?' intervenes Charlie. 'I was there, I saw it all and I remember it. Will was there, but not in his right mind.'

'Explain yourself, boy,' orders Forbes, intrigued.

'You gave us instructions – Will, Miss Mayer (God rest her) and me – to see the Pretender safe off these shores, ain't that so?'

'It is,' replies Forbes guardedly. 'But that did not imply permission to fight and kill His Majesty's troops in the process.'

'Nor did we, yer Honour. I swear on my life, s'welp me God, that neither Will nor me lifted a finger 'gainst Captain

Scott's men. And anyone 'oo says we did is a damned liar,' retorts Charlie indignantly.

Forbes's brow creases. 'You accuse Captain Scott of lying?'

'No, sir. The most o' what you just read out is true enough as far as the bare bones go. The rebels, what we'd travelled there with, *did* fight Captain Scott's redcoats for sure. And did it long enough for the ships carryin' the Pretender to set sail. But Will an' me, we weren't among 'em. We was on the shore, more'n thirty yards at least from any action. Will 'ere was 'avin' one of 'is fits o' blubbering, like what e'd been 'avin since poor Miss Mayer's death, an' I was doin' what I could to keep 'im from rushing into the sea and drownding 'isself.'

He then proceeds to inform them further of my debilitated state of body and mind whilst I listen in wonder and embarrassment at the full extent of my incapacity during those two days.

When Forbes turns to me and asks if it is true, it is words declaimed by Mr Garrick in his role of King Lear that come first to my mind. 'To speak plainly, sir, I fear I was not in my perfect mind,' I say apologetically.

'His mind was unhinged by Miss Mayer's death, sir, and by nearly dyin' 'imself in the fight with John Ross, the murderer.'

'Ross is dead?' says Hervey, looking up and speaking for the first time.

Charlie gives them an account of our final encounter at the waterfall. 'Alexander MacDonald and I came up just in time to see Miss Mayer fall and to see Will and Ross tussling wi' each other. I shouted and Xander fired a shot, an' then the two o' them went over the edge. We ran forward and managed to rescue Will, but it was too late for Ross. He was lyin' dead at the bottom o' the cliff.'

'You're absolutely certain he was dead?' asks Hervey.

'Certain as a great pool o' 'is blood and all 'is limbs twisted at impossible angles can make me,' says Charlie.

Hervey nods, satisfied. 'That solves the problem of one Pretender at least,' says he. 'But what of the other? Are you sure he was actually on that ship?'

'Saw 'im with mi own eyes, sir,' replies Charlie. 'Later that day of the fight at the waterfall, we arrived at the coast. Will was away with the fairies, so 'e knew nothin' about it. But there was two ships lyin' at anchor in the bay.'

'*Le Prince de Conti* and *L'Heureux,*' I interrupt, remembering, as if from a dream, the message that had come to Cluny's Cage with Cameron of Lochiel.

'Anyway,' continues Charlie, 'at a signal from the shore, a skiff sets out to pick up the Pretender. He and three or four other gentlemen got into it...'

361

'Did these gentleman have names?' inquires Forbes.

'Not ones that I knew,' says Charlie, 'but if I describe 'em, 'appen Will might know. 'E was with 'em longer'n me. There was one wot seemed like a cripple...'

'Donald Cameron of Lochiel,' I say.

'...an' a tall, dark gennelman 'oo seemed to be 'elpin' 'im...'

'Likely his brother, Dr Archibald Cameron.'

'...an' the third one was a dapper little cove, dressed to the nines like a peacock...'

'That would be Captain John Roy Stuart. '

Forbes notes down each of the names, then looks up again, inviting Charlie to go on with his account.

'Well, as I was saying,' continues Charlie, 'once they was all in the skiff, the Pretender, 'e stands up and addresses all 'is followers who're standin' on the shore – it's evenin' by now and the sun's settin' red be'ind 'im, lightin' up 'is hair in a kind o' halo. Easy to think o' 'im as a real Prince, lit up like an angel,' he says with a cheeky grin. '*My lads, be in good spirits,* says 'e, for there was a tear in many an eye. *It shall not be long before I am with you again, and shall endeavour to make up for all the loss you have suffered.* Then they all cheered and waded into the water to shake his hand and make their farewells. And then the oarsmen plied their oars and carried 'im off to the waiting ships. But by then the wind 'ad dropped and the tide wasn't right, so it wasn't till next day that they could sail – and that's when Scott and his redcoats arrived.'

'Did you shake the Pretender's hand, Master Stubbs?' asks Lord Justice Forbes sternly.

'Weren't my place,' Charlie replies. 'I'd only been with them a couple o' days. 'E didn't know me from Adam. 'Sides, I was dealin' wi' Will. John MacDonald tried to get Will to go forward, sayin' 'is supposed 'Ighness was askin' for 'im, but 'e was in no fit state an' fought and cried, cringin' away till the gennelman desisted.'

'Well,' says Forbes with a conspiratorial glance at Hervey. 'That all seems very satisfactory. I can find no proof of any traitorous intent or action here.'

'Indeed not, Mr Forbes,' agrees Sir William. 'You dispatched Mister Archer and Master Stubbs, together with the late Miss Mayer, to deliver a message to Lady Margaret MacDonald in Skye, I believe? If I am not mistaken, their route back would have put them in the vicinity of these events, would it not?'

'It is very likely, Sir William,' replies Mr Forbes. 'And, by the way, I have received word that Miss Flora MacDonald and her kinsman, Alexander MacDonald of Kingsburgh are shortly to be released without further charge, so I may contact Lady Margaret again to give her the good news.'

'Good news indeed, Mr Forbes,' agrees Sir William. 'So, to get matters straight, it would seem that the presence of Mister Archer and Master Stubbs was an unfortunate coincidence. And Captain Scott's decision to arrest them a regrettable, though perhaps understandable, mistake?'

The two of them share a self-satisfied, complicit smile.

'Most succinctly reasoned, Sir William. In which case I see no further reason to detain these two gentlemen and am happy to give them over to your charge.'

Lord Justice Forbes accommodates us for the night and next day Sir William, after requesting a full account of our pursuit and apprehension of John Ross and a repeated account of his demise, offers us a seat in his coach for the return journey to London.

An offer which I politely refuse.

Much as I want to be back in my own house in Soho and renew my acquaintance with Mr Garrick, I am not ready.

I need time to come to terms with my loss, to be among those I love and who love me. So I humbly crave his indulgence to let me and Charlie make our own way back to London via my family in Yorkshire.

'Aye, my lad,' says he. 'In your present state, you're no use to me.' The sentiment is blunt, but there is an unspoken sympathy behind his eyes.

'Can I ask another favour, Sir William?' says Charlie.

Hervey cocks an eyebrow at his temerity. 'You may ask, Master Stubbs. And I may grant it as you have proved yourself useful in this business. But do not presume too much.'

Charlie's request is simple. He asks if Sir William can prevail upon Mr Forbes to reassign Tom Hooper to be our escort back to London. In my present fragile state of mind, he says affectingly, he cannot be sure of delivering me safely back into Sir William's service by himself.

Hervey laughs heartily at his effrontery but accedes to his request.

I learn later that Tom has asked Charlie to do this and that he has an ulterior motive. 'I've had word that my elder brother is ailing and cannot manage the farm back in Dorset. I've had enough o' soldiering. Unlike that devil Scott, I've no appetite for harrying innocent folk out o' their livelihoods. So, with your permission Will, once I've delivered you and Charlie back to London, I'll carry on down south and be obliged if you deny all knowledge o' me should anyone come asking.'

What more is to tell?

The three of us ride leisurely through a country healing

itself from the recent divisions. I spend several weeks with my family in Yorkshire. My mother, older but happily acting as surrogate grandmother to Col and Sarah's growing brood of children. And Col himself, my longtime friend, who manages my estates and does more than any to assuage the grief of Agnes's loss, coaxing me gently back to an appreciation of life and love. Persuading me that I must move forward with my life. But to hold Agnes in my heart, remembering all that was good between us.

Two months later, as the oncoming winter is frosting the city streets with silver, we arrive back in London.

Where I discover that Susan is now married to Joseph and big with his child.

Where Mr Garrick, my erstwhile master, now has the patents for Drury Lane and is making plans for his first season as manager.

And where my house in Soho that I have hardly spent any time in, welcomes me back to the brief promise of peace and security -

Until I receive, as receive I will, my next summons from Sir William Hervey.

Historical Notes

The Jacobite Rebellion of 1745

The opening pages of this novel are an almost complete transcription of Henry Fielding's apocalyptic vision of a London overrun by wild, rapacious Highlanders and controlled by Protestant-burning Roman Catholic priests, that was published in *The True Patriot,* a brief-lived (November 1745 – April 1746) weekly periodical, on Tuesday November 19th 1745.

Written to alert an overly complacent Government to a very real Jacobite threat, it panders in an extreme manner to the fears and prejudices current at the time. But, as with all matters of great political and national importance, things are rarely as simple as some people would have us believe.

This is not the place for a detailed history of the rise of Jacobitism and the intricacies of national and religious allegiances which contributed to it. Some of these are touched on in this narrative, and if my readers want to know more there are many books on the subject by authors much more learned than myself.

Whether Charles Edward Stuart (grandson of James II) really was a romantic, heroic figure or a deluded chancer is open to debate. As is whether the Duke of Cumberland's actions after the Jacobite defeat at Culloden (which earned him the nickname 'Butcher Cumberland') were unnecessarily and indiscriminately revengeful, or a genuine attempt to restore national security.

Whichever view one takes, the 1745 Jacobite rising was a significant point in the relationship between England and Scotland,

368

the repercussions of which may still be felt until the present day.

David Garrick

1745 and 1746 were troubled years for Garrick. Disputes with management, the breakdown of his love affair with Peg Woffington and the further souring of his relationship with Charles Macklin. All contributed to the breakdown in his health. And the Jacobite invasion didn't help!

Details of his illness, his visiting family and friends away from London, his short season in Dublin and his taking over the patents , enabling him to become manager of Drury Lane Theatre are all based on fact. His residence in Soho Square, however, is my own invention.

People

Many of the people Will meets on his travels really existed and what they say is taken directly from diaries or accounts they wrote at the time. My fleshing out of individual character traits in this novel is based upon their 'voice' in those writings.

Hugh Bateman was a journalist with the *Derby Mercury* at the time the Jacobite army was in Derby.

The Widow Ward hosted the Prince at Exeter House and was rewarded with a diamond ring. Her son, Samuel, acted as the Prince's food-taster and later became a prominent businessman whose portrait was painted by Joseph Wright of Derby.

Beppy Byrom, 23 years old at the time, was enthusiastic about the Prince's visit. Almost everything she says here, relating to those events, is shamelessly lifted from her journal written at the time.

Her father, John Byrom, was a less committed Jacobite than his daughter. A noted poet, he also invented a type of shorthand which was suspected to have been used for secret messages between him and Queen Caroline whose one time lover he was rumoured to be.

Dr Thomas Deacon, non-juring Bishop of Manchester, lost all three of his sons to the Jacobite cause. The fate of two is mentioned in the narrative. The third was transported to the colonies. When his executed son Tom's head was displayed on the Manchester Exchange, he stood in the square, looked up at it, then removed his hat and bowed with great reverence. He was later accused of worshipping his son's remains like those of a martyred saint.

Cluny MacPherson, John and Alexander MacDonald, Cameron of Lochiel and his brother Dr Archie Cameron, MacPherson of Breakachie and John Roy Stewart all figured in the Prince's final flight and escape. In the absence of personal journals, their words and characters have been imagined here.

Captain John Fergusson and Captain Frederick Caroline Scott really were as nasty as they are painted here. Today they would be accused of war crimes.

Places

Descriptions of the Derby Silk Mill, Exeter House and notable buildings in Manchester are all based upon contemporary accounts of those two cities.

Though Cluny's Cage undoubtedly existed, its precise location has never been verified. My description of it, and of the journey across the moors, owes as much to Robert Louis Stevenson's 'Kidnapped' as to contemporary accounts.

I have at all times endeavoured to be true the historical accuracy of events and their sequence. Any lapses are in the interests of the fictional narrative.

Acknowledgements

Jacobites: a new history of the '45 rebellion

Jacqueline Riding   Bloomsbury 2016

Bare-Arsed Banditti: the men of the '45

Maggie Craig   Mainstream Publishing 2010

An Account of John Lombe's Silk Mill at Derby, 1791

William Hutton, _The History of Derby_ (1791)

David Garrick and the Birth of Modern Theatre

Jean Benedetti   Methuen 2001

and, of course, that invaluable source: the Internet.

Printed in Poland
by Amazon Fulfillment
Poland Sp. z o.o., Wrocław

54796080R00210